jim thompson
now and on earth

James Meyers Thompson was born in Anadarko,
Oklahoma, in 1906. In all, Jim Thompson wrote
twenty-nine novels and two screenplays (for the
Stanley Kubrick films *The Killing* and *Paths of
Glory*). Films based on his novels include: *Coup
de Torchon (Pop. 1280), Serie Noire (A Hell of a
Woman), The Getaway, The Killer Inside Me, The
Grifters*, and *After Dark, My Sweet*. A biography
of Jim Thompson will be published by Knopf.

Also by Jim Thompson, available from Vintage Books

After Dark, My Sweet

The Alcoholics

The Criminal

The Getaway

The Grifters

Heed the Thunder

A Hell of a Woman

The Killer Inside Me

Nothing More Than Murder

Pop. 1280

Recoil

Savage Night

A Swell-Looking Babe

The Transgressors

Wild Town

now and
on earth

now and on earth

jim thompson

VINTAGE CRIME / **BLACK LIZARD**

vintage books • a division of random house, inc. • new york

First Vintage Crime/Black Lizard Edition, February 1994

Library of Congress Cataloging-in-Publication Data
Thompson, Jim, 1906–1977.
Now and on earth/Jim Thompson.
— 1st Vintage Crime/Black Lizard ed.
p.   cm. —(Vintage Crime/Black Lizard)
ISBN 0-679-74013-9
1. Authors, American—California—Fiction.   2. Alcoholics—California
—Fiction.   3. Family—California—Fiction.
I. Title.   II. Series.
PS3539.H6733N62   1994
813′.54—dc20   93-27537   CIP

Manufactured in the United States of America
10 9 8 7 6 5 4

big jim thompson: an appreciation

IF YOU PUT ME UNDER THE GUN (AND I GUESS, CONSIDERING the subject, the pun is intended), I could probably name twenty great novelists of the "hardboiled detective" school within half an hour. It would be *my* list, granted; purists might not like the inclusion of such writers as Ed McBain and John D. MacDonald, but it would also include those of whom even the purists would approve—Dashiell Hammett, Raymond Chandler, Ross MacDonald, Robert Parker, and so on. If you put me under the gun and asked me to name those American novelists who I believe have written great novels of the criminal mind, my list would be much shorter, and half the people on it only wrote one. Theodore Dreiser (*An American Tragedy*); Frank Norris (*McTeague*); Elliot Chaze (*Wettermark*). The three who wrote more than one are Shane Stevens, James M. Cain, and Big Jim Thompson.

Was Thompson physically big? You got me. He was from Texas or Oklahoma or somewhere like that, so I *imagine* him as big, but authors are a lot of times like the fat disc jockey with the thin voice—the ones who write the most virile prose are the ones who, when you finally see their photos, turn out to be pasty pudgy types who look like insurance adjustors. Never mind; he'll always be Big Jim to me, because he *wrote* big.

Although that needs a bit of explanation.

The *settings* of his novels were never big; the *characters* were rarely big (Doc McCoy of *The Getaway* may or may not be an exception); the crimes themselves were never the grand-scale jobs readers have some to expect from fellows like Frederick Forsythe with his Jackal or Jack Higgins with his Nazis out to get Winston Churchill—Big Jim's criminals, like James Cain's or Shane Stevens's, were usually caught in a web of cheap bucks and cheap fucks. But Thompson's books were daringly, breathtakingly big in scope and risk and point of attack. Edmund Wilson (who also wrote a wonderfully acerbic and totally wrongheaded essay called "Who Cares Who Killed Roger Ackroyd?") once condemned James Cain's *The Postman Always Rings Twice* as nothing more important than a jungle-beat in a lunchroom. It wasn't that he was wrong; it was just that it was a comment from a guy who had never spent much time in The Lunchrooms of America.

Nevertheless, lunchrooms did and do exist; small towns such as the one so devastatingly depicted in Thompson's *Pop. 1280* did and do exist; smalltime hoods and desperate people on the run did and do exist. They may not dine at the Waldorf, but the intellectual businessmen and menopausal women who do are not all of the world.

Wilson once took Nelson Algren to task for his "cloacal approach to literature," as though shit did not exist . . . but as those of us who are regular would willingly attest, it does. And not all of it is in the toilets and sewers. Sometimes it overflows into the streets, the lunchrooms, and the human mind.

Big Jim Thompson was and is big in my own mind because he wasn't afraid of the jungle in the lunchroom, wasn't afraid of the shit that sometimes backs up in the sewers underlying more ordinary social consciousness and interaction. No one likes it when the doctor puts on his rubber glove, asks him to bend over, and then goes prospecting . . . but *someone* has to look for those irregularities that may signal tumors and cancers—tumors and cancers that may exist in the bowel of society as well as that of the individual. Dreiser knew it; Melville knew it; B. Traven knew it; Dostoyevsky knew it. Thompson also knew the truth: the literature of a healthy society needs proctologists as well as brain surgeons.

Know what I admire the most? The guy was over the top. *The guy was absolutely over the top.* Big Jim didn't know the meaning of the word *stop*. There are three brave lets inherent in the foregoing. He let himself see everything, then he let himself write it down, then he let himself publish it.

His novels are terrifying cameos of small-town hurt, hypocrisy, and desperation. They are urgent in their ugliness, triumphant in their tawdriness. He wrote goddam good stories, but goddam good stories are not literature. Who knows that better than I do? What makes Thompson's books *literature* is his unflinching flatly lighted examination of the alienated mind, the psyche wired up like a nitro bomb, of people living like diseased cells in the bowel of American society.

Thompson was not always great—but at his best he was

the best there was . . . *because he wouldn't stop*. The reader is captured by Thompson's feverish tales, carried on by the understanding that he will go on until the end, however ugly, mean, or horrible that end may be (and if you have only seen the film of *The Getaway*, you have no idea of the existential horrors awaiting Doc and Carol McCoy following the point where Sam Peckinpah ended the tale).

Someone has to examine the stool samples of society; someone has to describe those tumors from which more cultured people shy away. Jim Thompson was one of the few.

He's dead, and he doesn't backlist well, but not everyone has forgotten—thank God, they never do. The great ones seem to always find their springs and channels. And I think that is why you are here. Now, my friend, buckle your seatbelt and grab your gas-mask.

You are going into the darkness without me, without Eudora Welty, without John Updike or Truman Capote or Edmund Wilson. You are going there with a genuine maniac of the human underside. You may be revolted. You may turn away, gasping with a sickened sort of laughter. But Big Jim Thompson will not stop . . . and my guess is this: neither will you.

Stephen King
Bangor, Maine
September 1985

now and
on earth

I GOT OFF AT THREE-THIRTY, BUT IT TOOK ME ALMOST AN hour to walk home. The factory is a mile off Pacific Boulevard, and we live a mile up the hill from Pacific. Or up the mountain, I should say. How they ever managed to pour concrete on those hill streets is beyond me. You can tie your shoelaces going up them without stooping.

Jo was across the street, playing with the minister's little girl. Watching for me, too, I guess. She came streaking across to my side, corn-yellow curls bobbing around her rose-and-white face. She hugged me around the knees and kissed my hand—something I don't like her to do, but can't stop.

She asked me how I liked my new job, and how much pay I was getting, and when payday was—all in one breath. I told her not to talk so loud out in public, that I wasn't getting as much as I had with the foundation, and that payday was Friday, I thought.

"Can I get a new hat then?"

"I guess so. If it's all right with Mother."

Jo frowned. "Mother won't let me have it. I know she

won't. She took Mack and Shannon downtown to buy 'em some new shoes, but she won't get me no hat."

" 'No hat'?"

"Any hat, I mean."

"Where'd she get the money to go shopping with? Didn't she pay the rent?"

"I guess not," Jo said.

"Oh, goddam!" I said. "Now, what the hell will we do? Well, what are you gaping for? Go on and play. Get away from me. Get out of my sight. Go on, go on!"

I reached out to shake her, but I caught myself and hugged her instead. I cannot stand anyone who is unkind to children—children, dogs, or old people. I don't know what is getting the matter with me that I would shake Jo. I don't know.

"Don't pay any attention to me, baby," I said. "You know I didn't mean anything."

Jo's smile came back. "You're just tired, that's all," she said. "You go in and lie down and you'll feel better."

I said I would, and she kissed my hand again and scurried back across the street.

Jo is nine—my oldest child.

I WAS TIRED, AND I HURT. THE LUNG I'D HAD COLLAPSED during the winter seemed to be filled with molasses, and my piles were torturing me.

I hollered when I got inside the door, but no one answered so I supposed Mom was gone, too. I went in the bathroom and washed, and tried to do something about my piles, and washed again. No good. I went at it again, and I washed some more. And then I remembered that I'd already done the same thing about six times, so I stopped.

The refrigerator did have some ice-cubes in it. Nothing but ice-cubes, and some old celery, and a few grapefruit, and a stick of butter. But that was something. Mom has a hard time getting the trays out, and when she does she usually leaves them out. Roberta never puts any water in the trays. She'll take them out, remove all the cubes, and put them back without a drop of water. Jo and I are about the only ones in the house who always fill the trays and put them back where they belong. If it wasn't for us, we'd never have any ice.

God, listen to me rave! And about ice-cubes. I don't know what's getting into me.

While I was standing there drinking and scratching and wondering about things in general, Mom came in from the bedroom. She'd been asleep, and she was still barefooted. Mom has varicose veins. She's always had them as far back as I can remember. Or—that's not true either. Her legs were never real good, but she didn't have those veins until I was nine years old. I remember how she got them.

It was about a week after Frankie, my younger sister, was born. Pop was down in Texas, trying to complete an oil well. We were existing in a shack deep down on Oklahoma City's West Main Street. A tough part of town in those days; I guess it still is.

Margaret—that's my older sister—and I were sort of living off the neighbors, and Mom wasn't eating much. So that left only Frankie to take care of. But she couldn't eat handouts, and Mom couldn't nurse her, and we only had fifty cents in the house.

Well, Margaret and I went down to the drugstore after a jar of malted milk, and on the way back a group of the neighborhood hoodlums chased us. And Margaret dropped the bottle. It was all wrapped up in that tough brown paper, and we didn't know it was broken until Mom unwrapped it.

No, she didn't scold or spank us—to the best of my recollection we never received a real spanking—she just sat there among the pillows, and something terrible happened to her face. And then she placed one starved hand over her eyes and her shoulders trembled and she cried.

I think an artist must have been peeking in the window that night, for years later I saw a painting of Mom. A painting of a woman in a torn gown, tangled black hair and thin hand concealing her face but not hiding—oh, Jesus, no! not hiding but pointing at—wretchedness and pain and hopelessness that were unspeakable. It was called *Despair*.

But the artist should have stayed for the sequel.

We got some newspapers and spread them out on the bed, and dumped the malt out on it. And then Marge and I and Mom began to pick the glass out of it. We picked and sorted and strained our eyes for an hour or more, and just when we had a few spoonfuls without any glass in it, Frankie woke up with one of those wild kicking fits which characterized her awakenings. She almost bounced us off the bed. Somehow we held on, keeping the glass from being re-mixed with the milk. But it didn't do any good. Frankie had only been limbering up for the main event. Her nightdress had gone up with the first kicks, and now her diaper slipped down. . . .

Well, we threw the papers away and mopped up a little —it was so funny we all had to laugh—and Mom asked us what we thought we'd better do now. Marge, who was twelve, said she'd brought some chalk home from school; maybe we could grind that up and put it in hot water, and it would take the place of milk.

Mom was afraid it wouldn't.

I didn't have any ideas.

Frankie was squawling her head off, and it was impossible not to sympathize with her. Mom said, "Well if I write a note to Mr. Johnson will you take it down and—"

Marge and I began to whimper and whine. The boys would chase us if we went out again and we'd just break the next bottle of milk like we had the first; besides, Mr. Johnson was a mean ol' man and wouldn't trust anyone for anything. He had big signs up all over the store saying he wouldn't. "You just go down and see for yourself, Mom."

Mom said she guessed she'd have to.

We got out her old black serge dress and a shawl and some houseslippers, and Marge did the best she could with pinning up her hair. Then we wrapped Frankie up in a blanket and started out. We took Frankie because Mom wouldn't leave her alone, and she needed me and Marge to lean on.

It was bitterly cold, and I thought that was what was making Mom shiver. But it wasn't—not entirely. It was just the pain of her legs going to pieces beneath her. It was only a block to the drugstore and a block back, but, as I say, her legs weren't good to start with, and she'd just had Frankie, and she hadn't been eating right for years.

We got the milk. Johnson wouldn't have given it to us, but there was a whore and her pimp in the place—swell customers—drinking coke and paregoric, and he didn't want to show himself up for what he was. He even threw in a small bottle of soothing syrup which, no doubt, he would have had to throw out in the alley before long anyway. It had a little label under the regular one—rather, part of a label; most of it was torn off. The remaining letters read OPI—

We got back to the house, and went into the kitchen. The gas hadn't been cut off yet, although I can't figure out why. Mom put Frankie down on the table, and sat down herself; and Marge and I fixed the milk and filled the bottle. I'll swear to this day that Frankie rose up out of her blankets and snatched it from our hands.

She took a big swig, and said "Gush," and gave us a tight self-satisfied Hoover smile. Then she closed her eyes and got down to business.

Mom said, "That milk looks so good I believe I'll have some. You kids ought to drink some, too."

We kids didn't like milk. We never liked anything that was good for us, probably because we so seldom had the opportunity to acquire the liking.

"You like ice-cream sodas, don't you?" said Mom. "I could fix it so it'd be sweet and nice. You'd sleep better if you had something warm on your stomachs."

Well . . . an ice-cream soda—that put the matter in a different light.

We heated another pan of milk, and filled three glasses. And Mom put a third of the bottle of soothing syrup into each one. It was such a little bottle, and Mom didn't know any better. Pop said afterwards that she should have, and that Johnson ought to have been horsewhipped. But Pop wasn't there that night.

I remember, dimly, in the haze-filled passages I fled slowly through, a white face that kept rising up before me—a white face and long black hair and warning terror-stricken eyes that kept forcing themselves open with the invisible fingers of sheer will. And when I saw that face, I retreated and was somehow glad.

Once I had wandered deep along a subterranean corridor, following an odor, a sound, a vision—I do not know what it was but it was irresistible. And I had come to a carved archway, and there was a laughing little girl on the other side, holding out her hands to me. Jo. Jo holding out her hands and trying to grasp mine.

No. I mean it. It was Jo. That was more than fifteen years before Jo was born, but I knew at once that it was Jo, and she knew that I was her father.

I said, "Where's your mother?" And Jo laughed and tossed her hair, and said, "Oh, she isn't here. Come on in and play with me."

I said, "All right," and stepped toward her, and she bent her little face to kiss my hand.

And then Mom appeared between us.

She struck Jo—struck her and kept striking her. And Jo screamed at me for help, and I stood motionless and horrified, sad yet relieved. I stood there until Mom had beaten Jo to death with her bare fists. And then Mom motioned for me to precede her back up the passageway, and I obeyed. I went back up the passage, leaving Jo dead there in the little room.

Jo has never liked Mom. . . .

There was a large white pavilion with a small circular pool. And strong hands kept pushing me toward the pool, and I did not want to go into it because it was black and bitter. I wondered why Mom didn't save me, and I cried out to her, and a dozen voices shouted back, "He's coming out of it! He's going to be all right, Mrs. Dillon. . . ."

I opened my eyes. The black coffee rose lazily from the oil cloth and I drank. I had been asleep thirty hours, seven more than Marge. Mom had shaken off her stupor as soon as Frankie began to holler for more milk.

A few nights later Pop came home. He came in a taxicab, and it was filled with packages. He had a new coat for Mom—she hated it always and wore it about as long—a suit for me, dresses for Marge, shoes for all of us (none of them fit), toys, watches, candy, rye bread, horseradish, pigs feet, bologna—God knows what all.

Marge and I danced around Mom's bed, laughing and eating and unwrapping things, while Mom lay there trying to smile and Pop looked on in happy pride. Then I noticed the little black grip he was carrying.

"What's in that, Pop? What else you got in that, Pop?" I yelled, Marge joining me.

Pop held the bag up over our heads and giggled. And we stopped yelling and jumping for a moment because the giggle startled us. Pop was such a big man, and so dignified even in his amusement. I think he was the only man I ever saw who could look dignified with his pants torn and chili on his vest. Pop always wore good clothes, but he was a little careless about their upkeep.

He unfastened the catch on the bag and turned it upside down, and a shower of currency, money orders, and certified checks floated down to the bed and floor.

His oil well had come in. He had already sold a fraction of his holdings for 65,000 dollars. And here it was.

The artist should have stayed for that picture, too. Mom with her legs as big and black as stovepipes, and 65,000 dollars on the bed. . . .

Well, her legs are still like that. And Pop is still drilling oil wells—very real oil wells, to him at least. As for me—

As for me. . . .

3

"HOW DO YOU LIKE YOUR NEW JOB?" MOM ASKED. "DID you have to work very hard?"

"Oh, no," I said.

"What did you do mostly? Bookkeeping and typing?"

"Yeah," I said, "bookkeeping and typing." Then I lost my temper and told her what I really had done.

When I finished she said, "That's nice," and I-knew she hadn't really heard a word.

"Eating out tonight, are we?" I asked.

"What?" said Mom. "Oh. Well, I don't know, Jimmie. I don't know what to do. Roberta went off to town and didn't leave any money or say what she wanted or anything. Jo hasn't had a bite to eat all day but a peanut butter sandwich. I haven't had anything either, but of course—"

"Let me have a dollar," I said. "I'll go get something. I'll pay you back as soon as Roberta gets here."

"I could have got something myself," Mom said. "But I didn't know what—"

"Just give me a dollar," I said. "I'll go get some potatoes and bread and meat. That's what we usually have."

Mom went and got a dollar. "I will have to have it

back, Jimmie. Frankie has to get a permanent, and some new stockings, and we don't have a cent to spare."

"I'll pay it back," I said.

I saw it was almost six so I ran all the way to Safeways. The strongest butchers' union in the country is in San Diego. If you want fresh meat, you buy it before six. Otherwise you buy bacon, or lunchmeat—which is two-thirds cereal and a fourth water—or do without.

I reached the store at six sharp. I bought a pound and a half of lunchmeat—forty-five cents—some canned beans, and potato chips. I studied the wine counter a moment but decided I'd better not buy any, even if it was only fifteen cents for a short pint.

When I reached the corner, Roberta was just getting off the bus. Mack was asleep and she was carrying him. Shannon, for one of the few times in her life, was behaving herself.

Roberta said, "Hi, honey. Take this lummox, will you? I'm worn out."

I took Mack, and Roberta took the groceries. Shannon, with one of her lightning fast and unpredictable movements, leaped up and grabbed me by the elbow.

"Carry me, Daddy," she demanded. "You can't carry Mack unless you carry me."

"Go on," I said. "Go on. I can't carry both of you."

"Daddy's tired, Shannon," said Roberta. "Now stop swinging on him or I'll blister you. Why don't you show Daddy your new shoes? Show him how you can dance in them."

Shannon dropped loose, pirouetted, and was twenty feet down the sidewalk via a shuffle-off-to-Buffalo before I could take a deep breath. Shannon is four, but she is not as large as Mack who is eighteen months younger. She sleeps an average of seven hours a night, eats almost nothing, yet has more energy than either of the other children. One minute you see Shannon; the next she is three blocks away.

She posed for a moment, then, with her usual unpredictability, burst out with:

> My name is Samuel Hall,
> And I hate you one and all.
> God damn your eyes!

"Shannon!" I said.

"Shannon!" said Roberta. "You get right straight home! Get! One more word out of you, and I'll blister you till you can't sit down."

Shannon took a notion to mind. She wasn't afraid, understand. I gave up long ago trying to do anything with her, and Roberta is beaten too, but won't admit it. Shannon is not disturbed by dark closets. She does not mind cold showers. You can't punish her by depriving her of a meal, because she'd as soon do without as not. You can't spank her because, ordinarily, you can't catch her. And, anyway, she is always hoping a little that you will try to spank her. You are then in the position of an aggressor, and she fights best when she has been attacked. And there is nothing she loves more than a good fight.

The last time Roberta tried to spank her she—Roberta, not Shannon—had to go to bed. And while she was lying there, Shannon sneaked into the room and began beating her with a toy broom. It was all Mom and Frankie and I could do to pull her away.

Frankie exercises an occasional control over her by treating her with contempt. Mack's way is to catch her in an unguarded moment and to sit down on her. But neither Roberta nor I can do much with any method.

"How do you like your new job, honey?" said Roberta. "Have a hard day?"

"Not very," I said.

"What did you do?"

"Most of the day I went around on my hands and knees chipping up plaster."

Roberta stopped. "Wh-at?"

"Yes. They're building an extension to the plant, and a lot of plaster is scattered around the floor. I went around with a little thing like a cold chisel and chipped it up."

"But didn't you tell them—didn't they know—"

"They don't give a damn. They've not got any editorial work down there. They're building airplanes."

"But, couldn't they—"

"I don't know anything about airplanes."

Roberta started on, her mouth set in a tight line. "You're not going back," she said. "You just go down there in the morning and get whatever you've got coming, and tell 'em they can keep their old job."

"Thought of how we're going to eat? And—incidentally—pay rent?"

"Jimmie. The kids just had to have shoes. I know we're hard up, but—"

"Okay, okay. But how are we going to pay the rent? I suppose you told the landlady we'd have it at the end of the week?"

"Well," said Roberta, "we will, won't we? Don't you get paid on Friday?"

"O Jesus," I said. "O Christ and Mary. O God damn!"

Roberta got red, and her nostrils trembled. "Now James Dillon! Don't you dare swear at me!"

"I'm not swearing. I'm praying for forebearance."

"And don't get smart, either."

"Dammit," I said, "how many times have I asked you not to talk about me getting smart? I'm not six years old."

"Well—you know what I mean."

"I don't know what you mean," I said. "I don't know half the time what you mean. Why don't you ever peek inside a dictionary? Can't you ever read anything besides the *Catholic Prayer Book* and *True Story*? Why, Jes—my God, honey. . . . Oh, God! Don't cry out here on the street! Please don't. It seems like every time I open my mouth lately someone starts bawling."

She pushed on ahead of me into the house, letting the screen door slam in my face. Mom opened it for me.

"Now don't say anything," I said. "She'll be all right in a minute. Just don't pay any attention to her."

"I'm not saying anything," said Mom. "What difference would it make if I did? Can't people open their mouths around here any more?"

"Please, Mom."

"Oh, all right."

I put Mack down on the lounge and went back into the bedroom. Roberta had taken off her dress and hung it up, and was lying on the bed, hands over her face. I looked down at her and began to tingle. I knew how it was going to be, and I hated myself for it. But I couldn't help it. Roberta didn't need to do anything to win an argument with me but let me look at her. I knew it from the moment I saw her. She knew it after a few years.

I sat down and pulled her head into my lap. And she turned, so that her breasts pressed against my stomach.

I wish, I thought, that Mom could understand what Roberta means to me—why I am like I am with her. I wish Roberta could understand what Mom means to me. Maybe they do understand. Maybe that's why things are like they are.

I said, "I'm terribly sorry, honey. I'm just awfully tired, I guess."

"I'm tired, too," said Roberta. "It's certainly no fun to drag that Mack and Shannon around all day."

"I'm sure it isn't," I said.

"I am worn out, Jimmie. No fooling."

"That's too bad, dear. You've got to get more rest."

She allowed me to stroke her for a few moments; then she sat up brightly and pushed me away.

"And you're tired, too," she declared. "You've already said you were. Now you lie down while I help Mom get dinner."

She pulled an apron over her head, and I flopped back on the pillows.

"Give Mom a dollar," I said.

"What for?"

"For the groceries I got."

Roberta seemed to see the sack for the first time. "What'd you get that stuff for? We've got two pounds of beans up in the cupboard. Why didn't Mom cook them?"

"I don't know. I wasn't here."

"They were right there in the cupboard. She must have seen them."

"No harm done. We can eat them some other time. Now please go on and do whatever you have to do, and give Mom that dollar."

"I'll think about it," said Roberta.

Somehow I was on my feet, and the veins in my throat were choking me.

"*God damn it! Give Mom that dollar!*"

Mom opened the door.

"Did someone call me?" she asked.

"No, Mom," I said. "I was just telling Roberta about supper—about the groceries. To give you the dollar I borrowed."

"Why, I don't need it," said Mom. "If you're short why don't you just keep it?"

"Oh, we've got plenty, Mom," said Roberta. "We've got all kinds of money. You just wait a minute."

She began fishing around in her purse, fetching out nickels, dimes, and pennies, and spreading them out on the dresser.

"Why don't you give her a dollar bill?" I said.

"Now I'll have it for Mom in just a moment," said Roberta in a neat voice. "I'll get it, all righty . . . here you are, Mom. There's twenty. Twenty-five. Forty. Sixty. Eighty-three. Ninety-three. Oh, I guess I'm seven cents short. Do you mind if I give it to you tomorrow?"

"Just keep it all until some other time," said Mom.

Roberta picked up the change. "You can have it now if you want it."

Mom went out.

I lay staring at Roberta in the mirror. She met my eyes for a moment, then looked away.

"How much were the groceries?"

"Seventy cents. I've got thirty cents left, if that's what you're driving at."

"I suppose you're going to buy something to drink with it?"

"I won't disappoint you. I'm going to get a quart of wine."

"You shouldn't, Jimmie. You know what the doctor told you."

"Death, where is thy sting?" I said.

Roberta went out, too.

Pretty soon Mack came toddling back, rubbing the

sleep from his eyes. There isn't an ounce of fat on him, but he's practically as broad as he is long.

"Hi, Daddy."

"Hi, boy. What's the good word?"

"Save-a money."

"What'd you do downtown? Ride an airplane?"

"Yop. Saw a bitey, too."

"A real honest-to-God bitey?"

"Yop."

"What'd he look like?"

Mack grinned. "Look like a bitey."

Then he went out. I have bitten on that joke of his a thousand times, but it is the only one he knows and I think a sense of humor should be encouraged.

Roberta shut herself up in the bedroom with the kids about nine, and Mom was busy in the bathroom working on her bunions. Frankie was still out, so I had the front room to myself. Not that I minded. I arranged a couple of chairs—one for my feet—just like I wanted them. Then I went around to the liquor store and bought my wine.

I thought the clerk was rather patronizing; but it could have been my imagination. Wine-drinkers aren't regarded very highly in California—not when they drink the kind of stuff I bought. The better California wines are largely exported. The cheaper ones, sold locally, are made of dregs, heavily fortified with raw alcohol.

In Los Angeles there are places where you can buy

stiff drinks of this poison for two cents and a full pint for as little as six. And you can count as many as fifty addicts in a single block. "Wine-o-s," they are dubbed, and their lives are as short, fortunately, as they are un-merry. The jails and hospitals are filled with them always, undergoing the "cure." A nightly average of forty dead are picked up out of flophouses, jungles, and boxcars.

So—I got home, sat down with my feet up, and took a big slug. It tasted watery, but strong. I took another slug, and I didn't mind the taste. I was leaning back against the cushions, smoking and wiggling my toes and anticipating the next drink, when Frankie came in.

She made straight for the divan and took off her shoes. She is the big hearty perfectly composed type, the counterpart of Pop except for her blonde hair.

"Drunk again?" she inquired conversationally.

"Getting. Want a shot?"

"Not that stuff. I've already had three Scotches any-way. 'S'matter? Roberta?"

"Yes—no. Oh, I don't know," I said.

"Well," said Frankie. "I like Roberta, and I'm crazy about the kids. But I must say you're a fool. You're not being good to her. She doesn't like things like this any more than you do."

I took another drink. "By the way," I said. "When is your husband joining you?"

"I guess I asked for that," said Frankie.

"I'm sorry," I said. "I'm just feeling mean."

"That wine won't make you feel any better. You'll have the grandfather of all hangovers in the morning."

"That's in the morning," I said. "Tonight—here's looking at you."

Frankie snapped open her purse and pitched me a half-dollar. "Go get yourself a half-pint of whisky. It won't tie you up like that wine will."

I looked at the money. "I don't like to take this, Frankie."

"Oh, go on. Hurry up and I'll have a drink with you."

I put on my shoes and went out. When I came back Frankie was holding a letter in her hand, and her eyes were red.

"What do you think about Pop?" she asked.

"What about him?"

"Didn't Mom show you this letter she got today? I thought she had."

"Let me see it," I said.

"Not now. I want to take it back to the bedroom with me. You can read it tomorrow."

"Look," I said. "Whatever it is, it won't worry me any more to know about it than not to know about it, now that I know there's something wrong. Please don't argue. And if you're going to bawl, go hide some place. I've been laved in tears ever since I came home."

"You're a dog," said Frankie, wiping her eyes. She chuckled. "Did you hear the one about the rattlesnake that didn't have a pit to hiss in?"

"Shut up a minute."

I skimmed through the letter. It didn't say much. They didn't want to keep Pop at the Place he was in any longer. He was—he was too much trouble.

"We'll have to take him away, I guess," I said.

"Bring him out here, you mean?"

"Why not?"

Frankie gave me a look.

"All right, then," I said. "What do you suggest?"

"We can't have Mom live with him. Even if we did have the money for a place in the country and everything."

"What about his own folks? They've got dough."

"They were holding on to it, too," said Frankie, "at the last writing. You know how they are, Jimmie. You write one of 'em a letter, and he reads it dutifully, writes a note of his own, and sends the two on to another twig on the tree. The note, incidentally, begins exactly five spaces from the top right of one page, and ends five spaces from the left bottom of another. And of course it doesn't—it wouldn't—refer to Pop at all. That would be indelicate. Long before the sixteen-hundred-and-eightieth Dillon is reached, our letter is worn out and nothing but theirs remains. The result? Well—Aunt Edna's third-oldest girl, Sabetha, has her adenoids removed, and Great-Uncle Juniper gets a copy of *Emerson's Essays*."

That's about the way it would be. I've always believed that the Dillons originated the chain-letter.

"Let's have a drink and sleep on it," I said.

"Just a short one," said Frankie. "How do you like your job?"

"Swell."

"Got a good bunch to work with?"

"Oh, swell."

"Such enthusiasm. Let's have all the lurid details."

"Well, there are six of us altogether, counting the foreman—or leadman, as they call him. The stockroom is divided into two departments—purchased parts, that is, parts manufactured outside the plant, and manufactured parts—but we're all inside the same enclosure. The two fellows in Purchased Parts are Busken and Vail. Busken is dapper, very nervous. Vail is the sure, enigmatic type. They're two of a kind, however."

"O—oh," said Frankie.

"I was on my hands and knees all day, and naturally I was sweating a lot. At some time during the day these clowns in Purchased—they've got the stenciling machine in their department—taped a neat little chromo upon my buttocks. I must have worn it for hours. It said, WET DECALS. NO STEP."

Frankie laughed until the seams of her dress threatened to split.

"Why Jimmie! That's clever!"

"Isn't it? Then, there's Moon, our leadman. He came around tonight at quitting time and gave me a few words of comfort. He said not to worry if I didn't seem to be doing anything; the company expected to lose money on a man for the first month."

Frankie slapped her knees. "And you getting fifty cents an hour!"

"Oh, 'it's funny," I said. "Now for a really brainy fellow we have Gross, the bookkeeper. He's a graduate of the University of Louisiana and a former All-American. I asked him if he knew Lyle Saxon."

"Well?"

"He asked me what year Lyle was on the team."

"So that fixes him in your book." Frankie didn't laugh this time.

"The remaining member of our sextette," I said, "is named Murphy. He was laying off today so I didn't meet him."

Frankie picked up her shoes and got up. "You'll never make it down there, Jimmie. Not the way you feel. Don't you really think you can write any more?"

"No."

"What are you going to do, then?"

"Get drunk."

"Good-night."

"Good-night. . . ."

I thought about Pop: Now what the hell will we do, I thought. I thought about Roberta, about Mom. About the kids growing up around me. Growing up amidst this turmoil, these hatreds, this—well, why quibble—insanity. I thought and my stomach tightened into a little ball; my guts crawled up around my lung and my vision went black.

I took a drink and chased it with wine.

I thought about the time I'd sold a thousand dollars' worth of stories in a month. I thought about the day I became a director for the Writers' Project. I thought about the fellowship I'd gotten from the foundation—one of the two fellowships available for the whole country. I thought about the letters I'd got from a dozen different publishers—"The finest thing we have ever read." "Swell stuff, Dillon; keep it coming." "We are paying you our top rate. . . ."

I said to myself, So what? Were you ever happy? Did you ever have any peace? And I had to answer, Why no, for Christ's sake; you've always been in hell. You've just slipped deeper. And you're going to keep on because you're your father. Your father without his endurance. They'll have you in a place in another year or two. Don't you remember how your father went? Like you. Exactly like you. Irritable. Erratic. Dull. Then—well, you know. Ha, ha. You're damned right you know.

I wonder if they are mean to you in those places. I wonder if they put the slug on you when you get to cutting up.

Ha, ha-ha, ha, ha. They'll give you a spoon to eat with, bud. And a wooden bowl. And they'll cut your hair off to save on shampoos. And after the first month they'll make you wear mittens to bed. . . . They can't get you there? They got Pop there, didn't they? Not *they.* You. You and Mom and Frankie.

Remember how easy it was? Come on, Pop, we'll have a bottle of beer and go for a little ride. Pop didn't suspect. He'd never think his own family would do a thing like that to him. You had to? Of course you did! And they'll have to. And you won't know until it's too late—like Pop did.

Remember the startled look on his face as you sidled out the door? Remember how he knocked upon the panels? Knocked; then pounded? Clawed? Remember his hoarse voice following you down the hall? The quavering and cadenced tones—"Frankie, Jimmie, Mom, are you there? Mom, Frankie, Jimmie, are you coming back?" And then he began to cry—to cry like Jo might. Or Mack or Shannon.

Or you.

"M-mom. I'm afraid, Mom. Take me out of here. *T-take—me—out—of—here!* Mom . . . Frankie . . . Jimmie. JIMMIE! *Take—me out. . . ."*

I screamed and sobbed and my head rose to a peak and flopped back in a sickening mush.

"I'm coming, Pop! I won't leave you! I'm coming!"

And Mom was shaking me by the shoulder, and the clock on the mantel said five-thirty.

The whisky flask was empty. So was the wine bottle.

"Jimmie," said Mom. "Jimmie. I don't know what in the world's going to become of you."

I staggered to my feet. "I do," I said. "How about some coffee?"

4

WE DIDN'T HAVE ANYTHING IN THE HOUSE TO TAKE WITH me for lunch, and I lost my coffee before I'd gone a block. I coughed and choked and vomited, and then I began to cramp and I knew I ought to go to the toilet. But I was afraid I'd be late, so I went on.

It wasn't so bad going down the hill. All I had to do was stand still and keep lifting my feet and the sidewalk rolled under them. But when I reached Pacific Boulevard, I began to have trouble. They've got six-lane traffic on Pacific, and every lane was filled with aircraft workers going to the plants. Most of them were in jallopies because cars are higher than get-out on the West Coast, and you knew their brakes couldn't be too good. And they were all traveling fast, bumping and crowding into each other to get to the plants ahead of the others. It was still early, but you have to get there early if you want a parking space within walking distance.

It would've been hard for me to get through that traffic even if I'd felt—well—normal, and I didn't. I wasn't just so sick and tired I wanted to lie down in the gutter and go to sleep. The wine was playing tricks on me. I couldn't co-ordinate my impulses with my limbs and muscles.

I'd start to step into the traffic, but my reactions were so slow that I couldn't move until the opportunity was gone. Several times I was unable to halt the impulse I'd started, and I walked into moving cars, banging my knees against fenders and wheels. I couldn't judge distance at all. A car that seemed to be a block away would, in the same instant, have its bumper against my legs, its driver shouting what the hell.

I can't say exactly how I got across. I remember falling down and skinning my knees and rolling, and there were a lot of horns blowing. And then I was on the other side. It was a quarter of seven, and I had a mile to go.

I started off at a trot down the dirt road that curved around the bay. There was a steady procession of cars passing me, moving not a great deal faster than I was and so close that they brushed my clothes. But none of them stopped. Their passengers looked out at me phlegmatically, and looked away again. And I jogged on and on, red-faced, nervous, tongue hanging out—jogged along like a hound dog with a threshing crew. I wanted to spit through their windows, or grab up a handful of rocks and stone them. Most of all I wanted to be some place else. Where it was quiet and there were no people.

Of course I knew why I wasn't asked to ride. No car could very well stop in that traffic. The cars behind would push it ahead, even with the brakes on and the motor off. And practically all of them were loaded; and they couldn't let me ride on the running board because there is a severely enforced ordinance against that.

Nevertheless, I hated them. Almost as much as I did myself.

I reached the plant just as the five-minute whistle was blowing. Actually, you're supposed to be inside, standing ready at your station when the five-minute blows; but there were hundreds besides myself who weren't. I fell into line in front of the gate that held my clock number. I was weak but I felt better. The sweating had done me good.

There was a steady snapping of metal and rustling of paper as the gate guards examined each man's lunch. One man, a new one doubtless, had his lunch wrapped in a newspaper. The line was held up while the guard untied the strings and unwrapped it.

When I reached the guard in our line, he glanced at my badge and pass. Then, holding the pass in his hand, he plucked the badge from my jacket and gave me a shove through the other lines.

"Over there. Chief's desk."

I didn't ask why. I thought I knew. For a moment it was in my mind to run. Then I thought, Well, if they really want me they'll get me. So I stood at the desk until the chief in his military cap and Sam Browne belt looked up. His face was fat and cold; his eyes shrewd.

"What number?"

"Huh?"

"Number, number. What's your clock number?"

"Oh." I told him what it was.

He reached into a drawer and pulled out another badge and a yellow isinglass enclosed card. It bore the picture they had taken of me the day before, my name, age, and a detailed physical description.

"This is your permanent badge, and number. Punch it hereafter. This is your identification card. Don't lose, lend, or forget either one. You'll need them to get through the gate and while you're inside. If you leave them at home, it'll cost you fifty cents for us to send a messenger after them. If you lose them, it will be a dollar. Understand? All right. Good luck."

I punched in, and walked through the crowded yard to the plant entrance. . . . Relieved? That's not the right word. Maybe I'll tell you why some time.

The stockroom gate was locked, as usual. I could see Moon and Busken and Vail up in the Purchased-Parts section talking, but evidently they didn't see me. Gross, the bookkeeper, was on his stool, absorbedly manicuring his fingernails. I walked around to the window.

"How about letting me in?" I said.

He looked up. He is a handsome fellow, with his well-shaped head, dark eyes and hair, but so ruggedly built that he appears awkward. He was dressed impeccably in a doeskin jacket and brown whipcord pants.

"Crawl through the window," he suggested, pleasantly enough.

"How about the sign that says not to?"

"That don't mean anything. I crawl through all the time."

I scrambled through just as the seven-o'clock whistle was blowing, and bumped into Moon as I swung my feet to the floor.

"I wouldn't do that any more if I were you," he said. "There's a rule against it."

I looked at Gross. He was uncovering his typewriter, his back turned toward us.

"All right," I said. "What would you like to have me do today?"

"Get these parts off the floor the first thing."

"What—"

But he had turned away. Moon is something over six feet tall, very dark, and so thin that he seems to float rather than walk.

There was a short squat young man who looked like a Mexican moving around in the paper-carpeted area which held the night's accumulation of parts. As I came up, he picked up an armful and headed back toward the racks. I picked up another armful and followed him.

He disposed of his load, moving quickly along the shelves and cribs, and was going to pass me by on his way to the front.

I stopped him.

"Where do these go?" I said.

He glanced at them, pulled several pieces from my arms, and put them up.

"The others don't go here," he said, moving away again.

I moved along with him. "Where do they go, then?"

"Tank flanges to Welding; straps to Sub-assembly; compression-rib brackets to Sheet-metal."

"How come they were brought in here?"

"Oh, I don't know. Those straps used to be ours; used to put 'em on out in Final Assembly. Routing's wrong on the others."

We were back at the front now.

"Just put 'em down on the floor," he said. "I'll grab a move-boy pretty soon. Want to stack those ribs? They're all ours."

He pointed them out to me and indicated the racks in which they belonged. I loaded a hand-truck, wheeled them back to the racks, and began to unload. It was pretty slow work, and not entirely because of my hangover. The ribs had a tendency to catch on the paper, which had to be put down between layers, and shove it out the other side. And, despite their size, they were so light that a push on one would put the entire stack in disarray.

When noon came I hadn't disposed of more than two-thirds of the ribs, and I was so nervous that I forgot how weak and hungry I was. I went to the toilet and washed, and I had a couple of cigarettes in the yard. Then I came back in and went to work again.

I guess it was around one o'clock when the dark-skinned fellow dropped by. He seemed to have a few minutes to spare.

"How you doing?" he inquired. And, before I could answer, "Say! You're not mixing those together, are you?"

He fingered along the shelves, sliding out one here, one there. "Can't you see the difference in those two? One's slotted on one side and one on the other. And these—see?—the rivet holes are spaced differently. On one kind they come in pairs. In the other they're evenly spaced."

Well, and why the hell didn't you tell me there was more than one kind, I thought. But I just thought it.

"Any others I've mixed up?" I said, weakly.

"You ought to put part of these in your opposite rack. They're a right-hand rib, all right; but they use one of them in each left wing. The same thing goes for the left-hand rib of this type. You've got one left-right rib, and one right-left rib in each wing."

"Here's where I give up," I said. And I meant it.

"You'll catch on in time," he grinned. "That's all it takes is a little time."

"How am I going to straighten this out?"

"Well—" he looked over his shoulder, "I've got an order to throw out to Tailcone, but—but, well, I'll help you."

It must have taken him all of thirty minutes to do the job.

Moon came around just as he had finished.

"Got that tailcone stuff out yet, Murphy?" he said. "They're hollering for it."

I glanced at my dark-skinned acquaintance. Now I might make a mistake on ribs, I thought, but I know a Mexican when I see one. At least, he's certainly no Irishman.

"It's my fault if there's any delay," I said, as he hurried off. "I mixed these ribs up and Murphy was straightening me out."

"How'd you happen to mix 'em up?" asked Moon. "Where's the travelers on them?"

"I don't know," I said. "I don't know what a traveler is."

He turned and jerked his head for me to follow him. At the front counter he stopped, and I stopped. He reached down to the shelf beneath it, opened his lunch pail, and took out an apple. He bit into it, chewed and swallowed, and moved over to Gross's desk.

"Gross," said Moon—chomp, chomp—"did you find any wing travelers kicking around today?"

"Yeah," said Gross. "I picked up three—four, I guess it was."

"Let's see 'em."

The travelers were blue cardboard squares covered from top to bottom with print. "They carry every process that goes into the making of a certain part," Moon explained. "They follow the parts right down the processing line, and when they get here we put our count on

'em, and give 'em to Gross who enters 'em in the books.
... Yeah, those ribs you put up will have to be counted.
Gross can do it after while."

"Why I can do it, " I said. "It was my mistake."

"Gross can do it. He's not very busy."

"I'll do it," said Gross.

Moon took a final mouthful of apple, pulled a wooden
box up to the fence, and stepped up on it. About fifty
feet away a guard was leaning against a pillar, his back
to us. Moon took a slow unhurried look around the plant,
brought his arm back deliberately, and hurled the apple
core. It struck the guard on the framed front of his cap,
pushing it down over his eyes, bounced high into the air
and landed in the cockpit of a plane.

Moon stepped down, unsmiling. "Now, let's get busy,"
he said, "and sweep this place out."

5

GROSS WAS DIRECTLY BEHIND ME WHEN I PUNCHED OUT my card, and he followed me through the gate.

"Got a ride home?" he asked.

"No, I haven't," I said.

"Why don't you walk down here with me to my car?"

I said thanks, I'd appreciate it, and we walked along together, working our way through the double stream of traffic that was already beginning to flow toward Pacific Boulevard.

"What do you think of that guy, Moon?" he asked. "Did you ever see anybody so screwy in your life?"

I laughed. "He's got his peculiarities, all right."

"He's crazy," said Gross, "and I don't care who tells him I said so. He's been riding me ever since I went to work here."

I was rather anxious to divert the conversation to another subject. "Have you been here quite a while?"

"I've been in the plant four months. I only started in the stockroom three weeks ago. I worked down in Drop-hammer the rest of the time."

"You like this work better?"

"I'd like it if Moon wasn't so crazy and wouldn't ride me all the time. I ain't used to that riding. He don't like me because Personnel put me in there without asking him about it. I went over and talked to the personnel man, see; told him about my education, and how I wanted a chance to use it. We had a real nice talk. He's a nice fellow. He's quite a sports fan, and when he found out I was All-American, he really got interested. A few days after that they fired the bookkeeper they had in the stockroom—even Moon admits he wasn't any good —and gave me the job."

He stopped and opened the door of an old Chevrolet sedan.

"What do you think of Murphy?" he said, one foot on the running board.

"How do you mean?" I said.

Gross snorted. "Did you ever see anyone that looked more like a Mexican in your life?"

"Well—no."

"And he calls himself *Murphy!* I think they ought to do something about that, don't you?"

"Why—I don't know."

"Say," said Gross, "didn't you just get through saying he was a Mexican?"

"Yes," I said. "I mean—"

"Well, all right, then," he said.

He climbed into the car, settled himself, and looked at me with veiled amusement.

"Oh, I forgot to tell you. This isn't my car; it belongs to another guy. I don't know just when he'll be out, and I think he's going to have a load. Maybe you'd better go on."

"Thanks," I said. "I'll do that."

"Any time I've got my own car," he called after me, "I'll be glad to give you a ride."

"Thanks," I said, without turning around.

I knew he was laughing, and it embarrassed me. It always embarrasses me to see meanness in others, even when it is directed at me. I wince for them.

It wasn't until late that night that I thought about what I'd said and how it would sound repeated to Murphy. And I was confident that it was going to be repeated. It was, because it just isn't natural for me to do or say anything without trouble ensuing. Of course, I could protect myself by going to Murphy first and explaining that Gross had put words in my mouth. But then what if Gross didn't intend to tell Murphy, after all? I'd have started something. Murphy would confront Gross with my story, and I would be called as a witness. If Gross admitted it, I'd be a tattletale. If he said I was lying—well, what could I do?

I don't think I'm actually afraid of Gross. I've had my ears batted down so many times that I know there's nothing to be less fearful of than physical pain. I am only afraid of him in that he can worry me, and I do not know how I can stand much more. I've got to pull myself together.

The next morning, right after I had crossed Pacific and started down the dirt road, a car began to honk behind me. To hear a car horn in San Diego is an unusual thing; I think there's an ordinance against it. I looked around; it was Moon. He was driving a late model Buick, and the front door was swinging open. I hopped in.

When we reached the plant, he parked in a reserved space. And I thanked him and started to get out.

"Wait a minute, Dillon—Dilly. It's only six-thirty."

We lighted cigarettes, and he looked at me appraisingly. He is about thirty, I think.

"We're about the same size, Dilly."

I said yes, we were, wondering what was coming next. I don't think Moon is screwy, as Gross puts it. I think he simply says and does whatever is on his mind.

"I've got the edge on you for weight, though," I said.

"I can't put on any weight," he said. "I can't stop sleeping with my wife."

I laughed.

"Every time I think I'm going to," he said, "she fixes me a big batch of egg sandwiches. I told her last night that that was going to have to last a while, and this morning she fixed me six egg sandwiches for my lunch. You'd think *she'd* been living in China instead of me."

"You were in China?"

"Eighteen months in the interior. Petty officer. The last of my hitch in the navy. . . . Ever do any clerical work, Dilly?"

"Yes. It's not in my line, but I've done it."

"The trouble with keeping records in a place like this," he said, "is that you've got to know parts. Just being a bookkeeper and a typist and so on isn't enough. Now Gross had four months' experience in another plant before he came here, so he knows parts pretty well. At least he should know them pretty well."

"I certainly don't know much about them," I said.

"I'll have to show you around a little," he said. "I've been pretty busy before or I'd've already done it. You remind me of it some time today."

I went into the plant feeling, somehow, better than I had felt in a long time. Of course, I should know, by now, that no one is going to do anything for me unless there is a catch to it. But I keep right on getting caught with my guard down.

The boys in Purchased Parts had received several kegs of bolts and washers, and we had got in very few parts; so I was delegated to help them put their parts in the bins. Thus I witnessed another example of the humor of Busken and Vail.

All these small parts are magnafluxed; that is, they are dipped in a blue-dye bath. Partly to prevent corrosion, I believe; partly to show up any flaws which they may have. Of course, the dye rubs off easily. By the time I had worked five minutes, my hands were dripping with the stuff.

Well, a youth in a white shirt came up to the counter. One of the stock-chasers. Vail quickly slipped on a pair of gloves. Busken darted around behind the racks and went through the gate.

"Why, if it isn't my old pal, Jack!" said Vail heartily, striding forward with his right hand extended and tugging at the glove thereon. "Where you been keeping yourself, Jack?"

"Now, none of your jokes," said Jack, extending his hand nonetheless. "I'm in a—"

Vail immediately shed his gloves and seized the outthrust hand, massaging it vigorously.

"How are you, Jack, ol' boy, ol' boy?" he demanded, rubbing in the dye. "I say, ol' boy, do you think it'll rain? Do you think—"

"You son-of-a-bitch!" snarled Jack. "Leggo, goddammit! I told you I was in a—"

Busken stepped up behind him, and slapped him on the back, clamped two blue palms against the white shirt-sleeves, giggling.

"Why, what's the matter with Jack—he, he?" he inquired. "He, he, he—did 'oo get 'oo 'ittle hands dirty?"

"Yes, I did!" snapped Jack. "This crazy son-of-a-bitch —" Then he saw the havoc that had been done to his shirt. "Why, you bastard!" he yelled. "Look what you done to my shirt! God damn you, if I—"

Vail seized the left hand also; held both in a firm grip.

"Jack's just tired," he informed Busken. "He's been out in the heat too long. You come inside, Jack. It's twenty degrees cooler inside."

He leaned back and pulled, trying to pull the hapless

Jack across the counter. Busken was almost dancing with glee.

"Throw me the broom, Dilly!" he chortled. "We'll give ol' Jack—he, he—a prostate. Want a nice massage, Jackie? He, he!"

I handed him an ordinary kitchen broom, and, standing well out of kicking range, he drew the worn straws slowly between Jack's buttocks. Jack writhed and shrieked with laughter and rage. Busken tickled him delicately upon the testicles. Jack leaped high into the air.

As Busken worked the tormenting broom—and I have never seen anyone put more enthusiasm into a task—Vail tugged. So, gradually, Jack began to slide across the counter.

Midway in the process, Moon came up and stood watching, neither amused nor unamused. Vail turned to him, inquiringly.

"Want something?"

"How long you going to be busy here?"

"Oh, we'll have him over in a minute."

"Better hurry it up. It's about time for the guard to come around."

A moment or so later, Jack was pulled inside. He was a wreck. He could do nothing but stand and curse, and even that not very effectively.

"You'd better get on out of here," observed Moon. "No one's supposed to be in here but employees of the department."

"Damn it!" screamed Jack. "Didn't you see what happened? Do you think—?"

"Well, you go on, now," Moon repeated. "I'm supposed to keep you fellows out of here, and I'm going to do it."

Jack went out the gate muttering, tucking in his ruined shirt.

"You come with me, Dilly," said Moon. "I want you to do some typing."

I walked around to Gross's desk with him. "Let Dilly have your stool, Gross," he said. "I want him to do some typing."

Gross got to his feet. "I can do it."

"You go help Murphy take those propellers over to Service."

Gross reddened. "I thought I was supposed to be the bookkeeper around here."

"Who said you weren't?"

"Well—what're you—why are you— Oh, hell!" He strode off, scowling.

"Now this is a shortage report you're going to type, Dilly," said Moon, handing me two hand-inscribed pieces of paper. "A first-release shortage report. The first release is for twenty-five ships, the second for fifty, and so on. As we really get organized and step up production the size of the releases gets bigger."

"Then, this shortage report," I said, "it's intended to show the parts you need to complete twenty-five ships?"

"That's it. Ordinarily you'd have to take the shortages

from the books, but since you're new, I've done it. Look. Here's your first item—a bulkhead bracket, Number F-1198. We use four of those to a ship. We've issued forty to Final Assembly, and we have forty-three in stock. That gives us a shortage of seventeen. Twenty-five ships would require a hundred parts, and eighty-three from a hundred leaves seventeen."

"I get it," I said.

"Good. Give me an original and four copies, and let's see how fast you can turn them out."

I scoured my hands on my pants, fitted carbon and paper into the typewriter, and got to work. I was nervous, naturally, and the typewriter wasn't all it should have been. But I knocked out that shortage report—composed almost entirely of symbols and figures—in less than half an hour. And it didn't have a single mistake in it.

Rather proudly I handed it to Moon.

He looked at it, looked at me. "What are these smudges?"

"Why, I guess they're from the bolts I was handling," I said. "They're not very bad, are they?"

The question was rhetorical as far as I was concerned. The pages were practically spotless.

"I can't send anything to the office that looks like this," said Moon.

"Well," I said, "I'll wash my hands and do it over."

"Let it go."

"But I don't mind," I protested. "If I haven't done it right, I want the chance to do it over again."

"Let it go," he repeated. "I'll have Gross do it."

"But, listen—"

"I've got another job for you, anyhow."

I spent the rest of the day making parts boxes—probably the most unpleasant job the mind could conceive. The boxes are shipped to us in the form of flat cardboard cutouts. You take one of these, crimp the ends and sides, and smear the back flap with glue. Then you bring the flap over quickly, smearing yourself to the elbows, weight it with sandbags, and stand it on the floor to set. When the back flap is firmly attached, you shake out the sandbags, apply glue to a tough board which fits beneath the front flap, and do the same thing all over again. The box is then complete except for attaching the handle. The screws for the handle, of course, usually split the wood, since you have inserted it with the grain the wrong way, and the job has to be done over.

That glue was like some a guy was supposed to have sold at Ranger, Texas, during the boom; Pop told me about it. Some old farmer had made it up from a secret recipe, and he used to drive around the drilling wells in a horse and buggy peddling it. It would stick anything together. If a man got his hand cut off, he could stick it on with this glue and it would be as good as it ever was. If a string of pipe parted, a little glue would patch it up. The way Pop told it—and I heard the yarn so many times I used to get up and walk out when he'd start on it—it was like this: One day when the farmer was passing a well the driller pulled the rig in, and one of the guy-wire stakes whizzed through the air and hit the farmer's horse, slicing it in two. The farmer wasn't alarmed, of course; he knew what the situation called for. He simply got out a pot of glue and stuck the horse together again. As it happened, however, he didn't stick the two halves together as they originally were. He got two legs pointing one way, two another. But it worked out all right. After that the animal was indefatigable. When he became tired of walking on two of his legs, the farmer would turn him over and let him walk on the other two.

Well . . .

By noon I looked like I was wearing yellow gloves. And the stuff wouldn't come off, as I've implied. I had to eat my sandwiches out of the palms of my hands, and the only way I could get a cigarette was to lift it from the package with my lips.

Gross was vastly amused, although he sympathized with me orally, and reiterated his conviction that Moon was crazy.

When I got home that night, Roberta took me into the bathroom and soaked and scrubbed me. She cried real tears. And after supper she was still so sorry for me that we went over to Balboa Park and sat until we were sure that everyone had gone to bed.

We came home. Everything was quiet. I went into the kitchen and got a drink of water, and I heard her drawing the shades and slipping a chair under the door-knob. I waited a minute before I went in. I left the kitchen light on. Roberta knows how she looks, and she likes a little light. She is the only woman I have ever known who did.

I went in. She had put the pillows from the divan upon the floor, and was lying upon them and her slack suit was by her side. She looked up at me and smiled and cupped her breasts in her hands. And she was more white, more beautiful and maddening than I had ever seen her.

I had seen her that way five thousand times, and now I saw her again. Saw her for the first time. And I felt the insane unaccountable hunger for her that I always had. Always, and always will.

And then I was in heaven and in hell at the same time. There was a time when I could drown myself in this ecstasy, and blot out what was to follow. But now the epigamic urgings travel beyond their periphery, kneading painfully against my heart and lungs and brain. A cloud surrounds me, a black mist, and I am smothered. And the horrors that are to come crowd close, observing, and I feel lewd and ashamed.

There is no beauty in it. It is ugly, despicable. For days I will be tortured, haunted, feeble, inarticulate.

And yet, even during those days. Even tomorrow morning when I first awake. Yes, even an hour from now. . . .

6

I DIDN'T GET PAID FRIDAY.

About two o'clock in the afternoon, Gross asked me if I wanted to get in the check-pool. I asked him what it was.

"Check poker," he explained. "Each check has a serial number on it, and the man with the best serial—the best hand according to poker rules—wins."

"How much does it cost?"

"Two-bits. There's about a hundred in our pool—in this stockroom, and Sheet-metal, and Sub-assembly, and Receiving. Better come in. You might win twenty-five dollars."

"Can you wait until I get my check cashed?" I asked. "I don't have any change."

"Yes, we can do that," he said.

He started to walk away, hesitated: "Say, you only went to work here Monday, didn't you?"

"That's right."

"Well, hell. You won't get any check today. They hold back a week on you."

I couldn't believe him, reasonable as it was. Probably

because I needed that money so badly. I asked Moon about it.

"No, you won't get any today," he admitted. "The time is always made up a week late. You'll get paid for this week next week."

My face must have shown my feelings.

"What's the matter?" he said. "If you absolutely can't make it, Personnel might advance you five or six dollars. They don't like to, but they will sometimes."

"I guess I can make it," I said.

"It seems kind of hard, now, but it's a good thing in the long run. It's pretty nice to know that you've always got a week's pay saved up."

I hated to go home that night. More than usual, I mean. I knew no one would blame me; that is, I couldn't pin them down to blaming me. But there would just be general hell.

When I turned the corner at Second Avenue, I saw a car I recognized sitting in front of the house. So I slipped across our neighbor's yard and went down the driveway until I came to our bedroom. I scratched on the screen, and Roberta came to the window.

"Is that the landlady in there?"

"Yes. Did you get your check cashed?"

"I didn't get any check. I—"

"You didn't get it! Jimmie! Didn't you tell them—"

"Look," I said. "Now stop shouting and listen a minute. They hold back a week's time on everyone. There's nothing I could do about it. It's a company policy. The question is—"

"But didn't you tell them you had to have it? They can't expect you to live on nothing!"

"They don't give a damn whether I live or not. Now the thing to do is go in and tell the old girl what's happened, and that we'll pay her next week."

"Oh, I can't do that, Jimmie!"

"You put her off once, didn't you?" I said. "You rented the place from her. She's never met me. If I go in, she'll think it's a run-around sure enough."

"How are we going to buy groceries?"

"Let's not worry about that now. Go in—"

"But we don't have anything for supper, Jimmie. I don't know what we'll do—"

"Are you going in there and tell her?" I said.

"No, I'm not," said Roberta. "Tell her yourself."

"Well call Mom back then and have her tell her."

Roberta's face hardened. "I'm not asking Mom to do anything! She's already taken my head off once today. Just because I said Frankie didn't wash the bathtub out —and I wasn't mad at all, Jimmie—I was just as friendly as could be. I just remarked that it would make things so much easier on all of us if each one would—"

"Roberta," I said, "are you going to do what I asked you to, or not?"

"No, sir, Jimmie. I am not."

"That's fine," I said. "See you in the morning, maybe."

"Jimmie! *Jimmie!* Where do you think you're going?"

"What's it to you?"

"Jimmie! You can't—"

"Good-by," I said.

"You can't do this, Jimmie!"

"See if I can't!" I said grimly.

And Fate accepted the invitation.

Mack, Jo, and Shannon came roaring around the corner of the house and threw themselves upon me.

"Daddy!" they shouted. "Daddy! Daddy! Daddy! Did we get paid? Can we count the money? Can we have some—"

Above the turmoil I heard Mom's voice, starched with amusement. "I believe Mr. Dillon's here now. If you'll just wait a moment . . ."

I went in. It wasn't as bad as I expected. In one way, that is.

The old girl is one of those people who are nuts about writers—any kind—and she'd actually read some of my stuff. So, instead of being a deadbeat, I was an eccentric. I was working in aircraft to get material for a book; she said so herself. As for the money—well, of course, I will have to have it, Mr. Dillon, but next Friday will be perfectly all right. I know how it is with you writers. You're always forgetting and mislaying, and—ha, ha, ha—oh, yes, indeedy! I know how you are! Ha, ha, ha.

Ha, ha, ha. . . .

I sat there smirking, nervous as a worm in a fish pond,

hoping to God that Shannon wouldn't take a notion to beat up on her, or that Mack wouldn't do something in her hat, or that Jo wouldn't say something scathing.

Finally, about six, I laughed her out the door.

It was lucky I got her out when I did. At five after six Frankie and Clarence arrived. Clarence is Portuguese, an ex-fisherman now employed as a carpenter in the ship-yard where Frankie works. They had an unknown quantity of beer inside them, and they were carrying a sixty-pound tuna.

I HAD TO WORK SATURDAY. WHEN I WAS HIRED, I WAS TOLD
that I would work five eight-hour days a week. But Moon
says we will probably be working every Saturday, and
perhaps some Sundays from now on. The Government
wants planes and wants them now.

That is all right with me. I'd as soon—rather—stay at
the plant than go home; and anything over forty hours
a week pays time-and-a-half. And I must have more
money.

I've said that I wasn't happy when I had money any
more than I am now. That's only relatively true. As I
remember, Pop didn't get along much better with us
when he had money than when he was broke, although
God knows that wasn't our fault. But we were a little
more chary about jumping down his throat, and the
same thing applies in my case. Things weren't as bad
when I had money. Roberta had some way of entertain-
ing herself besides keeping me in an uproar. I could give
Mom a lift instead of saying I don't know what to do
either. When things got too bad, I could hide out in a
hotel for a day or two. Or take a trip. Or—well, just get

up and walk around the block and come back when I got ready.

No, I can't even do that now. It sounds ridiculous, but I can't. I've tried it, and there's always trouble. Of course, if I will explain the exact route I am going to take, and why I want to go out, and when I will be back, and allay any suspicions arising from the fact that I want to be alone, then I can go. If I want to.

Roberta and I have been over and over this matter, and it is always the same:

"But, Jimmie. What if I just got up and walked out? What would you think?"

"Do you really want to do things like that, too, Roberta?"

"I feel like it sometimes. What would you think if I got up and walked out, and didn't say where I was going or when I was coming back? You'd think it was mighty funny, wouldn't you?"

"I suppose I would."

"Don't you see that when I want to know where you are it's just because I love you so much? You wouldn't like it if I didn't care, would you?"

"No."

"I get awfully tired sitting around the house all day, too, Jimmie. I don't think I'm asking too much when I want to go walking with you."

"Oh, of course you're not, honey—"

"And the children just worship you—you know that—

and they get to be with you so little. Don't you like to be around them any more?"

"Oh, Roberta!"

"Well?"

Well?

I don't know.

I think money would help.

Frankie gáve us an extra week in advance on her board, so, what with the tuna, we had enough to scrape by on. We had an awfully good dinner Saturday night—baked tuna, and whipped potatoes, and avocado salad—the first good meal we've had since I don't know when. I'd had a good bath and put on my suit of clothes. Frankie'd brought home half a pint of gin someone had donated to her, and we'd all had Tom Collinses. The children were so busy stuffing themselves that they couldn't start anything, and—well, everything was swell. I had a week's work behind me, and Roberta's thigh was pressing against mine, and she was laughing at some joke Frankie was telling, and Mom was getting off some wisecracks of her own. And—it was simply swell. I felt so good that tears came into my eyes.

Then Jo said, "Will you please transmit the tubers?"

Roberta looked at her and stopped smiling. "Now none of your smartness," she said. "If you want something, ask for it right."

Jo stopped smiling also. "I want some potatoes, please."

"Why don't you ask for them, then?"

"All right, Mother," said Jo. "Please pass the potatoes."

I passed them. I was mad, but I wanted to get over it, and I thought I'd better pass it off as a joke. Jo can take a lot if you give her a joke to chase it with.

"We don't allow foreign languages around here," I said. "Absolutely no English."

She grinned half-heartedly, watching Roberta out of the corner of her eyes.

"That's right," said Roberta. "Go ahead and laugh. You and your daddy think you're awfully smart, don't you?"

"Leave her alone, honey," I said. "Let's finish one meal in peace."

"Jo didn't mean anything, did you, Jo?" said Mom.

"I meant what I said," said Jo.

"I know what she meant," snapped Roberta. "She can just stay in after dinner and do the dishes. That'll take some of the smartness out of her."

"May I go out afterwards?" asked Jo. "I'm supposed to practice a play with—"

"No, you may not go out afterwards! You'll go to bed. I'm getting tired of you gadding around all hours of the night."

"Mama mean to Jo," Mack observed wisely.

Roberta whirled and slapped him, and his fat face puckered and he bawled. Shannon's eyes flickered dangerously. She will beat the stuffing out of Mack herself, but it infuriates her to see anyone else touch him. She slid under the table. Roberta knew what was coming, and she tried to kick her chair back; she even kicked Shannon. But, of course, that wouldn't stop her. In a split second Shannon had buried her teeth in Roberta's leg.

Roberta let out a scream that they must have heard down on the waterfront. She got to her feet—or rather foot—stumbled, and fell backward. And Shannon slid out from under the table, following her, and there was blood trickling from the corners of her mouth.

I grabbed her by the legs and pulled, and Roberta screamed louder than ever. She dropped down on the floor, shrieking hysterically, and began striking Shannon in the face. Shaking her by the hair. Clawing, and scratching, and screaming. Screaming for us to do something. To stop standing around and do—OoooooOOO! JIMMIE!

I got Shannon by the nose, and shut off her wind. But she merely held on with her middle teeth, and began to breathe out of the corners of her mouth. Her eyes were wide open, unblinking, and there was a fiendish animal joy in them. I could have choked her loose of course. Or, rather, some people could. I couldn't.

Jo tried tickling her. Mom poured ice water on her until the floor was covered an inch deep. We all threatened—and tried—to blister her. It was useless. It looked as though we were settled there for the night—Roberta sobbing and pleading; Shannon, jaws set, laughing hilariously inside her tiny body.

It was Frankie who got her loose.

"All right, Shannon," she said. "The next time I bring any boys home, just don't expect to be introduced."

Shannon looked at her, hesitated, and opened her mouth. And Roberta jerked free. She had been bitten badly. I know it must have hurt a great deal.

"You've got to spank her, Jimmie," she wailed. "You've just got to take her in hand!"

"Dammit," I said. "I can't spank her!"

And I certainly couldn't have by that time. Shannon had got to the open door and was standing with her back to it.

"Why won't you introduce me, Frankie?" she said.

"Huh! Think I'm going to introduce a cannibal like you to anyone?"

"What's a cannibal?"

"That's what you are. Someone that eats people."

Shannon threw back her head and her falsetto laugh filled the room.

"Jimmie!" snapped Roberta, rubbing her leg. "Are you going to punish that child, or not?"

I got up; and Shannon took pity on me. She ran. By the time I got to the door she had disappeared. I went out and looked around the house and called her. But there wasn't any answer.

I went back inside. "She's gone," I said.

"She'll be all right," said Mom. "She's probably gone

over to the drugstore. She hasn't been over there yet today."

"What's she doing over there? That's three blocks away."

"They give her a nickel's worth of stuff every day to leave them alone."

I turned on Roberta. "You pay them for it, don't you? You don't let her go around blackmailing people?"

"No, I don't," said Roberta. "I didn't ask 'em to give her anything."

"Give me some money," I said.

"What for?"

"What for? Good God, Roberta! What's getting into you? How many other places is she pulling this stunt?"

Mom and Roberta looked at each other.

"Out with it," I said.

"Well, I don't believe she has any other place but the grocery store," said Mom. "And it was—"

"Oh, my God!"

"It was just once, Jimmie," said Roberta. "Just this morning. She wanted some bacon for breakfast, and we didn't have any. So—she went down to the store and got a half-pound."

"Oh God damn!" I said. "Well, I'm going after her. If I've got to bring in the money and buy the groceries and do every other damned thing around here—"

"Keep your shirt on," said Frankie.

"But, Frankie!" I said. "The child isn't five years old yet. What'll she be like when—"

"I'll go get her," said Frankie. "I've got to get a neck-clip, anyway. She can sit in the beauty parlor with me until I'm through."

"Yes, but the money—"

"If you want something to worry about," said Roberta, "you might look at my leg."

And I gave up. Mom and I helped her back to the bedroom and doctored her leg.

Jo went to practice her play.

Frankie went after Shannon.

About ten-thirty, after the others had gone to bed, she and Shannon came in. Shannon threw her arms around me and kissed me and said she was going to be good all next day. And I was relieved, because I knew that she would remember and keep her promise. A promise is a sacred thing with Shannon. I think one reason that she has so little use for us is that we have made so many promises to her that we haven't kept. But that may not be it. If I were she, I'd dislike us just on general principles.

She unfolded one tiny fist and dropped something into my lap. A nickel.

"I didn't get candy," she explained proudly. "I told the man I wanted a nickel. For you to buy whisky with."

I choked and started to swear, and then I thought, Oh, hell, what *is* the use. So I kissed her good-night again, and she and Frankie went to bed.

About fifteen minutes later, when I was settling down

with a magazine, Mom came in wearing the old wrapper she sleeps in and sat down on the lounge.

"I thought you'd gone to bed," I said.

"Frankie woke me up. . . . I wish you'd speak to Frankie, Jimmie."

"What about?"

"You know. About her drinking, and everything."

"Frankie can carry liquor," I said. "She's the one person I've seen that it really did good. She never drinks to keep from feeling bad. It's always to make her feel better."

"Well, it's a bad thing, anyway. It's cheapening and coarsening. She's going to take one drink too many with some of these fellows, and it'll be too bad."

"Frankie's not like that."

"You don't know what she's like. No one does."

"Oh, all right," I said. "I'll speak to her."

"I wish you would. . . . What do you think we'd better do about Pop, Jimmie?"

"Oh, I don't know, Mom," I said. "Look. Haven't we had enough trouble for one evening? Do we have to thresh out everything now?"

"We are going to have to do something, Jimmie."

"Don't I know it? Am I holding back? But I can't think tonight. I just can't."

Mom looked down at her hands. "Do you suppose if I rented a typewriter—"

"Please don't ask me that, Mom."

"Don't you think it's a lot in your own mind, Jimmie? Don't you think that if you really tried—"

I laughed. "That's it," I said. "I haven't really tried. Not really. You get me a typewriter Monday and I'll go to work again."

The sarcasm was wasted on Mom. I might have known it would be. I'm always broadcasting when I should be receiving.

"That's a bargain," she said, getting up. "I'll get the typewriter and have the table cleared for you right after supper. All you'll have to do is write."

All I'll have to do is write. . . .

So I had that to worry about.

I thought I was hungry. I told myself I was. I threw down the magazine and went into the kitchen. I made a big pot of coffee and a plate of tuna sandwiches. I started to eat.

The first sandwich started coming up as I was biting into the second. I kept right on eating. Take it, damn you, I said, you've had your own way long enough. I swallowed, and stuffed a whole sandwich down my throat. I threw my head back, and tossed down a cupful of scalding coffee.

That did it. I strangled and a geyser spewed out, splashing over the walls and floor. I got over the sink, and there was a tidal wave of it. I couldn't stop. I couldn't breathe. There wasn't any more fish in me, but there was plenty of blood. I brought up a cupful with every gasp. I didn't have to cough. A deep breath was enough to start it rolling.

Then Roberta was there with her arm around me. She sat me down in a chair and fed me cold water.

"What have you been doing to yourself, Jimmie?"

"Nothing," I whispered.

"Did you really want a drink that bad?"

"No," I said. "I just thought I wanted one. Besides, we don't have the money to throw away."

"You sit there," she said. "Don't move. I'll be right back."

She went back into the bedroom, and then I heard the front door close. And through the dinette window I saw her hurrying down the sidewalk, her fur coat over her nightdress.

She was back in a minute—not more than three, anyway—with a pint of whisky. I took a stiff drink before I told her that she shouldn't have bought it.

"It was my money," she said. "I'd been saving it to take to church. It's been so long since I took anything— anything like that—Jimmie. And you're supposed to, and I hated to go any more without doing it. And— and—"

"Honey," I said. "Oh, for Christ's sake. . . ."

I guess I had forgotten how much Roberta did and does love me. I guess I have wanted to forget. You cannot fight a person who loves you, and I have had to fight.

But, now. Well, I know what the Church means to Roberta, and I knew that in her own mind she had damned herself a little by diverting that dollar from its original destination. That dollar—the seven cents she had chiseled from Mom was probably part of it. I remembered all over again.

I was going to school at the University of Nebraska, and Lois, my partner in so many nights of love, had been married a month. And I was, to put it politely, on the make. I met Roberta at a school mixer (they were not exclusively for students). I rubbed her and felt her, and she didn't seem to mind. So the next night I took her for a ride; and the night after that I took her to another dance. It was still all right. I could go as far as I liked.

Well, I had observed the best fraternity traditions. I'd shown her a good time. I hadn't got her drunk or told her she'd have to walk or ride. It was just a case of two people wanting something they knew would be good. Or so I thought.

We went up to my room.

I said, "Don't you want to take your dress off? It might get wrinkled."

She took off her dress and lay down again.

I said, "How about those other things? Can I help you?"

She said, "Does it hurt very much?"

I didn't get it for a minute. "You're not sewed into them, are you?"

"You know what I mean," she said. "I don't mind, but if it's going to hurt I want to know. So I won't holler."

"Look," I said, "are you a—haven't you ever done this before?"

"I certainly have not!"

"Well—well, what the hell are you doing here then?"

"Why you know. I love you."

"Well, look, honey," I said. "I appreciate it, and all that, but—but I don't want it that bad. You'll love some other guy later on, and—"

"No, I won't. Now, show me how."

"But—but, baby," I said. "I won't let you do this."

And she said, calmly, "You may as well. I'll never love anyone but you. No one will ever have me but you."

I was never any good at arguments.

Two months later when Jo was conceived, we got married. I didn't have to marry her; she made that very clear. But she also made it clear that wherever I was, there she was going to be, forever and always. I thought it might be inconvenient to have her and children around without a marriage license. So—

But, as I was saying, there is one thing I am sure of. Roberta loves me. She loves me so much that she doesn't give a whoop whether I go to heaven or hell if she can go along. She would, in fact, prefer hell. I would need her there. I might not—I might see someone I liked better—in the other place.

That is Roberta. I didn't mind so much that Saturday night.

We moved in to the lounge, and she took a nip or two from the bottle so that the whisky on my breath wouldn't bother her. And then we sat and talked about everything under the sun. I said I was going to get ahold of myself, and be different, and she said I didn't need to be different. However or whatever I was, she'd love. She said she was the one that was going to be different—"I know I'm hateful and cross and mean, Jimmie, but it seems like I just can't help it. I'm always sorry afterwards, but I can't help it at the time. But I'm going to be different from now on; really, I am."

That's the way the evening ended. Not quite, but we've covered the other matter.

There was an armistice all day Sunday.

I almost felt good Monday morning. Mom fixed my breakfast, and I actually ate some.

"You still want me to get the typewriter, Jimmie?" she said.

"Sure. I'm going to sit down tonight and beat the holy hell out of it."

Gross picked me up in a new Ford just as I'd crossed Pacific.

"You see, that really wasn't my car the other night," he said. "This is my car. I mean it's the one my wife's folks bought for her."

"It's a nice car," I said.

"Yeah," he said. "I already heard plenty about how nice it is. I wish I could tell 'em to take it and ram it."

"In-laws are funny people," I said.

"They ain't to me. I don't know what to do sometimes. I thought, maybe, if I could get a little clerical experience I might get some kind of civil service job. That would be nice and dignified, and it would pay pretty good."

I kept him talking about himself. I knew, if I didn't, the conversation would turn to my private affairs.

When he left college, he said, he'd played pro football for two years. Then he'd begun to lose his speed, and they'd canned him, and he'd joined the army. They discharged him after eleven months because of a permanently disabled ankle. . . . He received a seven-dollar compensation check from the Government every month. He'd gone from the army into aircraft work. He didn't say so, but it was apparent that he was fit for nothing but manual labor.

We walked into the plant together. Moon was at the desk examining the books.

"I see you haven't straightened these out yet, Gross," he said ominously.

"I'm making headway," Gross protested. "The things are crazy, Moon. And you know how it is—half the time I don't know when stuff is brought in or taken out of here."

"Dilly," said Moon, "do you think you can handle these books?"

"Why—" I began. "Why, I—"

"I think you can," Moon said. "Gross, show Dilly the ropes. When you get through, you can start dusting the racks."

EARLY LAST WINTER I WAS COMING OUT OF THE POST office in Oklahoma City when I ran into Mike Stone. I told him I'd just been up to the recruiting station, trying to join the army.

It was the day Mike had been released under 50,000-dollar bond on a criminal syndicalism charge, and he undoubtedly had many things on his mind. But he stopped to inquire into my troubles, regardless.

"I don't think a change of scenery is going to help you, Dill," he said. "But—but if you've just got to go some place, how about the West Coast? Our attorney borrowed a car from his brother at San Diego when he was out there on vacation, and he's got to send it back. If you want to take it, your transportation won't cost you anything."

It sounded pretty good. If I got out there on a limb, sort of, maybe the foundation would extend my fellowship. Or maybe I could connect with one of the Hollywood studios. I went home.

"Well," said Roberta, "where's your uniform? I thought you'd be on the way to Fort Sill, by now. They didn't turn you down because you had a wife and three children, did they?"

"Jimmie was probably afraid they'd make him sleep on the ground," said Mom. "I never saw such a boy always to be afraid he'd get an ant or a little worm on him or something."

"You ought to join the Foreign Legion, Jimmie," said Frankie. "You could get some good material for stories."

I said, "Get my things packed. I'm going to California."

"Ho-hum," said Roberta. "Can you folks eat macaroni and cheese for lunch?"

"I'm going in a car. Mike Stone's lawyer is going to give me his car to go in."

Roberta came alive then. So!—I'd been chasing around with those filthy Reds again. Well, she hoped they'd send me over the road with the rest of the crowd; it'd serve me right.

"Jimmie, you mustn't have anything to do with them," Mom said. "We've already got about all the trouble we can stand."

Frankie said, "I always liked Mike. What's the deal? Maybe I'll go along. I'm getting doggoned tired of cashiering for fifteen a week and getting docked for shortages I don't make."

"I'm going by myself," I said. "As soon as I get settled and see how things are, I'll send for the rest of you. Roberta, when my check comes, wire me forty and keep the rest."

"You're not going any place but to jail," said Roberta. "I warn you, James Dillon: If you even look like you're going to—"

"I don't know, Roberta," said Mom. "It might be all right. There's really nothing I've got to stay here for, and Frankie ought to get away from Chick. I don't see how she stands him slobbering and sulking around all the time."

"Oh, Chick's all right, Mom," said Frankie. "He just doesn't know quite how to take you people. And he gets blue and disgusted because he doesn't have a better job."

"If he goes, I'm not," said Mom. "The reason he doesn't get anywhere is because no one likes him. He's just a big sulking calf."

"No one's going but me," I said.

"Don't be such a pig, Jimmie," said Frankie.

"You wouldn't want us to stay here, just barely getting by, if we could do well out there, would you?" asked Mom.

"I've been trying to think what I could wear," said Roberta. "I guess my green slack suit would be the best."

"Now, look here!" I said. "You folks just can't get up and tear off like this. It's absolutely crazy!"

"Well, of course if you don't want us—" said Mom.

"He's always trying to get away from me, Mom," said Roberta. "Ever since we got married. He's not going to, though."

Well—we came to California.

I felt pretty sorry for Chick. Chick is an expert mechanic on pin-ball machines and other gambling devices; it's probably the only thing he's any good at. Since they were outlawed in the Southwest, he's had to work at anything he could get at about a fourth of what he used to make. There really wasn't room for him in the car, and we did promise we'd look out for him. But, after we got here, we were so busy looking out for ourselves that we couldn't be bothered a great deal. He wrote Frankie a rather nasty letter, then one to the family in general. So now none of us knows quite what to do. Frankie wants to see him, I'm sure. But Mom and Roberta are so angry still that seeing him would mean not seeing them. So—

I don't know why the family is so damned casual about some things and so intense about others.

I couldn't get an extension on my fellowship; they were afraid that the war would so change things that any material I gathered would have no value. Or so they said. I wrote to a couple of Hollywood writers I'd corresponded with. They didn't reply. (And I didn't blame them.) Fawcetts was willing to give me a try at studio gush and gossip, but the Hays office wouldn't accredit me. There were too many writers only half-living in Hollywood already.

In the end, I went out to the aircraft factory, hoping they wouldn't hire me and wondering what I'd do if they didn't. And that's about all.

It's hard to say how I feel about the place. I'd like to

be disinterested, but I can't and hold my job. And, as jobs go, it's no worse than any would be that I *had* to hold. It's just something to endure, something to live through, numb yet painfully aware of what is going on around me. It's like—well, I'll try to give you an example.

Three months after Mack was born a doctor acquaintance of mine performed a vasectomy on me. It was around Christmas, and the only payment he exacted was ten fingers out of a quart of rye; in advance, yes. I think he must have served an apprenticeship at cutting out baseball covers, because I was going around in a sling for weeks afterward. But what I started to say was—to strike a parallel with my job—it drove me nuts without actually hurting at all. I was so shot full of local that he could have trimmed out my appendix without hurting me. But that snipping and slicing finally got me so bad that I raised up and whanged the hell out of him, and he had to sit on my chest to finish.

9

THE PLANT, IN THIS, MY FOURTH WEEK, IS BEGINNING TO make a little sense. There is still a great deal that confuses me, but I am getting a vague idea of what it's all about. I should have sooner, but for my timidity.

On the day I took over Gross's job, Moon remembered his promise to show me around. We went down to the Drop-hammer Department, first, and watched the manifolds and other castings being pounded out. They are as large as a small room, some of these hammers, and when they are dropped the concrete floor shakes for hundreds of feet around. The men are the huskiest I've seen, and you can see just about all of them because they're practically naked. Their bodies, and particularly their arms, are covered with scars from the splattering metal and from cleaning out the hot pots.

I didn't think that was as it should be. There are very few things with which I can't find something wrong. I suggested to Moon that it would be better if they bundled themselves against the heat and other hazards of their work as cooks do.

He replied, "These men have been working this way a long time and they probably know what's best."

We only looked through the door of the Plannishing Department, and that was enough to give me a headache for the rest of the morning. Here the castings are run back and forth through a series of rapidly moving hammers until they are beaten smooth; and the noise is too frightful to describe. It has no cadence; you can't accustom yourself to it. Every one of the hundreds of thousands of blows of the hammers rips right through you.

Through a side door leading into the yard, I noticed several men wandering idly around, massaging their ears and heads, smoking but not talking.

"Some of the plannishing boys," said Moon. "They get a rest period every half-hour or so. Have to have it or they'd go nuts."

"I suppose they get pretty good money," I said.

"Not so much. They're here because they can't get out of it. At least, most of them are. They're put in here, not knowing what plannishing means, and pretty soon they begin to build up seniority so they hang on, hoping they'll get a break and be transferred to some other department. If the company gives you a transfer, you know, you don't lose your seniority. But if you demand it, they can start you in in a new department at a beginner's rate. That's pretty hard to take. When you've been in a department four months, you draw twelve and a half cents an hour above the minimum—a dollar a day more.

A man with a family is going to do a lot of thinking before he gives that up."

"But most of these fellows are just kids," I said. "They're not old enough to have families. I should think—"

Moon gave me one of his solemn looks which, someway, have the effect of making me feel even more the idiot than I am.

"Ever hear of the draft act, Dilly?"

"Yes. Of course, I have."

"Well, where do you think these young fellows would be if the company didn't want to have them deferred?"

Well . . .

I didn't have any suggestions that time.

We went out to the carpenter shop where the wing spars are made, and then we came back inside and started up the sheet-metal forming line. It's called a line, but it's actually four, each about fifty yards long. Each line consists of possibly a hundred benches and workmen; practically every operation is done with handtools. At the beginning of the "line" is a metal-crimping machine, from which the parts come in rough form. From this they go from bench to bench, each man doing his particular little task, until the last bench is reached. There, the move-boys pick them up and trundle them off to the paint and dope shops.

That is as far as I got. In fact, I didn't get quite that far; I progressed only far enough to reach certain conclusions. Midway in an explanation of one of the processes, Moon abruptly excused himself and hurried off. And in something less than five minutes a company guard had me by the elbow and asked me what I was doing.

10

"I'M A NEW MAN," I SAID. "MY LEAD-MAN HAS BEEN showing me around."

"Who is your lead-man?"

I told him.

"Where'd he go to?"

"I don't know."

"Let's take a look at your identification card."

I gave him my card, and he studied it carefully, looking now and then from it to me. Rather reluctantly, I thought, he handed it back.

"I guess it's all right," he said. "But don't waste any time. We're all here to work."

I went on by myself, and the fifteen minutes or so I spent wandering around before I returned to the stock-room were, of course, absolutely wasted. I didn't take time to see very much, and what I did see meant nothing. I was that badly frightened. I naturally told Moon I'd made out all right; I didn't dare risk another interview with a guard.

So, as I say, I've had to pick up little by little what I should have known at the start.

Only a relatively small number of the parts which I

saw being made that day reach us. Hundreds of them come through as parts of assemblies. Others are being made for other plants. For instance, we make manifolds for several factories; we have the men and equipment to make them with and they don't. For the same reason we have to buy stuff from them. No aircraft factory is self-sufficient. The items which we sell or buy vary from day to day, depending upon the availability of labor, equipment, and materials.

I have, in all, four types of parts to keep record on: assembly, sub-assembly, and regular assembly-line issue. The fourth consists of parts such as cowling and fire-walls, which, because they are bulky and difficult to handle, go direct to the assembly line—a fact which does not excuse us from keeping track of them. When a plane reaches a certain stage, it has a definite number of parts. We—I—am supposed to know what those parts are, regardless of whether I have seen them, and to show them as having been issued.

There is something screwy about this. When I think of what it is, I will tell Moon about it. I am also going to find out why we are constantly short on some parts and invariably long on others.

We issue, or try to issue, parts in units of twenty-five. Not twenty-five pieces of each part, but enough for twenty-five planes. A flap requires only one nose-cover, but it uses sixteen ribs of a certain type. So the unit number on the nose-cover is 1, but it is 16 on the rib.

The release books are, at first glance, the ultimate in

simplicity. The first, which is our major concern since we have not yet completed twenty-five planes, consists of twelve bills-of-material, one for each station. On the left side of the bill is the part number, its description, and the unit number. On the right, opposite each number, are twenty-five squares. When a part is received—say, forty-eight pieces of L-1054, which has a unit number of six—I draw a wavy line through eight of the squares opposite that number. When the forty-eight pieces are issued, I merely block the squares in.

But—instead of getting forty-eight pieces I may get forty-nine. Then I must carry my wavy line through eight and one-sixth squares, and they are extremely tiny. If six were the maximum unit number, I might stay somewhere near straight, as far as this particular difficulty is concerned. But the unit number on some parts runs up to one hundred and sixty-four. And there's no way on God's green earth of splitting the squares that fine.

I told Moon about it; and a lot of good that did.

"Well," he said, feeling in his pocket for an apple, "a few pieces like that don't make much difference, Dilly. Just do the best you can."

"But it's not just a few pieces," I said. "You've got seven releases—seven hundred and fifty ships—or a total of thirty bills of material for each assembly station. By the time you multiply even a very small error by thirty you're going to be in one hell of a mess."

"Well," he said again, "what do you want to do about it?"

I didn't know. "I'm just trying to explain why the records are off," I said. "I just didn't want you to think it was my fault."

He climbed up on my stool on his knees and hurled the apple core over the fence. And far down the line, above the whine of unishears and the boop-boop of the rivet guns, there rose a yell.

"Well, as long as it's only a few pieces, Dilly—"

"But, Moon. I just got through saying—"

"—we don't care."

He sauntered off.

That was in my third week here, and this is the end of my first month. And I'm beginning to catch on to things better. But it seems like the more I understand, the less I know—the more trouble I find.

The design for our plane hasn't been frozen yet. Engineering changes are being made every day—almost every hour. And they're completely balling up our records system which is static in design. We're getting through dozens of parts that aren't on the bills of material. Some of them are effective on the first plane; some on the tenth; and so on. And I don't know how the hell to show the things. I don't know whether they're replacing other parts or whether they're outright additions.

Moon says if they're not on the bills of material, why to hell with them; and I have let a lot of them slip. But that isn't going to do. The stockroom is getting filled with parts that we have no record on, and consequently when we make our issues we're not throwing them out.

This is going to mean only one thing in the end. The Government will reject the planes because they do not meet specifications; and a certain stockroom bookkeeper is going to be on the spot.

And, still, that isn't all.

When a part is replaced or supplemented by another, the unit number on the original part is naturally changed. For example, where, at one time, seventy-five pieces of a part were required to complete twenty-five ships, we may now use only fifty. But—but what in the hell are you going to do when your records show that you've already issued more than enough of the first part for twenty-five planes? Where are you going to put the supplementary or additional parts?

I can see where the difficulty is. The fact that we have issued parts for twenty-five planes doesn't necessarily mean that the assembly station has put them to productive use. They've been ruined, or rejected by inspection. Knowing this, however, doesn't help.

I talked to Moon about it (and he, by the way, seems to be getting a little weary of my talking).

"Well, what do you want to do about it, Dilly?"

"The office must keep a record on scrapped and rejected parts. I want to see it."

"They don't know anything up there. The only way they know about scrapped parts is when they start running short. And you can't prove they've been scrapped, then. The guys out in Final will say that our records are wrong—that they never got the parts."

"But the office would know by checking on raw stores—"

Moon shook his head complacently. "No, they wouldn't, Dilly. You've got Experimental and Testing to reckon with. And then we're swapping and lending stuff all the time to other plants. Up in Purchased Parts this morning I noticed we had an invoice for forty static-ground tailwheel tires. We paid for 'em and we received 'em, but we don't have them on hand and Final Assembly doesn't have them. God knows where they are."

"If I could just get a report on rejections, then—"

"Wouldn't do any good. When a part is rejected, it goes to the chief inspector. If he rejects it, it goes back to the department responsible for the flaws. They let it lay around a while, and then if it can't be reworked and sent back to Final, they scrap it and send the rejection tag up to the office. Or, maybe, if rejections have been running heavy against them, they throw it away. Anyway you look at it, though, we don't learn about the rejection for weeks, and it's too late then to help us."

I didn't say anything, but I guess I looked a lot.

"Don't let it get you down, Dilly," said Moon ."You're doing all right. As well as could be expected."

So that's the way things are. Or were. For they're getting worse by the moment. I can't say that I'm bored any more. I don't say that the work is beneath me. It would take a genius to work his way out of this mess.

I don't know what in the name of God to do. I've

been cutting down on the liquor at night, so that my head will be clear, but it makes me so restless and sleepless that I'm not sure it's a good idea. I've tried to talk to Roberta about it, and Mom, and Frankie, but they're no help. Some of Roberta's old prophecies are coming true, and she's more interested in seeing me repent than anything else. Anyway, she doesn't know anything. Mom says I worry too much. And Frankie says they really can't pin anything on me, if it comes to a showdown, and just to tell 'em all to go jump in the lake. Jo, for one, has made a sensible suggestion. She says I ought to get some books on accounting. But—I don't know. I'm afraid it would take me so long to learn anything that it would be too late to help. And, anyway, I've got to write at night. I told Mom I would and I can't let her down. She's already making over her old suit to go back and see Pop in. I don't know what she'll do after she sees him, but—

The hell—the bad part about it is that I can't quit. There was a young fellow over in one of the other plants who had a grudge against his foreman. He thought a good way of getting even would be to change the labels on a number of the parts' cribs. He did it, and then he quit. And three months later the FBI picked him up on the East Coast. I don't think they'll be too hard on him because he comes from a good Republican family, and his father's a Legionnaire. But me— Oh, good God Almighty! The stuff I've written; my friends and asso-

ciates; the car I came out here in. If I mess things up—
or if things get messed up where I am—what'll it look
like?

Don't tell me.

I've studied and I've thought and I've worn a path in
the concrete sidewalk around our house from walking at
night. And still I don't know what to do. Jesus, I don't
know—

If I could just calm down. If I could just do that. And
I have tried, and you see how it turns out. I used to
work as a posting-clerk for a seed and nursery company.
When our books wouldn't balance, we'd start copying
from one ledger into another until, when we reached
our mistake, our pencils warned us of it. And I've tried
to do much the same thing here. Without anticipating
any problem, I've tried to—

And it's no go. I've just wound up as usual. Too rat-
tled to know my head from my hatband.

You're probably wondering about Gross. So am I.

All I can say is he's been a lot more decent—on the
surface—than I would have been in the same circumstances; and that I feel tremendously sorry for him.

When I left the plant today, Saturday, he said that
he had to go to town anyway and that, if I wanted him
to, he'd drive me home. I accepted. I wouldn't have, if
Moon had been around, because I'm pretty sure that
anyone who is friendly with Gross won't be with Moon.
But Moon had already gone.

On the way Gross said, "I'm glad you took over the books. I wanted Moon to let me off of them."

"Glad I could help you out," I said. "They are pretty much of a headache."

"Haven't got them straightened out yet, huh?"

"No."

"I thought Moon said you were an A-1 bookkeeper."

I didn't say anything.

"I guess you think I don't know how to keep books. I suppose you told Moon you couldn't fix up the books because I made so many mistakes."

"I haven't discussed you with Moon," I said. "If you want to let me out I'll walk the rest of the way."

"No, you won't either," he said. "I was just talking."

When we reached the house, I thanked him and started to get out.

"Wait a minute," he said. "I want to show you something."

While I watched, he took an old envelope and a fountain pen from his pocket, and, after several preliminary gyrations of his hand, executed a picture of a bird with one flourish.

"Can you do that?" he asked.

I admitted that I couldn't.

"Well—keep that, then," he said regally, and tossed it into my lap.

Of course, I had to ask him to autograph it. And I'll be damned if he didn't do it!

MY FIFTH WEEK—MORE ACCURATELY, THE BEGINNING OF the sixth.

Things at the plant are in a worse tangle than ever; I've got a raise; Shannon has been very sick.

There's not much use talking about the first item.

The raise I got last Friday. I was working away at the books for dear life—I mean that literally—when Moon and a little fellow I'd seen wandering around the plant but had never paid much attention to came up to my desk.

"Dilly," said Moon, "Mr. Dolling wants to talk to you. Mr. Dolling is the superintendent of all the stockrooms."

There wasn't the slightest change in his voice or expression, I'm positive; he was as lackadaisical and phlegmatic as always. And, yet, somehow, I sensed a sneer, and I think Dolling sensed it also.

Dolling is barely five feet tall, pot-bellied, sandy of hair (what little he has), and he has a voice that would awaken any dead who weren't completely decomposed. There is a rumor that he owns a big slice of stock in the company, but I don't know whether it's true.

He looked at Moon sharply. "All right. Thank you."

Moon said, "Don't mention it," and walked away.

Dolling turned back to me. "Mr. Moon," he said, in his rodeo-announcer's voice, "tells me that you are a very conscientious worker."

"Well—thank you," I said.

"I've noticed a small improvement in things myself," he continued, bellying up to the desk so that he was at my side instead of facing me. "Did you understand the conditions under which you went to work here?"

"Why, I don't know exactly what you mean," I said. "I believe I understood them."

"According to company policy—a long-established policy—any man who passes our thirty-day probationary period is entitled to a four-cent raise. We state this very clearly in the company rule book. But we don't run this company any more; the union runs it. They gave us a contract and we signed it with a gun at our heads. And the contract—the union contract, mind you, not ours—specifies that any man who has worked here sixty days and is not drawing fifty-eight cents an hour is entitled to demand a raise to that amount. It says nothing whatever about raising you to fifty-four cents after thirty days. Now I have nothing against the union whatsoever. If a man in this company wants to join the union, I will not persuade him to do otherwise. I definitely will not say, and I am not saying, anything against the union. Understand?"

"Of course," I said.

"I'm just explaining our position. Before, it was our policy to raise all approved probationers to fifty-four cents. Now, since the union doesn't care, why should we?"

"I suppose you shouldn't," I said.

"But Moon tells me you're a good man," he said. And paused for confirmation.

"Thank you."

"And I must say that in this case I believe Moon is right"—pause.

"Thank you, sir."

"You seem to be the type of man we like to have around. Industrious"—pause.

"Yes, sir."

"Sober."

"Yes—sir."

"Conservative."

"Y-yes, s-sir."

"So we are raising you to fifty-four cents an hour, effective this pay period. That's all."

He paced away, hands folded behind his back.

When Moon showed up again, I started to tell him about the raise, but he'd already heard about it he said.

"I was just down in Plannishing," he said. "I didn't

have any trouble hearing while he was talking to you."

Well—four cents an hour isn't much, only a couple of dollars extra on the week, but it did make me feel kind of good. And I suppose the folks saw how I felt and they didn't kid me about it even when I invited it by kidding myself. Everyone said that the company must think a lot of me to make an exception like that.

After a good deal of very friendly debate we decided to spend the extra two on a Sunday dinner, with me planning and preparing the menu. I can cook, you know; I mean I did it, many years ago, for a living.

I started for the store, and Shannon asked me if she could go along. And of course I said she couldn't, because I was afraid she might start something. I should have known that there was something wrong with her or she wouldn't have asked; she'd've just gone. But I didn't think, and surprisingly enough she didn't come anyway. She just got up and went back into the bedroom and closed the door.

She wasn't around at supper time, but we didn't think anything of it; she's in the habit of keeping her own hours. But along about eight o'clock we began to get worried and we started looking for her. I won't tell you where all we looked—I even went clear down to the bay. To make it short, I found her in the closet in our bedroom. I'd gone in there to get a jacket because it was getting kind of cool, and when I lifted it off the hook I knocked some dresses down and I saw Shannon.

She was way back in the corner, sitting on the floor. She'd got Frankie's manicure set and some lipstick and other cosmetics and she was a sight.

"Oh, my God," I said. "Now, what will your mother say? Don't you know we've been looking all over the country for you? Can't you ever behave yourself? Come on out of there!"

She got up and held out her hands, and like a damned fool I didn't understand. "Now don't daub that stuff all over my pants! For Christ's sake come on out and wash yourself and eat something if you want it, and go to bed."

"Don't you think my hands are pretty, Daddy?" she said.

And then I began to catch on. But at that moment Roberta came up. She let out a wild shriek.

"Shannon! Look at your dress! And you've got that stuff all over my suede shoes. And—"

She grabbed her and began to slap her, and Shannon didn't fight back. And then she, Roberta, began to understand and she got down on her knees and hugged and kissed her.

"Of course you're pretty! You're the prettiest girl in this whole wide world! Wasn't that nice of her, Daddy, to make herself so pretty for us? Just think! All this time she was b-back—"

We were all crying—even Jo and Mack. We were all thinking. A little girl, a four-year old, back in that dark closet for four hours. A little girl who had never been wanted—and who, I realize now, knew that she had never been wanted—trying to make herself wanted; fighting at the last ditch with a weapon she had always scorned to use. Trying to make herself pretty. I thought of her fierceness, how with the animal's desperate impulse for survival, she had struggled against neglect and slight. The tantrums she had thrown to secure a new dress or a warm coat; her swiftness in striking before she could be struck; her dogged determination to have the food she desired—and needed. Yes, and her wakefulness, the fear of attack in her sleep.

And I thought of how, during those four years that she had been with us, she must have wept in her heart, even as she fought and screamed; the loneliness that must have been hers; the fear and dread. And I thought Why did it have to be this way, and, as with everything else, I could find no answer. . . .

I was a 125-dollar-a-month editor on the Writers' Project that year. And Pop was losing his mind and I didn't know it. He came to me with a proposition—a lease deal—and it looked good. And I borrowed 250 dollars to swing it. Pop could never give a coherent explanation of where the money went. But it did go, never more to return, and I had fifty dollars a month to pay back out of my salary.

Our rent was forty dollars. You can see how it was.

One night I found Roberta in a faint on the bathroom floor, a swollen twist of slippery-elm bark protruding from her. And I thought she would be pulled apart before we could remove it. But Shannon—the bubble, the egg, whatever you want to call it—held firm. We went to see a woman down in Southtown. She took fifteen dollars from us, and prodded and poked Roberta with something that looked like a bicycle pump. She poked and pulled and pushed for more than an hour, and Roberta bled and fainted and writhed with the knowledge of the damnation that was to be hers. And Shannon fought again and won.

She fought the sitz baths, the cotton root and ergot, the quinine. She fought the jolts that came from Roberta jumping off the divan, from climbing stairs, from hanging up clothes. No, I'm not being romantic. She did fight. You could feel her indomitability. Feel it and hate it as you would hate a drowning person who threw his arms around your neck.

Then the doctor said it looked like she would be a Christmas baby—yes, sir, it did. And, finally, as the days passed, he became sure of it. And Roberta and I became ashamed of ourselves, and silently we prayed to Shannon for forgiveness. It would be all right now. We wouldn't starve. We could pay the doctor and the hospital. We'd always wanted her, we said. It was just that we didn't see how we could. Now, it would be all right.

I should explain that Christmas babies in our town were sort of municipal property. All the banks and loan sharks made up cash purses. The stores donated clothing and furniture and food. You got a year's supply of milk and ice and stuff like that for nothing. You got—well, you got just about everything. You know. They probably do things the same way all over the country.

At eleven o'clock on Christmas Eve I was sitting at Roberta's bedside in the hospital. The local florists had got wind of what was up, and flowers were already beginning to arrive. There was candy, too, and a big cake from one of the bakeries with "Happy Birthday Xmas Babe" spelled out on the icing. Even some reporters had been there to interview Roberta and snap her picture for the morning papers. Of course, the doctor was there, pacing back and forth and gloating over all the free publicity he was going to get, and asking the "little lady" how she felt.

She felt fine. Not too good understand. But good enough. She felt, in short, like she was going to have the baby on Christmas day.

Maybe it was the excitement. Maybe Shannon, distrusting us, sensed our will and rebelled against it.

But at eleven-thirty Roberta's lips stiffened, and she groaned.

The doctor wasn't alarmed. It wasn't a real bearing-down pain. He was sure that—

She groaned again. Her stomach revolved like a football being rolled inside a sweater. She clutched herself, and the involuntary spasms of her stomach rocked her back and forth.

"I won't!" she screamed. "I won't, I won't, I won't!"

They wheeled her out to the delivery room, the doctor

pathetically tagging along behind the nurses, and the closing door cut off Roberta's hate-filled and outraged protests. . . .

Shannon was born at twelve minutes of twelve.

I cannot say that we were cruel to her. Roberta may sometimes have neglected to heat her milk or change her diapers, but Roberta was sick a great deal. I may have smoked too much too close to her, and kept her awake with my typewriter. But I was trying to write a novel, the advances on which were necessary for our existence. I suppose that the worst I can say is that our kindness and attention were deliberate. We had to think about doing things for her. Occasionally, conscience stricken, we'd smother her with gifts and caresses. But we always had to think—we never did it automatically. And to Shannon, I guess, it seemed a long time between thoughts.

Our spasmodic fits of affection upset her, and she learned to fight against them. She distrusted us, so she ordered her own life; and, all things considered, I think she did well.

There was a summer evening, when she was about two, when we were all sitting out on the lawn of our home. Shannon suddenly announced that she had to go to the toilet. Roberta declared that she didn't.

"She's just trying to make me get up, Jimmie," she said. "I never sit down for a minute that she doesn't think of something."

"Have to go," said Shannon.

"Well do it in your pants then," said Roberta.

"Hurt bottom," said Shannon. "You take me, Daddy."

I started to get up, but Roberta said, "No, don't you give in to her now, Jimmie." So I sat back down again.

"You don't really have to go, baby. Wait a minute and you'll get over it."

"Have to go," she repeated.

"Go by yourself then," snapped Roberta. "All I hope is that a big bitey gets you."

Shannon looked toward the dark house, and her knees shook a little. And then her head went back and she marched up the steps and through the door.

She was still gone after fifteen minutes, so I went in, and there she was sitting on the stool and grinning toothlessly to herself. And she had had to go; there was no doubting that.

"Stink the biteys," she said. "Stinkem to def."

Fighting, fighting. . . .

Shortly before she was three we took a house adjacent to one of the parks. One day when I was escorting her and Jo there, we saw an old man approaching, and Jo shrank behind me.

"That man," she whimpered, "he said he was going to cut my ears off."

"Oh, he was just joking," I laughed. "You're not afraid, are you, Shannon?"

"Uh-uh," said Shannon. "I fix him."

She was carrying an enormous rag doll with a china head. Before I could stop her, she was down the sidewalk, had drawn the doll back over her shoulder, and had hurled it with all her astonishing energy straight into the old man's solar plexus. I'm not exaggerating when I say it almost killed him.

You couldn't scare her by the mention of policemen. The mere fact that we told her they would get her for her misdeeds was proof to her that they were vulnerable. It got so bad that we couldn't take her downtown. At the sight of a cop she was off, fists flying, mouth open to bite and slash. And even at two and three she could inflict serious damage. We were warned officially, more than once, that if we didn't do something about her, it would be just too bad.

She wasn't afraid of—well, she just wasn't afraid. In her lonely friendless world she had survived the horror of not being wanted, and she knew there was nothing worse to fear.

We tried, we tried very hard to make things up to her. Remembering, we would buy her some trinket or article of clothing that Jo actually deserved. But with the coming of Mack, with his square shoulders and low chuckle, it was harder to remember.

And Shannon made overtures which we seldom understood. Like the time she washed Roberta's bedspread in the toilet. Or—well, like the other night when she brought me that nickel "to buy whisky with." (I'm glad I didn't bawl her out for that.)

After the sound and fury had died Roberta might say, "But why didn't you ask Mother and Daddy first?" And

Shannon, not knowing how to translate the whisper of her instincts, not knowing how to say that she did not ask us because she did not think we knew, would stand mute. Grinning or glaring; furious, and amused, and sick. But never defeated; ready to fight until the last tick of her tiny heart.

She wouldn't eat any supper that night. She kept saying that she was tired, and she wanted me to hold her. She didn't seem to have any fever, but after a while she began to complain about being hot. So I picked her up—she weighs almost nothing—and walked outside with her. I carried her over to the park, then down to the bay, her fingers twined in my jacket, her great blue eyes reflecting the stars. And when I wanted to sit down on one of the pilings she still fussed that she was hot.

"Look, baby," I said. "Daddy's hot, too. How about going home, and getting a bottle of beer, and we'll sit out on the steps together."

She deliberated a moment, staring blankly at me. "Go to my store," she said.

"Oh, now, baby," I said. "Not tonight. Daddy's—"

"You go to my store," she said. "You hear? My store, my store, my—"

"All right, all right," I said. "Just don't get excited. We'll go. We're going right now."

So we went. And I will never be happier or more sad over an act of mine.

It had never occurred to me, I suppose, that Shannon

would be welcome any place. But here she was more than welcome. The car-hop girl, who had been slouching in front of the place, seemed to come alive when she saw her. She came rushing over and wanted to take Shannon out of my arms, but Shannon wouldn't go, so she contented herself with pinching her cheeks and running her red-fingernailed hands through her hair.

"How's my brat, tonight?" she cooed. "Wanta fight me, brat? Huh? Wanta fight Alice?"

She went inside with us and called to the soda jerker, "Hey, Ray. Here's our brat. Draw us a tall carbolic and arsenic without ice."

"Now, don't you call Shannon a brat," admonished Ray. "Shannon's my sweetheart. We're going to get married, aren't we, Shannon?"

And before Shannon could do anything more than grin wisely, the proprietor was there, seating us, and saying, no, Shannon couldn't get married because she had to work for him.

He introduced himself, and I said, rather embarrassed, that I hoped Shannon hadn't given him too much trouble.

"Trouble?" he appeared astonished. Then he laughed. "Well, we did have a painful few days before we learned how to take her. She came in here and demanded some chewing gum, and she raised so much—well, we finally had to give it to her. And the next day it was the same old story, and the next. It was cheaper to give her the coke or the candy or whatever she wanted than it was to argue about it. After we'd paid our toll, she still wouldn't leave, but she was quiet. She'd go over there to the magazine rack and fuss around, and we all thought she was looking at the comics. And then Ray noticed—"

"It wasn't Ray, it was me," said the car-hop.

"Well, then, Alice—Alice noticed that Shannon was arranging the magazines. She'd looked all around and decided that was what needed doing worst; so, by George, she'd taken on the job. And a darned good job she was doing, too! I—can she read?"

"I don't know."

"I think she must be able to. I don't see how she could remember the looks of things well enough to do what she does. Why I've got almost 150 magazines and periodicals there, Mr. Dillon, and Shannon knows them all. She never makes a mistake. She'll come over here in the morning and open up twenty or thirty bundles and rack every one in the right place." He laughed and slapped his knee. "Oh, Shannon's worth her weight in gold. These high-school jellybeans that used to come in and buy a coke and thumb through the magazines for half a day don't hang around any more. Shannon's got them all spotted. She'll give 'em about five minutes, and then—"

"I want some beer," said Shannon.

"Now, baby," I said. "How about a nice ice cream—"

"Beer!"

Of course, she has drunk beer. We have it around the house, and there's no way of stopping her. But out in public like that . . .

The druggist felt her pulse and laid a hand over her heart. His eyebrows went up.

"If you don't mind, a little beer might help her. She needs to sleep."

They brought a fresh bottle; Shannon wouldn't take mine. She lay back in my arms, nursing it, sipping daintily and licking at the foam.

"Yessir, Shannon's a great girl. I only wish she was mine," said the druggist.

And I didn't say anything, but I thought. I thought, well, why couldn't you have had her? Why couldn't you, instead of us? Or why couldn't we have had your security, so that we could have wanted her as you want her. For, oh, Christ, as she lies here in my arms, exhausted but afraid to sleep, living on hatred, even the thought that we did not want to want her makes me feel a criminal. And I am not. And Roberta is not. We wanted Jo, and we wanted Shannon, and we wanted Mack. Six in all, we had dreamed of; and a big white house with a deep lawn and many bedrooms and a pantry that was always full. We wanted them, but we wanted that, too. Not for ourselves, but for them. We wanted it because we knew what it would mean if we didn't have it. I knew how I was, and Roberta knew how she was. And we knew how it would be: As it had been with us.

We did want her. Goddammit, I say we did! We

want her now. I was crazy to say that we didn't or hadn't. But we are getting tired, and we are so cramped, and there are so many things to be done.

Why? I ask, why is it like this? Not for Roberta, not for myself; but for all of us.

Why, Karl? And what will you do about it? Not twenty years from now when Shannon and all the other Shannons have bred, and a plague spreads across the land, and brother slays brother.

Not then, when it is too late, but now!

And you, God? What have you to offer? Sweet music? Pie in the sky? Yes. But, on earth . . . ?

Now and on Earth?

"Yes, sir," said the druggist. "A great girl. You should be very proud of her."

"I am proud," I said. "I did not know just how proud I was or how much I loved her until tonight."

The bottle slipped from Shannon's hands and crashed to the floor. Her head fell back against my arm, and a tremor ran through her fragile body. And then she was asleep. And try as I will, I cannot describe the beauty of her smile.

12

THAT WAS LAST SATURDAY, AND SHANNON HAS BEEN SICK all week. We've had the doctor twice—and I don't know how in the hell we're going to pay him—but about all he could tell us was that Shannon was overwrought and undernourished. We are supposed to keep her quiet, and we have some vitamin tablets to give her. And that's about all we can do.

We have been very quiet, all of us. For a week now we've not had a single brawl. But it doesn't seem to help much. Shannon is getting more listless every day. She sits for hours, looking off into space, and she seems to be listening for something. And every once in a while she will get up and prowl around the house, looking, I don't know for what.

We've offered her everything we could think of and tried to find out what the trouble was, but it doesn't do any good. If we talk to her too much, she begins to cry, and it is terrible when she cries. Jo has no sympathy for her; she has the idea, apparently, that Shannon is putting on and she gets pretty sarcastic. But Mack seems to know what it is all about. He is becoming as silent and distraught as she, and he seldom leaves her for more

than a few minutes. When she sits, he sits, as close as
he can get to her. And when she starts looking, he looks
with her.

It is an eerie thing to see these two tots wandering
from room to room, eyes vacant, hands tightly clasped.
Roberta says if it doesn't stop pretty soon, she won't be
able to stand it. But she is so afraid I think she will
hold in a while longer.

We're being as quiet as we know how. I said that
already, I know, but we don't know of anything else to
do and it is a comfort to know—to keep thinking—
that we are doing something.

But Shannon isn't any better, and the thing is getting
ahold of Mack. I've stopped using the typewriter. I've
stopped drinking, almost. We don't even keep a light on
after nine o'clock.

But—well. . . .

Yesterday we had a letter from Marge. I'll give you
the letter. It'll explain about Pop, and Marge, too.

Dear Mama & Frankie & Jimmie, Roberta & Kids:
  Thought I'd better drop you a line before you thought
I was dead. Tell Roberta I will write her a long letter
just as soon as I get around to it. (Mom, does she still
fuss at Jimmie? I think what they both need is a vacation.
I was reading the other day about two people like that
who took a vacation from each other, and when they
went back together they were happier than ever. I'll try
to think of the magazine and send it to you. What do
you think? Maybe I hadn't better.)

Mrs. Pinny was here. You remember her. She always wore that footie little green hat that made her look like one of Robin Hood's men. And she stayed and she stayed, and Walter came home and he was so unreasonable about everything as if it was my fault that she came in and I hadn't got supper. Anyway, he came home early. And I was terribly upset. I don't know what makes him act like that. You know he's superintendent of all the stores here now, and he had a nice raise and he should be feeling awful good. But he's just as cranky as some old bear. I told him he was simply going to have to snap out of it or I was utterly through with him. He never takes me to a dance or anything, and everyone's talking about it.

The other night he brought a boy home from one of the stores, his name is Johnnie, and he's real tall and has dark hair, and he's a marvelous dancer. I tried to get Walter to dance with me, but he said he was too tired, so Johnnie did. After while Walter wanted to go to bed and he said it would be all right for Johnnie and me to go out and dance some place. Johnnie kind of hung back, but Walter insisted, and we finally went. He's a marvelous dancer. He said he was going to come back again tonight, and if he doesn't I'm going to make Walter call him up. He had kind of a hard time with Pop last night and he was pretty mad about it. But I told him it would just do him good to think about someone but himself for a change and it will. I guess if I can look after Pop all day he can do it for a few hours at night.

I told you that I'd gone and got Pop, didn't I? I'm sure I did. As soon as I received your last letter, I got out the car—my car, I mean; Walter has a new Pontiac coupe he uses himself—and I went right up there and got him. Mama, I don't think there is anything wrong with Pop. I charged a new suit of clothes for him and got him fixed up a little, and he looks just like he always did.

Now, Pop's not a bit of trouble, Mama, and we're delighted to have him. But I think you'd better write him a long letter about certain things. I don't want to hurt his feelings, but you could do it. I think you ought to tell him to go to church and read the Bible because they have got him in the habit of swearing a lot at that place he was in. I don't mind myself a bit, but Walter is always bringing someone home to dinner and I think it makes him mad to have Pop swearing so much. I told him that Pop never used to swear, and that it was just that place he had been in, but he simply refuses to understand.

I wish you would tell Pop about using the bathroom, too, Mama. I can't get him to do it. I guess he got so much in the habit of being out in the country when he was drilling oil wells that he doesn't think about other people being around. I don't think he sees very well, either. He usually goes out on the porch and does it, or if he has to—if he has to do something besides pee he uses the shrubs in the front yard. The other day I got out in the yard and stood a few feet away from him and waved my hands so that he could see that I could see him, but he kept right on. I think the whole trouble is that Pop is just forgetful.

Now, Mama, when you write him don't let on that I said anything, and don't say anything that will hurt his feelings. He's very sensitive. Just tell him to be sure and use the toilet. There's one right next to the telephone, downstairs, and there's another one upstairs right off the south bedroom. I believe that if you can make Pop understand that he's supposed to use them he will do so. I'd talk to him, but it's been so long since I was around him much that I hardly know how to any more.

I'm sending you a box of stuff. Nothing much, but I hope you can use it. They got in some imported Canadian hams at the No. 1 store the other day, and you ought to eat more meat, Mama, so I got one. Also put in some cigarettes and candy and other stuff because the box was too big and I had to fill it up, anyway.

Well, Walter just called and said he couldn't come home, so I guess I won't get to go out after all. I don't know why he does things like that. I think I'll just have Johnnie come over here, anyway, and Pop can watch us because he enjoys music and dancing as much as anyone else.

Now, write soon, Mama. And you too Frankie and Jimmie. I won't ask Roberta to write because I still owe her a letter. But I am going to write real soon. Would have before this, but it seems like I just can't get anything done. Love,

Marge

P.S. Don't bother to write Pop. He doesn't seem to be able to read any more.

When I finished that letter I said, "Mom, is that girl completely crazy?"

"What's the matter with Marge?" asked Mom, beginning to bristle. "It looks to me like she's doing all right. She's taking care of Pop. She's always been good to us. She's the only member I can think of, offhand, that ever remembered my birthday."

"I remembered it, Mom," said Roberta, "a good many times. It always worked out, though, that we had some old note or something to pay off at the same time."

"But look, Mom," I said. "You know Walter isn't going to put up with this. The last time I saw him he was getting pretty fed up, and Pop wasn't around then."

"I guess Marge can handle him," said Mom.

Frankie, when she came home, saw things my way. "Jimmie's right, Mom. You'd better write her to take Pop back."

"They don't want him back."

"They'll have to take him, anyway. They've got to keep him a little while until we can make some arrangements."

"What arrangements? I don't know of any."

"Well—until Jimmie sells a story."

"And when will that be? He's not written a line all week."

"Now Christ Almighty!" I said. "Why throw that up to me? You know why I haven't written. What do you want me to do? Sit out in the gutter and type?"

"Keep your voice down," said Roberta sharply.

"Well, what do you want me to do?" I repeated.

"Nothing," said Mom. "Absolutely nothing. But don't get in the way of people who are doing something."

She got up and plodded out, and Frankie told me not to pay any attention to her—she was just upset. I was pretty hurt. Marge, to the best of my knowledge, never contributed a dime of cash money to the family in her life. But, through her faculty for remembering Mother's Day and her habit of waking you up in the middle of the night to ask if you're sleeping well, she seems to be, in Mom's eyes, the trunk of the tree.

Mind, I'm not jealous of Marge, although she always got the best of everything when it was available. Long after Pop had more money than he knew what to do with, I carried a paper route, and worked for Western Union, and caddied, because Pop thought that a job— any kind of a lousy goddamned job—"gave character to a boy." And while I was doing that, Marge was taking lessons on the violin at rates up to thirty-five dollars an hour. And she hated the violin, and I loved it. . . .

I used to get her instrument out of its case, and run the scales, and saw out things like "Home Sweet Home" and "Turkey in the Straw"; and I guess it was pretty awful. And Pop would fidget, and after while he'd ask me if I didn't have some work to do. Or he'd dismiss me with: "That's good. Now let's hear you play, Marge."

I wanted to be a violinist. At least, I wanted to get away from jobs where people snubbed and swore at you. I wanted never to have to ask any one for money. I wanted attention, and admiration, and the chance to express myself. I started to write. You could get a pencil and a piece of paper anywhere.

Oddly enough, I sold the first thing I wrote, a sketch about a golf game; but it was a very long time between that first story and the second. And, although I never gave up writing, I kept at it largely from habit. Pop went broke and his was the irremediable brokeness of a man past fifty who has never worked for other people. I had to distinguish myself and support the family at the same time. And even at fifteen, a high-school freshman, I knew I wasn't going to do it by writing.

I got a job as a bellhop in the largest hotel in town. They didn't want me because I was so tall—they didn't have a uniform that would fit me. But I kept going down, standing around the lobby and looking wistful; and I dug up an old pair of blue serge pants and had some braid sewed on them. And, finally, when one of the night boys was careless enough to get himself arrested for pandering, they put me on.

My hours were from ten at night until seven in the morning. I went to high school from eight-thirty until three-thirty. I didn't think I could do it, at first. I wasn't even sure that it was worth the effort. You see I thought that a bellboy was supposed to carry icewater and baggage to the rooms. And my first month I barely made expenses.

When I found out about the other things, it made me a little sick. But I didn't know what to do then, any more than I do now; I didn't see any other way out. We needed money, and this, apparently, was the only way of getting it. I began to get.

Mom wasn't very worldly-wise, and I'm pretty sure she really did not know how those thick rolls of ones and fives and tens were produced. Pop—well, Pop knew.

And he came to despise me for it. But he didn't do anything about it. He didn't produce any money himself.

Well, I drank. "Give the bellhop a drink" was party etiquette in those Prohibition days. Most of the stuff was poison, but after a few drinks I began to forget my shame and my fear of exposure and arrest, and I could concentrate on the all-important business of making money. I bolstered myself with other things also. I bought Society Brand suits and twenty-dollar Borsalinos and Florsheim shoes. And I bought a snappy Dort coupe. But nothing took the place of drink. Some of the "boys" —they ranged up to forty-five in age—sniffed cocaine; and I tried it several times. But I always preferred liquor.

In my second year I was sick in bed for six weeks. I was delirious most of the time, and I burned and froze by turns. The doctors called it malaria. It was beyond their ken, I guess, that a sixteen-year-old boy could be suffering from alcoholism.

The 'twenty-nine boom was building up, then, and it cost me a hundred dollars to buy my job back, plus two dollars and a half a night to work. And I had to go after the money harder than ever. In my fourth year I broke down completely—tuberculosis, alcoholism, nervous exhaustion.

Marge was engaged to Walter then, and our home had to be maintained. And I'm sure—I have to be sure—that the family didn't know how sick I was. I struck out by myself. I got drunk in Mineral Wells and lost the little money I had, and I suppose I would have got a stiff jail sentence if they hadn't been afraid I'd die on them. As it was—

I'm a little blank on a lot of things. But I wound up, eventually, as a night watchman on a pipeline that was being built from Iraan to the Gulf. On the night that my high-school class graduated I was seated on a generator, far out on the Texas plains, and on the ground below me a huge rattlesnake listened raptly as I screamed and cursed and raved at him.

I'd never been particularly afraid of crawling things before. But after that, after those two years, a roach or an ant made me cringe, and, if I was not on guard, scream.

I had no rest from them, you see. While I tossed on my cot in camp, during the day, they were with me— the ones that were worse than the real ones. They ringed me in, the rattlers, the tarantulas—the great black-and-white tarantulas as large as saucers and with fur like rabbits—the ten-inch centipedes, the scorpions, the vine-garroons, and gilas. I say they ringed me in; everywhere I looked they were there, at my head, my sides, and feet. And then, before I could leap over them, always before I could leap over them—the thing happened to me ten thousand times, a dozen times in a day, but I could never bring myself to leap until it was too late—then, then, as I say, another ring would come up to reinforce the first. It would climb and slide and crawl on top of the first ring. And then another ring would climb and crawl and slide on top of it. And then there would be

another and another and another and ANOTHER!
ANOTHER! ANOTHER!

Oh, Christ. . . .

They rose to the top of the cot. They mounted higher
and higher around me. And as they mounted the rings
drew in to form a sort of beehive. Drew in. Drew in.
And, finally—finally—there was only a speck of light left
(they always left enough light for me to see by). And
then the pile began to sag, sag down.

I pleaded with them. I told them funny stories. I sang
to them. I pleaded and sang and told funny stories all
at once. And then they dropped down on me in a mass,
and their weight stopped my heart and I ceased to
breathe. . . .

Whatta they keep that crazy bastard around for?

*Ahh, he's a good kid. I been through this myself.
Come on, Slim. Snap out of it.*

He needs a drink. Anyone gotta drink?

Got a can of heat he can have.

*Well squeeze it out for him . . . Slim, goddam yuh,
get this down your gullet. Huh, huh! Don't yuh know
it's bad luck to die in a tent?*

At night, when I went out on the line, they were still
with me, the real ones, and the others, and I could never
be sure which was which. I had thirty generators to oil,
gas, and water; a ditcher and a dragline; so I needed to
keep moving. And I did not know when it was safe to
walk through the things in front of me and when it was
not. Sometimes, most times, my feet would melt through

their bodies. But—sometimes a diamond-shaped head would lash out at my eighteen-inch boot, or a great furry mass would leap straight toward my face. And then I would stumble backwards, run, knocking over fuel cans, tripping over pipe, battering myself against the generators; run and run and run until I could run no more.

Good men were scarce in those days; that's probably obvious. I was getting fifty cents an hour for twelve hours, seven days a week, with only a dollar a day out for board and flop. So I stayed on after I got well; after homesickness was beginning to take the place of the other. A hundred and fifty dollars a month clear to be sent home; so I stayed.

After two years—something more than two years— a few days before Thanksgiving, we put the button on the job, and I beat my way home. I got there Thanksgiving Day. The folks were over at Marge's for dinner, and I was broke, and there wasn't anything to eat in the house. I got cleaned up and put on some other clothes. An hour later I had bought back my job on the installment plan and was hopping bells again.

Yes, as the lawyers say, I'm going to connect all this up. I've laid the groundwork for it, or am laying one for something else.

I worked at the hotel another year and a half, and then the bug began to bite me again. I had to lay off a lot. Frankie was thirteen that summer and big for her age, and I got her a job slinging hash in the coffee shop. But it worried me so much to see her walking around in her sleep, to see her insulted and propositioned and bawled out, that I made her quit after a few weeks. So there we were. We had to make a jump and we didn't know which way.

Then, one evening while I was killing time in the library, I picked up a copy of the *Texas Monthly*. And there on the title page was a line *"Oil Field Vignettes . . . By James Dillon."* I had written that story almost a year before, one bitter night down on the Pecos—written it by lantern-light with the sleet beating down against the nickel tablet and my hands swathed in mittens. And I had sent it to town with the provision truck and promptly forgotten about it.

I called on the editor and we spent a whole afternoon talking—it was that kind of magazine. He couldn't pay me in money, but he had a lot of advice to offer, chiefly to the effect that I had better get myself some more schooling.

How? We-ell—he just might be able to help me there. His alma mater was Nebraska. He had a great many friends on the faculty. If he could arrange a loan for the tuition . . .

I told Pop about it that night. I wanted to hurt him, I guess. All I did was to prove something that I had always known down in my heart—that I was small and he was big.

"You'll go, of course," he said. "Don't let anything stop you. Go."

"But what about—about you?"

"I'll get by. I wouldn't want to live, anyway, if I thought I'd made you miss a chance like this."

And Mom and Frankie?

Well, Mom had a sister in Nebraska. She and Frankie could stay with her a while. I didn't want her to, because I remembered what that sister was like, but—

But the decision was taken out of our hands. I learned, one morning, that I had sold a quart of whisky to a Federal man, one of those singular prohibition agents who couldn't be bought off. A warrant was being drawn for my arrest. We were on our way out of town by noon. Destination, Nebraska.

Now, to connect up. . . .

I think I've explained or partially explained a number of things. How I came to be in Nebraska, and thus had the opportunity to meet Roberta. Why I was with her as I was. Why I am like I am and why Roberta is like she is, perforce. Why, in a way, we have had such a completely messy existence. Why I—we—are in a mess now. And why we will not get out of it, unless it is to get into something worse.

I haven't said anything about Marge? That is the only way I can say anything about her—to say nothing.

As far back as I can remember—not quite but almost —Marge was blinding herself to facts which she did not care to recognize. And at twelve, when the family's fortunes took a turn for the better, it was as if her mind had been swept free of what misery and poverty she had known before. Swept free, for that matter, of everything else.

A mean thing to say, but largely true. She had Bright's disease. She was an invalid for a couple years. It interrupted her schooling. She forgot things that she was never able to remember.

I shouldn't feel toward her as I do, because I recall with terrifying clarity how the disease was brought on. But, to use an oil-field phrase, I'd as soon be smothered with dung as wild honey. When I last saw her a couple of years ago, I was never sure whether I wanted to pat her head or wring her neck. Now I'm afraid the pull will all be in one direction.

She's incapable of doing anything useful. She has no idea of the value of time or money. And—and she insists on telling everyone she's three years younger than I am!

If she breaks up with Walter, I don't know what we'll do. Because she'll come here, of course. I'll ask her to come. I'll insist upon it, because she's my sister and I love her. But I don't know how we'll put up with it.

Mom will spend three-fourths of her time cooking special dishes for her, and the other fourth working over her clothes. And Roberta will be mad, boiling mad and jealous from one week to the next— "See here, James Dillon; if you think for a minute I'm going to do without just so your sister—"

I don't even want to think about it.

There'll be Turkish cigarettes everywhere you turn. The bathroom sink will be full of henna, always. There'll be fudge in the ashtrays, and lipstick on the drinking glasses, and moving-picture magazines from hell to breakfast. I'll never be able to write or read. The house will be filled constantly with the "handsomest fellow" and the "most refined man," and the phone will ring unceasingly and the doorbell likewise. And always, always in that timid half-hesitant drawl of hers Marge will give us her views, her advice, on everything from intercourse to the international situation.

Well—maybe Pop is better. After all it's been almost eight months since we saw him. But I don't think so. Things just don't work out that way for us. As soon as we straighten out one problem, we're faced with another. I sometimes wonder if we wouldn't do just as well if we simply sat back and did nothing.

I tried to discuss this with Mom the other night.

"Mom," I said, "what do you suppose would have happened back there when I was fifteen if I hadn't gone to work as a bellhop. What would we all have done?"

"Well, you know how I always felt about that," she said. "I knew it wasn't the right thing for a growing boy to be out all night. I didn't want you to do it. Don't you remember how I used to fuss at Pop, and—"

"Now, don't get on your high horse," I said. "Good God, Mom! Can't we talk to each other any more?"

"I guess I know what you mean," said Mom. "I used

to wonder the same thing. I don't think we should, though. When I think of how I used to take you kids to a five-cent movie and sit in it all day to save fuel. And of how we skimped on food. Do you remember the games we used to play? I'd break up the bread on your plates at breakfast, and pour coffee over it, and each piece would be a fish, and we'd be big sharks ourselves. And then at noon the bread and gravy would be cars and our mouths would turn into tunnels—"

I laughed. "Yeah. And where were we living when you chased down the alley that day and got those two road-workers for boarders? I remember Marge and I had a pet chicken named Dickie, and how we bawled when you took it to the store and swapped it for fifty cents' worth of groceries to give these guys their first meal with."

"Yes, and then Pop came home, and he never noticed anything, and he could talk with his mouth full. Our boarders didn't get anything but their coffee. They never came back."

We sat looking at the floor, not wanting to meet each other's eyes. Mom got up.

"I guess it had to be done," she said. "I'm going to fix myself a cup of tea and go to bed. I think I ought to be entitled to a cup of tea, at least."

I jumped up and followed her out into the kitchen.

"Sure it had to be done," I said. "It does make sense. It has to. Why, if it didn't—"

"Jimmie."

"Yes, Mom."

"Don't be like Pop was. Don't always be looking for an excuse to run away from your obligations."

"But, Mom, if it didn't make any difference—if everyone got along just as well—better—"

"Got along, how? By doing without food and clothes? By living with relatives and sponging off the neighbors? You mustn't even think about it, Jimmie."

13

I'M MAKING A LITTLE PROGRESS AT THE PLANT. I DON'T mean by that that the books are in anything like good order, but I am beginning to see daylight.

You remember that I mentioned certain parts which we never saw and yet were required to keep a record on? And that something seemed to be wrong with this if I could only think of what it was? Well, it finally came to me, and as a consequence I've got about fifty less parts to deal with.

If we know, say, that a fuselage must be equipped with a firewall before it reaches motor-preparation, what reason is there for keeping a record on firewalls? Absolutely none. You can forget about them.

Then I've got Moon to get the Chief Dispatcher to issue an order that all parts must clear the other stockrooms—Sub-assembly, Sheet-metal, and so on—before they touch us. This will, or should, stop parts that don't belong in our stockroom from getting there. At least, if any do get to us, we can lay the blame on the other stockrooms.

Finally, at my insistence, Moon has put Murphy to taking inventory along the assembly line, and as he finds out what they have out there, I am able to solve many of the tangles that had been baffling me. Vail was supposed to have taken the inventory, because he has more time to spare than Murphy, but he declared that Busken couldn't take care of the purchased end of things by himself, so Murphy got stuck. He didn't like it very well. He and Vail are barely speaking. But I don't see that that's my fault.

I have never worked in a place where it was assumed that I knew so much more than I actually did. Now Moon and Murphy—yes, and Gross—knew that a new part would be integrated in one ship before we received a quantity order of it. And, I suppose, common sense should have told me as much. All I had to do was to take the part and go up and down the assembly lines until I found a ship that had a part to match it. The part would be effective from that ship-number on.

Everyone knew this but me. And so sure were they that I knew it that they could not understand my fretting over the effective-numbers of new parts. Or, perhaps, they thought it would do me good to find out such things for myself. Every man is pretty much on his own here. Every man has just a little bit more to do than he can get done in eight hours, and there's no time to help another man even if you want to. You may give a fellow-worker a hand-up or a quick word of advice, but if he's slow to take either, you keep right on going. You have to. I've received much more assistance and co-operation than I'm entitled to by the rules of the game. Partly because,

I believe, they are getting tired of changing bookkeepers; largely because Moon can humiliate Gross by keeping me on. That was the catch in the job.

I have found out why Moon has it in for Gross.

Moon has been in aircraft work for almost five years; relatively speaking, he's a veteran. Not only that, not only does he have more experience than 95 per cent of the men in the plant, but he has a natural and unusual talent for the business. He's worked in Final Assembly, Sub-, Wing, even in Engineering. Part numbers don't bother him. He can look at one small part and reconstruct an entire assembly of several hundred.

A day or so ago, during the lunch period, he and Vail played a game for dollar stakes. By turns, one would go outside the fence and down the assembly line to a plane which the other could not see. Then he would call out something like this: "Six inches inboard from the right wing tip, and three inches down!"

And the other would answer, say (I can't produce their words verbatim): "Compression-rib bracket; one sixty-fourth of an inch dural with a quarter-inch hole and a one-coat green prime!"

Or: "Five inches up from tail-cone bottom, tail-fairing connecting?"

And: "That's easy. Aren's tab-control, minus control rod!"

Vail knows something about planes himself. He's got two years behind him and seventy hours in the air. Moon finally stuck him, though, on rivet sizes.

Now, a man like that is extremely valuable at any time and particularly at a time like this. It would actually be impossible to replace him. And Moon is not inclined to underestimate his worth.

About three months ago, or just before I came here, Moon was getting a dollar and four cents an hour, and he was none too well satisfied with it. But the company was negotiating with the union at the time, and he was content to wait for developments. Well, then, the agreement was signed and it specified that the wage of a leadman need be only 20 per cent higher than that of the highest paid worker in his department. In this case the highest paid was Vail, at eighty cents. So the personnel office, in their penny-wise fashion, cut Moon's wage to a dollar.

Moon made no complaint. He simply went over to another plant where he was promptly hired at a dollar-sixteen. Then he handed in his resignation here. Of course, Production had to hear about it and when they did, they hit the ceiling. What in hell was Personnel trying to do? Didn't they know we were here to build planes? Did they think five-year men could be picked up off the street every day? You guys had better wake up!

Moon was advised that his pay, from that moment, was a dollar-sixteen.

He called up the other plant. They offered him a dollar-twenty-five.

Our plant saw the raise and twelve and a half cents more.

The other made it one-fifty even.

Our plant began to see red. You can't do us this way, they declared. We'll report you to Knudsen. We'll make it warm for you in the Aeronautical Chamber of Commerce. It's bad ethics; it's sabotage; J. Edgar Hoover shall hear about it.

Well, the other plant didn't want that. They told Moon, very firmly, that they couldn't accept his application for employment—unless our plant decided they didn't want to keep him.

Moon started coming to work late. The timekeepers didn't notice.

He began eating apples and throwing cores at the guards. The guards were instructed to think this was funny.

He arranged the crates of pilot-seats into a pyramid, with an aerie at the summit, and he would lie there all day long, reading and eating candy bars and blowing smoke through the skylight. . . .

Officially, no one noticed. They didn't want to. They knew him, and they were sure that in time he would become bored by the game and give up.

Busken and Vail liked Moon and tried—unnecessarily—to cover for him. Murphy, who told me the story, was on the inside, and, at any rate, wouldn't have played stool-pigeon. Gross, however, didn't have the lowdown, and he didn't particularly care for Moon. It seemed to him that his good friend, the personnel manager, would be shocked if he knew what was going on; also, that with

Moon out of the way, he, Gross, with all his experience in football, would be the logical candidate for lead-man.

Well, it was pitiful in a way. Personnel had forgotten who Moon was. They sent him a discharge notice on the spot and a copy to Production. The latter caught Moon just as he was going out the gate, and they had to give him one-fifty to get him to come back. And ever since then they've had to let him do about as he pleased.

Moon found out about Gross. And, while Gross did do him a favor, he doesn't like him very much.

There is one thing about this place: If you are good enough at your job you can get away with anything.

Three weeks ago, the week Shannon took sick, we began moving into the extension to the plant. Everything was in twice the usual uproar. The production lines were running full blast; Final Assembly was running extra shifts; Engineering and Experimental were working as furiously as ever; we were receiving and throwing out parts more frantically than usual. And amidst all this we had to move. You'd see a fuselage roll by on a jig, with half a dozen men swarming over and inside it. We threw out and received parts while the racks were rocking along on the dollies. Nothing stopped for a moment.

Well, you might have thought that at such a time allowances would have been made for any disarray or untidiness. But the day we started to move the front-office announced a clean-up campaign. When we went outside at noon, there, suspended by his neck from one of the hoist-tracks was a dummy of a man—the ugliest most scabrous object I have ever seen—placarded SLOPPY SAM. Underneath his title was another placard that read I AM AT HOME IN THIS DEPARTMENT. On the adjacent bulletin board there was a notice saying that Sloppy Sam would be awarded to the department which was adjudged the dirtiest by a committee composed of so-and-so and so-and-so, the award to be made the following Monday.

I don't know just how far Sloppy Sam set back production, but it must have been considerable. Rivet guns were replaced by brooms. The unishear men went around picking up scraps. Moon wouldn't even let me post my travelers. I had to get a dust cloth and start polishing the racks.

When we came through the plant entrance Monday, we all shuddered a little because it looked like Sam was suspended over our space. But when we came closer, we saw that it was Tooling, the department next to ours, that had drawn him. And still there was no let-down. We'd got by this week, but we might get him next, and Moon, like any good lead-man, had his pride.

Now, tooling men, in their own eyes at least, are a race apart. They go around spitting out tobacco and fractions, and they sometimes—not often—become so absorbed in what they are doing that they don't hear the quitting whistle. Incidentally, there aren't many of them. Not nearly as many as the plant would like to have.

Living somewhat in a world above us, they were not

treated to the jeers and jokes that we doubtless would have received. But they were outraged nonetheless, and they brought all their fine art to bear to show just how they felt about things.

At some time during the morning they lowered the dummy. When they raised it again, it was equipped with a giant phallus—so gigantic, in fact, that Sloppy Sam required both hands to hold it upright. Or, to be more exact, outright. For, by changing a line here and shading one there, they had given the detestable creature a look of lewd beatitude that gave the lie to any innocent theory that he was urinating or acquiring a sun-tan.

Perhaps the high-hats didn't know about it. Perhaps they chose to ignore it. At any rate Sloppy Sam remained there until quitting time.

The following morning he had a companion. She was facing Sam, and her skirts were up, and so cunningly had the night-shift artists wrought rubber and red lead and excelsior that you could tell, from fifty yards away, why Sam was no longer using his hands.

Inside of a half-hour the chief of the company police was there. A moment later he was joined by the first vice-president, the second and third vice-presidents and the factory manager. The department foreman was called.

Who was responsible for this—this—this—

"That? Oh, I guess all the boys had a hand in it."

"So! Then you can inform your men—each of them—that they are to get a three-day layoff without pay."

"Well. I kinda think they won't come back if you

do that. Myself, I've sorta been looking around. . . ."

Baldwin, the production manager, came up, harried of face, prematurely gray, his pockets bulging with papers.

"Now see here! What the hell is this? Are we getting out planes or running a restaurant . . . what? What ! ! ! These men?! Well, you can write mine out, too. I go all the way to Jersey to get a good man—just one good man —and you . . . ! By God, I give up!"

They all walked away except the chief of police, who remained to cut the dummies down.

We've heard and seen nothing more of Sloppy Sam and the clean-up campaign.

I would like to be as indispensable as that. Not here. It is too much like home here; this is the one place I've been that was as crazy as my home. And I couldn't stand two such places very long. But if I could get back into writing again—real writing. . . .

I had about 750 words done when Shannon became sick. Since then I've only done around three hundred. The only place I could think of to write where the typewriter wouldn't bother her is the bathroom, so I've been trying to write in there, and I haven't been very successful. For one thing, there isn't enough room for a table and the typewriter is a little too large to fit over the toilet seat. For another, the family seems to have to go every few minutes. Before that, I'll swear that Roberta would go for a day at a time, and Mom and Frankie were in the same class. But, now, well, just let me get settled good and about ready to hit the keys, and there they are beating on the door. I told them last night that they were going to have to get some pots, but that brought up the question of who would form the sanitation detail. And no one would. So we're in the same shape we were.

I wish Shannon would get well. I don't think any of us can go much longer without letting off some steam.

And—I guess I've made a pretty bad show of being funny. I am worried about her. I couldn't write anywhere so long as she is like this.

Well, to mention something cheerful, I've got a ride to and from work now. I started riding with Murphy, Wednesday. Gross laid off that day, throwing us short-handed, so we worked overtime until five-thirty. Moon didn't have his car for some reason, and he asked Murphy to take him home. Murphy just about had to say yes, of course, and since the three of us were together, he also just about had to ask me to ride, too. Moon got in the back seat and put his feet up. Murphy and I rode in front.

We stopped in front of our house just as Frankie was going in, and she turned and waved.

"Your wife, Dilly?" said Moon.

"My sister," I said; and I added, "She's married."

"She and her husband live here with you?"

"She does."

"Oh," he said. "Look, Murphy," he said, "why don't you carry Dilly back and forth to work? It's not much out of your way. You'd help out on the gas, wouldn't you, Dilly?"

"I'd be glad to," I said. "I don't know just what you would have to have, but I could give you a dollar a week, Murphy."

"All right," he said.

"I don't want to force myself on you—"

"It'll be all right, Dilly," said Moon. And they drove off.

And it does seem to be all right. Murphy just doesn't have a whole lot to say. That is, most of the time he doesn't. I've learned that he originally came to the plant as a draughtsman and that he used to be a lightweight fighter; and he told me the story about Moon trying to get fired. But he's a moody cuss, and you get the impression that he'll be glad to leave you alone for the same kind of favor.

Or maybe that's just my imagination. I'm always going around reading things into people and their actions which are nonexistent.

At any rate, I do have a ride and it makes things much more pleasant than they were. That walk up the hill was getting me down. I haven't said much lately about being sick, because there's nothing new about it and it can't be helped; but I'm—I don't think I'm getting any better.

I get through the mornings pretty well, but along about one o'clock my body seems to increase in weight, and from then until three-thirty I have to fight to keep from dropping down on the floor and stretching out. I'm not sleepy; it's been a long time since I was. I just want to rest.

14

ROBERTA HAS BEEN VERY ATTENTIVE TO ME THESE PAST
ten days or so. Probably because the ordinary outlet for
her emotions has been closed. I imagine that has something to do with the way I feel, and my inability to
write, but—but I'm getting off on a sidetrack. I started
off to tell you about Shannon.

Tonight was Saturday, and I had intended going down
to the library to get a book or two on blue-print reading.
I need to know blue-print reading in my work. Well, I
made my intentions known to the family, and everyone
—that is, Mom, Roberta, and Frankie—discussed the
matter and decided it would be all right for me to go. It
is absolutely fantastic the debates that can be held over
such a thing as my going over to the drugstore after a
package of cigarettes. It isn't that they don't want me to
go; they simply have to discuss it. And if I don't wait
until the discussion is over, someone is hurt. It is crazy
but that's the way it is.

If I go without waiting, I'll discover when I return that
Mom wanted a spool of black thread, Number 50 ("but,
oh no, don't go back after it"); or Roberta *would* have
gone along if I'd just waited until she got her hair
combed ("but I've been in the house all week, one more

night won't kill me"); or Frankie will remember that if I'd just waited until five minutes after eight there was a place down the street where I could have got a free quart of beer with my fags ("I knew there was something I wanted to tell you, Jimmie").

I've always—the last couple years, at least—had to furnish Roberta with my itinerary and a timetable when I stepped out. But that's aside from and in addition to the debates.

But they decided I could go, and I got cleaned up so that I'd be ready to leave right after supper. If you don't get down to the library early on Saturday, it's hard to get waited on. Besides, I was afraid if I hung around too long there'd be an argument of some kind and I never would get there.

Jo was down the street somewhere practicing a play— she's always practicing with half a dozen groups—and she didn't come home until the meal was almost over. That irritated Roberta; her nerves have been worse than usual, anyway, what with Mack and Shannon glumly refusing food, sitting side by side in their chairs as listless as two statues.

Jo squeezed my hand and patted me on the shoulder before she sat down.

"Gee, you look nice, Daddy. Going some place?"

"Just to the library," I said.

"By the way, Jimmie," said Roberta, "pick me out a good mystery, will you? Something by—well, you know, something good."

"All right," I said.

Roberta looked at Jo and her nostrils started to tremble. "Now what are you snickering about? What did I say that was so funny? Answer me!"

"Why I wasn't laughing, Mother," said Jo, innocently. "May I go to the library with Daddy?"

"No, you can't. What do you want to go for, anyway?"

"There's a book I want. It's about early Elizabethan costumes. I really need it, Mother."

"Your daddy will bring it to you."

"But I don't know the name of it. I don't know what to tell him. I have to go down and pick it out myself."

Roberta finished a mouthful while Jo waited anxiously.

"May I, Mother?"

"Do you know your catechism?"

"Oh, of course!"

"Jo!"

"Well, I just said of course."

"For God—let her go, Roberta," I said. "What difference does it make?"

"She can go," said Roberta. "Just as soon as I hear her catechism."

Jo brightened. "Right now, Mother? I'm really not hungry. You can hear—"

"I'll hear it when I get ready to hear it and not one minute before. We're not running this house for your benefit."

I said, "Let her go, honey. She can recite her catechism when she gets back."

"Why don't you, Roberta," Frankie put in. "After we get 'em out of the way, you and I'll step out and get a coke."

Roberta didn't say anything.

"Well, I'm sorry, Jo," I said, "but I'm going to have to leave as soon as I finish eating. Perhaps you can go some other time."

"I need to go tonight," said Jo. "You ought to make Mother let me go."

Well, I should have. She was right. But—

Roberta laid down her fork. "Jo Dillon," she said, "just one more word out of you and I'll slap you to sleep."

Jo got up and started to leave the table.

"Excuse yourself," snapped Roberta.

"You told me not to say another word."

"Jo! Are you deliberately trying to get my—to make me mad?"

"No, Mother," said Jo. "Excuse me."

She gave me a peculiar lingering look which I could not interpret, but which, I know now, was meant as an apology for what was to follow. Then she went into the bedroom. When she came back, she was wearing a housecoat; and she had done something extraordinary with her hair and face. No—well, yes, she had been into the rouge and lipstick and bobby pins; but that didn't account for the change. It was the way she held herself, some alteration in expression. She looked, except for her size, a good ten years older. She looked very much like Roberta.

She sauntered over to the lounge and pulled the pillows off onto the floor.

"Now, what are you doing?" demanded Roberta.

"Why I'm just going to lie down," said Jo, looking at her levelly. "There's nothing wrong with lying on the floor, is there, Mother? Don't you think it's fun to lie on the floor, Mother?"

"Well," said Roberta. "Well, you be sure and put them back, now."

Jo lay down on her back with her knees in the air, and her housecoat fell down against the cushions, revealing that she had nothing on underneath.

"Jo," said Roberta, although not very severely. "Do you think that's—don't you want some pants on?"

"Ummm," said Jo, closing her eyes and rolling her body gently. "Ummm, Ooooh . . . uh, uh, uh . . . mmm."

"Jo," I said.

And Roberta said, "Jo, you get up from there this instant!"

Jo didn't get up. She knew that she would have to pay for this act of vengeance, and she intended getting her money's worth.

Roberta's face was fiery red, and she was shaking so that her chair creaked. Mom was looking—pretending to look—at her plate. Frankie was hiding behind a section of the evening paper, and, from the sound of things, slowly strangling.

And Jo—the Jo that was Roberta—kept on.

Fascinated, sick with shame, I watched the conclusion of the performance; thinking of the observations and study that lay back of it; of what a terrible thing it is to rear children in poverty and hatreds; how something that should have been beautiful and sweet to Jo must always be an indecent mockery.

She was on the small of her back, bottom upward, heels against her thighs.

And then Roberta had her. She grabbed her by the hair and dragged, hurled her against the wall. And she was screaming curses as she beat and kicked and slapped her all at once.

"You—you filthy little b-bastard! I'll kill you, you son-of-a-bitch, you you scum, you you GODDAM YOU I'LL KILL YOU! Do you hear me? I'LL KILL YOU! I will, I will, I will . . . !"

And I knew that she would kill her. And Jo was laughing so wildly that she could not fight back or get away.

I grabbed Roberta by the arms, but she had her hands tangled in Jo's hair, and I did not know what to do because she was so insanely angry that I was afraid she might literally yank Jo's scalp off. And, just to help out, Mom had to say that Jo deserved a good spanking.

"You just let Roberta spank her, Jimmie! The idea! A child doing a thing like that—"

And I lost my head, of course, and yelled goddammit,

did she want the kid murdered? and if she couldn't do anything wouldn't she at least keep still.

So that brought Frankie into it. "Don't you talk to Mom that way, Jimmie! She doesn't have to take it from you or anyone else!"

"Well, you take it, then!" I yelled. "If you don't like it—"

Jo broke loose from Roberta. She ran between her legs, I believe, because Roberta fell forward and banged her head against the fireplace. Not hard enough to knock her out. Just enough to make her madder.

Jo got behind me and kept moving me around as Roberta fought to get at her. And Roberta seemed to think that I was holding her off, which I suppose I was, and she started slapping me and kicking me on the shins. And Mom and I and Frankie were all screaming at each other. And—well, I do think it was about the worst brawl we have ever had.

Then Shannon took a hand. Yes, Shannon. She wasn't listless any more. Far from it.

Before I knew what was happening, I'd been hit about sixteen solid punches in the groin. I think Jo caught it next—a slashing bite on the rump—but I can't be sure, because she and Roberta, who'd had her corns stamped on, yelled at the same time. And then Shannon started going around us like a cooper around a barrel.

"You goddam mama. You goddam Jo. You goddam daddy. Beat the hell outta you. Fix you all. Beat the—"

Mack came rushing in from the bathroom, carrying the

toilet plunger. He knew his limitations in combat, knew that he needed a weapon. But Shannon was in so many places at once that he couldn't use it, so he kept proffering it to her.

"Heah, Shan'. Hit 'em wif a 'tick, Shan'!"

We got worn out.

Mack and Shannon discovered that they were hungry, and Mom had them go into the kitchen and stand on a chair by the stove so that they could supervise the scrambling of their eggs. I took Roberta into the bathroom and washed and bandaged her head, and made over her. And Jo came back and hugged us both and said she was sorry, and could she go to the library by herself? And Roberta said I think it'll be all right, don't you, Jimmie; and I said yes. Frankie hollered down the hall that she'd buy a quart of beer, and I hollered back get two and I'll pay for one. And Roberta hollered get some potato chips, too, Frankie, and I'll give you the money when you get back. And later on I told Mom I didn't know what I was saying, and she said, Oh, that's all right. So . . .

It is hideous when you think about it. A child—two children—sick without this insanity which is driving them insane. Lost and bewildered when it was withdrawn. Living in a malarial swamp and not daring to leave it. . . . I think, perhaps, if we could catch them now, change their environment by gentle stages if necessary, something could be done. But we cannot do that.

Nothing is settled, you see. We have spent something tonight that we can never replace—that I, I know, cannot replace—and we have solved nothing. It is futile to hope that we ever will. One of us—I think any one of us—alone, might solve something. But he would have to be alone, be far away. If we were away, where the poisons in us could not be refreshed and restored daily, there might be a chance. Or if I could change things so magnificently that we could have separate rooms, a separate way of life, freedom of action without impinging upon others, so that we would not have to struggle against one another to preserve our own identities, so that we could become acquainted gradually as strangers should. . . . But—there's no chance of that either.

I was sitting in the dinette late tonight, typing, when Mack came through to get a drink of water. I'd worked three hours and I must have had all of thirty words—I, who used to knock out five thousand in a day.

He pulled a chair up to the sink, turned on the faucet, filled a glass, and drank it. Then he brought one to me.

"Saw a bitey inna hall," he said.

"Yeah?"

"Yop. Inna hall, Daddy." He waited. "Saw a bitey inna hall, Daddy."

I turned my head away.

"You sick, Daddy?"

"You'd better learn a new joke, boy," I said. "Better learn a lot of new jokes."

The first time I called at Roberta's house she and her mother were in the kitchen. Roberta let me in and whispered I'll be right with you, honey; and then she went back into the kitchen and I could hear her and her mother talking in low voices. I wanted to smoke, but I couldn't find an ashtray; I looked around for something to read and there wasn't anything. Not a newspaper, not a book or a magazine of any kind. I began to get nervous. I wondered what in the name of God they were talking about, whether the old lady was trying to talk her out of going out with me. Lois' mother hadn't been exactly fond of me either, and her father, who was in the School of Economics at the college, felt that Lois needed someone a little more stable. But it hadn't been like this. . . .

There:

"My dear boy! Aren't you just frozen? Lois will be right down. She's had such a cold today; barely able to drag herself around. I don't suppose I could persuade you two to spend the evening here? The doctor and I are going out, and—goodness gracious! You're sneezing! Aren't you afraid that Lois will catch—?"

"It's nothing serious," I'd say. "Just t.b."

"Oh . . . now, you're teasing me, aren't you? By the way, I've a book you must take with you when you go. Dear, dear Willa! I do know you'll enjoy her. What sacrifices she must have made! What a lonely life she must have led!"

"Willa? Which Willa do you mean?"

"Why, Miss Cather!"

"Oh. I thought you were talking about the other one."

"Which—what other—is there another—?"

Then the doctor, chuckling: "Martha, Martha! . . . By the way, Jim. I've just received my copy of the *Prairie Schooner*. Your story is very well done. Too bad there isn't some money in that sort of thing. Too bad."

That's the way it had been at Lois' house. They didn't hide in the kitchen there. They seated you in a room with a baby grand and more books than a branch library, and then they pelted you with words until your hide became so sore that you began to shout and snarl even before you were touched, until you made such a fool and a boor of yourself that you could never go back.

But at Roberta's:

I got up and began to pace the floor, and finally, call it eavesdropping if you will, I stopped where I could hear:

"Why Mother! You don't mean it!"

"Yessir, that's just what she did! She took a little cornmeal and beat it up with some canned milk and water, and she dipped the bread in that. And it made the finest French toast you ever saw!"

I thought, well for the love of— But it went on and on:

"Mrs. Shropshire's husband came back."

"No!"

"Yes. I was standing out in the—no, I was coming up from the cellar—when I saw him getting out of the car. I don't know where he'd get the money to buy a car with, do you?"

"Now I just wonder, Mother."

And:

"You can't guess how much I paid for eggs today."

"Well, now—how much was that last dozen?"

. . . When we were outside in the car, I said, "Do you always keep your dates waiting while you discuss the price of eggs?"

Roberta said, after a minute, "I don't have very many dates." She flared out, too, with, "But if they don't want to wait, they know what they can do!"

"This one knows," I said, and I drove back around the block and opened the door of the car.

"I didn't mean to make you mad," she said, not stirring.

"It's hereditary. You didn't do it."

"You know what I mean. Mother and I have always been pals. I'm about the only person she really enjoys talking to. I'm away all day, and she looks forward to being with me at night."

"What about your father?"

"He's not much company. Anyway, he's on the night shift with the police department."

"Well, look," I said, "suppose I hadn't come around; suppose no one had come around. What would you have done all evening? Just sat there and talked about nothing?"

"We weren't talking about nothing. I enjoy being with Mother just as much as she enjoys being with me."

"But—but don't you ever read anything, girl?"

"Mother can't—Mother doesn't care much for read-ing."

"But, you! What about you, Roberta?"

"I guess I'd be a fine one to sit with my nose in a book when Mother couldn't—didn't have anyone to talk to! Now wouldn't I?"

She did like to read—I found that out after we were married—but nothing that would help her to a better understanding of herself and me. I was working on an assignment for a string of puff sheets—a cent a word six weeks before publication, and I had to pay travel out of that. Across Iowa, the Dakotas, and Missouri, down through Oklahoma and Texas. When we wanted amuse-ment, we had to fall back on the public libraries. And I was a long time in learning not to be exasperated; I sup-pose I never learned.

"But why can't I have what I like, Jimmie?"

"Why? Because Edgar Wallace is only a man, not a factory."

"Now you tell me why."

"Oh, my—! Roberta, here's an adventure story. It's all about a city way off in Africa, and goddesses, and battles, and stuff like that. A guy named Flaubert wrote it. I think he's going places. I think you'll like him better even than Max Brand. Now please read it, honey."

"I did read it."

"When?"

"Well—I sort of looked through it."

"Roberta! Why, in the name of God, won't you just once read a *book*?"

I knew why, in time—the why of the books and everything else. She was afraid. She wasn't sure of me, and she was afraid that in traveling those paths which might make her sure, which would bind us together, she would only fail in front of me. Now, I only thought —I didn't *know*. It was better to leave it that way.

She didn't mind my reading aloud. Not a bit. Not until Jo came.

"But, Jimmie, you're keeping her awake. You'll make her nervous."

"No, I won't. She'll go to sleep when she gets tired listening."

"Listening! A three-months-old baby!"

"What's the matter? Are you afraid she'll learn something?"

"Oh, go ahead. I suppose she may as well get used to it early."

Then:

A one-room apartment in Fort Worth, or Dallas, or Kansas City. Jo watching my face; Roberta, lying on the bed, watching both of us:

"Now, listen carefully, Jo. What's the little girl's name next door?"

"Woof."

"That's fine. Ruth. And the other little girl—the one down the hall?"

"Mawy?"

"That's right. You're all little girls, but you've got different names. Isn't that funny?"

"Mm-hmm."

"Three little girls, and . . . now look at this thing again—this thing here on the wall. Remember what I told you about the little girls? Three different names? All right, what is this?"

"Cwack?"

"Crack. We already had that. Now what's another name? Remember the three—"

"Kwe-vis?"

"Why of course! Crevice! One more, now. Fis— Fish—"

"Fis-ser?"

"Fissure! That's doing it! Want to see if you can find it in the dictionary?"

"Uh-huh."

"Well. . . . No, No! A-B-C-D-E-F— You remember that! You wouldn't look for my shoes up around my neck, would you? Well. Why look for an f with the a's."

And then:

"Ha, ha. Clever youngster you've got, Dillon. Very. Has she really read *La Fitte*?"

"Yes, and *Children of Strangers*, too."

"Poor child. Probably hold a grudge against me all her life—ha, ha. Very clever. Are you giving me dinner, by the way? I think I'll insist on it. I really shall. If I told you about the luncheon I had— Ugh! Revolting! Actually revolting, old man."

"Well—Mrs. Dillon won't be—I can get some stuff from the delicatessen—"

"Oh, horrors! . . . Ha, ha. Never mind. Just my way of speaking. Got to run, anyway. Really must."

And then:

"Of course he knew you were here. Do you think he's deaf? Why the hell did you have to start running the vacuum cleaner, anyway?"

"Because I wanted to, that's why. And I thought it'd be a doggone good hint to him that someone around this house had something to do!"

"I guess he took it."

"If you can't hold your job without feeding everyone that drops in from Washington or New York or New Orleans, you'd better get another one."

"I may have to."

"Jimmie—you don't mean that, do you?"

"What difference does it make? What difference does anything make? What's the use in having the best job I ever had in my life, in selling everything I can write? What's the use in anything? . . . Oh Christ! Let's take a drink and forget about it."

"I couldn't do it, Jimmie. I just can't do things like that. I can't sit there like a bump on a log and when someone says something not know what—I just can't, Jimmie!"

I'm not blaming anyone, unless it's myself. Not Roberta. I've only been telling you about Roberta, not blaming her. She couldn't have been any different, under the circumstances, just as Jo couldn't have been any different, or I couldn't have been any different. Abe Lincoln could have, but I couldn't. Maybe he couldn't. . . .

And, no, it would have been the same story with a different twist with Lois. We found that out the hard way.

One day, after she was married and I was married, we met on the street in Lincoln. And I undressed her with my eyes and she me with hers. And nothing mattered but that we should be together again. We drove to Marysville, Kansas, and registered at a hotel. We even wrote letters—unmailed, fortunately—explaining why we had had to do what we had done. Then the physical reunion, and after that, talk, lying there together in the dusk. She had it all planned. She had a sorority sister whose husband owned a big advertising agency in Des Moines, and he was a perfectly gorgeous person. If I would just be nice to him—

"What do you mean, nice? I've never spit in anyone's face yet."

"Well, that's what I mean, dear. You say so many things that are misunderstood. They give people the wrong impression of you. They think that—"

"—that I've been in some pretty nasty places. Well, I have been. And anyone who doesn't like it can lump it."

"Please, dear. I think it's marvelous the way you've worked to make something of yourself—"

"—with so little success, is that what you mean? Well, what do you want me to do? Never mind—I'll tell you.

. . . 'Ooh, my deah Mrs. Bunghole, what a delightful blend of pee—excuse me, tea! And what are your beagles doing this season, Mrs. Bunghole? Beagling? Why how gorgeously odd! Do tell me—' "

"Now you're becoming impossible!"

"Perhaps I always was."

"Perhaps."

We went back to Lincoln that same night.

Five years later I would have admitted, in the security I had then, that she was not superficial, and she would have conceded that the common streak in me was no broader than it needed to be. And each would' have borrowed from the other, and profited by it.

And yet I wonder. . . . I'm pretty sure that those five years did things to me which made her wince when she thought of our one-time intimacy. And I can say positively that I felt the same way about her. If I had been her husband, I think I should have put a saddle on her and trotted her around the countryside until she had worked off about forty pounds.

The fool shouldn't have let her get that way. She wouldn't have with me.

THIS IS A TYPICAL DAY FOR ME.

I arise at four, shave, wash and dress, and at four-thirty I start writing. Or, at least, I sit down to my typewriter. I sit there until six—and I usually get something done— by which time Mom has such breakfast as I care to eat. When I have eaten, I lie down on the lounge and rest and smoke until about a quarter of seven. Then I go outside and wait for Murphy to arrive.

He seldom gets here with any time to spare. (We've been more than five minutes late twice.) I can hear him coming several blocks away, and when I do, I get over on the other side of the street and hop in as he slows down.

I grit my teeth and close my eyes as we start down the hill to the bay, and I have a theory that he does, too. We make the descent in twelve jumps—one for each intersection. A good half of the time either the front or rear wheels, or both, are in the air. Stop-signs, children playing ball, switch engines across our path mean nothing. Maybe we jump over them.

At the boulevard he forces his left front wheel between the bumpers of two other cars. Usually, one is forced to give way. If not, he shoots the car into reverse, then darts ahead with the right wheels on the sidewalk and the others scraping fenders with those in the procession until he sees another "opening." And so on until he is able to crash through.

The road leading to the plant is only two-lane, and the night shift is coming off duty at the time. But Murphy doesn't mind them. He stays on the left side of the road, and if the night workers want to eat breakfast at home instead of in the hospital, they will pull off on the bay shore. Well, Murphy will give way, but I think he feels imposed upon when he has to. After all, he is only a few seconds in getting to the plant while they are minutes on the road.

We arrive at the plant midway between the first and last whistle and punch in as the last one is blowing.

He smiles with satisfaction. "Thought we were going to be late, didn't you?"

"I thought we were going to be dead."

"Ha, huh. Didn't scare you, did I?"

"Oh, no!"

The stockroom floor is covered with piles of parts that have come in during the night. I list the travelers on each pile, then check the list with my books. Any parts that are short on the assembly lines are sent out at once. I have to see that the travelers match the parts they accompany—the move-boys delight in dropping the right traveler on the wrong part—and that lefts and rights of a certain part have not come in on the same traveler. Frequently, a part that has been universal is changed into left and right or inboard and outboard without our being notified. Engineering forgets about it, or the office makes one of its many slips, and we have the same number on more than one part. This, obviously, won't do.

But my chief trouble is with the stockchasers or expediters.

There is one expediter for every two positions on Final Assembly, and one each for Wing and Control Surfaces. It is their job to see that there is a continuous flow of parts from the manufacturing departments to their assemblies or "projects"; to see that never, at any time, is there a delay in production because of parts' shortages.

It is my opinion and the opinion of every other stockroom worker that they are damned nuisances who actually slow things down instead of speeding them up. But I suppose we're prejudiced. Practically every defense plant has them; if they weren't a necessity, they wouldn't be there. Blueprints and work orders get mislaid; foremen keep putting off a difficult job for an easy one; parts become buried in the various stockrooms; move-boys pile finished parts in with unfinished. So the expediters, who speed from one end of the plant to the other, who keep themselves informed of plans before they are reduced to paper, who are bursting with knowledge of every phase of production connected with their project—they really are necessary.

Any shortage means a reproof for them. Many shortages mean dismissal. So shortages are their only concern.

They pour through the gate the moment it is opened, grab up such parts as they need to stay an immediate shortage, and dash out again—without the formality of telling me what they have taken.

I or Murphy or one of the others will call out:

"Hey, there! Where you going with that?"

"Position 4," the stockchaser calls back. "They're waiting for—"

"Let 'em wait. What you got, anyway?"

"Oh, hell. Just a half dozen pieces. I'll tell you about it after—"

"Half a dozen, hell! I can see eight from here. What are those anyway? Tank-support brackets?"

"Yeah. I'll give you the number after—"

"You'll give it right now. What's the matter with you guys? Don't you know we have to keep records here? That'd throw us off in two places. The traveler'd be short and Final'd be long."

Sometimes it will go like this:

"Now wait a minute! Wing's already got plenty of that! You tell 'em to look around down there."

"No, they haven't, Dilly. I'll swear to God they've been crying for this stuff for a week. Let me take it now, and if I find any down there—"

"Moon! Oh Moon!"

"What's the matter, Dilly?"

"Our friend here is trying to get out with these static tubes. Wing's got enough already."

"Put them back where you got them," says Moon, eyeing the stockchaser somberly.

"I can't, Moon. By God, I just got to have them."

"No, you don't. They've already got enough static tubes down there."

"Yeah, but they're short on pitots. I was going to—"

"Just what I thought," says Moon grimly. "You were going to change the tape on them and use 'em for pitots. Just wait until Material Control hears about this."

"Aw, now, Moon . . ."

"Put 'em down, then." And the old harried question. "What's the matter with you guys, anyway? Don't you know what that would do to our records? We'd show fifty statics out and no pitots when we'd actually have twenty-five of each."

One of the most infuriating tricks of the stockchasers is the taking of parts from the paint shop or plating direct to the assemblies without telling us about it. Another is to have parts reworked into other parts without a rework order. Yes, there are rules against this sort of thing, but the plant authorities wink at them. Anything to solve an emergency, regardless of whether the solution creates another emergency or not.

I suppose I should be glad that things are like this, because it would be extremely difficult to hold me culpable for any costly mistakes or delays that occur. I'm not breathing any too easily, but I think it would be. But, despite that fact, I would rather find some other way out.

I don't like so much turmoil; so many arguments. I think there is an easier, less nerve-wracking, and better way of doing things.

I think the essential difficulty is our system of keeping records. And I don't think there will ever be any improvement until we change it. As it is, the parts are classified according to positions and assemblies, and a part may be carried in one position one day and another the next. This makes for a lot of erasing and scratching out. It makes it possible for us to show a shortage on a part when we actually have more than we need, and vice versa. It means that the only way you can be sure that you have not overlooked a part is to start searching for it at the top of the first page of the release book and search right through to the last.

Worst of all is this business of breaking everything up into ship-units of twenty-five. What is gained by that? I wonder if the fellow who set up this system thought of the work it would involve? That to receive a quantity of only one part, the bookkeeper would have to make as many as thirty entries?

And there are no places to show dates of arrivals and issues. No wonder we can never win an argument with the other departments. It's simply our word against theirs, or, rather, their many words against ours; so we're always to blame.

But to get on:

I spend an hour or so out on the assembly lines, checking for parts that may have been short-circuited around us, and tracing out the effective numbers on new parts. I may have made this last seem a little too simple when I first spoke of it. You see, many parts on a plane are concealed.

I come back to the stockroom and usually find a number of parts which do not belong there. Yes, the move-boys did and do have instructions to bring nothing to us until it has been turned down by the other stockrooms; and they'll always swear that they've done so. But if they don't, and obviously they don't, there's little to be done. Moving is pretty much a beginner's job; few stay on it after their probationary period is over. By the time you reported a move-boy—and I've never done it—he'd probably be in some other department. So, to repeat, there's little to be done. And, of course, these mistakes aren't always the move-boys' fault. Probably not more than half the time.

Speaking frankly, Moon gives me more trouble than any man outside the department. He usually forgets to write down the parts he issues. Invariably, instead of setting down the part number, he uses the name. And, no, that doesn't do just as well. We've got three or four hundred different kinds of brackets, for instance, and it's impossible to distinguish one from the other by name or description. Particularly when your vocabulary is as limited as Moon's. You can do it by number.

Gross is a constant source of trouble, too. But with him it's deliberate. I can never take his count on anything. I have to make a re-check.

As for Murphy, well, he's careful and conscientious and he's friendly toward me. But there's a flaw in his vision, a peculiar quirk, which makes him write backwards and upside down: 31 for 13, and w for m.

In a way, of course, the situation has its bright side— in the same way that my difficulties with the expediters have their bright side. But I still don't like it. In fact, I feel some days that I can't stand it. I want to shake Moon, and tell Gross to straighten up or get out, and advise Murphy to see an oculist. But, of course, I don't. I've got to get along.

I never go to the toilet or take a drink of water on my own time. I don't have enough of it. The lunch period is only thirty minutes, and it takes about five minutes to get out of the plant and find a spot to sit, and another five to get back in again. Obviously, unless I want to swallow my food whole and do without smoking, I drink and go to the toilet on the company. Everyone does.

Well, the whistle blows, and I race for the door. And two thousand other men are racing with me. By the time I get outside, sitting space against the sheet-metal sides of the building is already at a premium. I see an empty space far down the wall and run for it.

"Hey, turd-head!" someone calls.

I don't look around.

"Hey, prick!"

I hurry on. By stopping I would admit that "I knew my name."

I go on down the wall, and if the space I come to is

not marked RESTRICTED AREA, I sit down. I unscrew the vacuum bottle as I reach into my lunch sack, so that not one of the precious twenty minutes will be wasted.

Yes, I mind.

The first time I was called by "name," I got white in the face and stopped and demanded to know "Who said that?" It was a boy of twenty or so, clean-cut, good will shining out of his face, embarrassed and very much astonished. He muttered something about kidding, and someone near by said, "Can't you take a joke?" So I went on, and I've never stopped since.

But I mind. It's not that I've never been called things like that before. You hear some pretty salty talk around hotel locker-rooms and in the pipeline camps. You hear so much that, if you are like me, you will do almost anything to get away from it. And when you do, and have to come back, it is all the harder. Particularly if you are thirty-five and see no way of getting away again.

While we are on this subject: In the ten weeks I have been here I have heard the word f—k used more often than I had in my life heretofore. Everyone uses it, from the factory manager down to the maintenance men. Upstairs in the office you will hear it fifty times in an hour, and the women and girls have become so accustomed to it that they never so much as raise an eyebrow.

A part is f—ked up. Sheet-metal is f—king around again. If those f—kers in Engineering don't do this, we'll do so and so. A design is f—king well all right (or not *all right).* If you're in error, you've f—ked *things.* You're f—ked *(stumped).*

I don't know why the word should be so much more popular in aircraft than it is elsewhere, but there must be a reason. I've been dallying with the idea of writing Ben Botkin about it—perhaps doing a little paper on it—but, of course, I won't. If I do any writing, it'll be on my story. It's about finished, and I can get some money for it. I hope.

Generally, you don't hear as much off-color talk around the plant as you would elsewhere. (I know I've given a contrary impression.) What you do hear is less sordid, seemingly, than the brand outside. There is something light-hearted about it. I have heard only one shady story since I have been here—only one that you couldn't tell in church.

San Diego, prior to the establishment of the aircraft factories, was not inappropriately dubbed the "City of the Living Dead." There were no industries, there was no construction; the town's one asset was its climate. If you were young and wanted excitement and had a living to make, why, the town wouldn't want you and you wouldn't want it. If you were old and had a small income or pension, you couldn't have found a more attractive place to live (or die) in.

Well, when the defense boom struck, the town just couldn't throw off its lethargy. It did ultimately, but for a long time the city fathers' idea of taking care of a 100 per cent increase in population was to up the price of rents and other living incidentals by a corresponding increase. Living isn't cheap here now, or even moderately reasonable, but the Government has stepped in and— But here's the story:

A newly arrived aircraft worker walked into a bar and ordered a cheese sandwich and a bottle of beer. The waitress took the dollar bill he proffered in payment and gave him back a dime in change.

Ruefully the aircrafter asked her if there wasn't some mistake.

Oh no. Sandwich, fifty. Beer, forty. No mistake.

"Funny," said the aircrafter in a tone that said it wasn't. And his eyes settled on the buxom mounds of her bosom. "What's those?"

The waitress colored. "Why they're my breasts, you fool! What'd you think they were?"

"Didn't know. Everything else is so high in here I thought they might be the cheeks of your ass."

Offhand, I'd say that two-thirds of the men are under thirty; half of them, probably, under twenty-five. And intelligence is much higher than the average. Once in a while a misfit like Gross or myself slips in, but not often. And you can be reasonably sure that the misfits are not without certain valuable talents. The plant believes that, in them, it has something to work on, and it is willing to risk a little money on the belief.

Practically every production worker who is not already a skilled mechanic must be a trade-school graduate, which means, invariably, that he is a high-school graduate also.

In non-production work, such as I am in, two years of college or the equivalent are required. Degrees are so numerous around here as to be commonplace. An average of only one out of every twenty-five applicants is given a job, and fully a fourth of those are discharged during or at the end of the thirty-day probationary period.

I mention all this, not by way of giving myself an indirect pat on the back, but because of the newspaper talk to the effect that the aircraft plants have made the WPA and other relief agencies unnecessary. Nothing could be further from the truth. You find no dispossessed share-croppers or barnyard mechanics here. They get no farther than the office-boy in the Personnel Department.

Well, there's the whistle. So a final drag on a cigarette and back we go again for four more hours. . . .

The office crowd has begun to get its breath by now and is hollering for something more to worry about. The auto-call roars. The phone begins to ring:

"Dilly? How about a shortage report on Position 4 by three-thirty?"

"I'll try. For how many ships?"

"Well—where are we now?"

"We've got fifty in the yard, but we're not through with 'em, you know. We need props on about fifteen, and the cockpit leathers and—"

"We've got an acceptance on fifty, though? Make it for the next twenty-five, then."

"All right. Say—I notice you're still figuring thirteen

wing inspection-hole covers to a ship. We're using twenty-two."

"We'll catch it. You'll get the report for us? Swell!"

One thing I like about this plant: You don't have to hem and haw and be sugar-tongued with anyone. They don't want you to. If you've got a criticism or some information to pass on, you do it in the quickest possible fashion, and no formalities. I "Mister" our superintendent, Dolling, and try to choose my words because, without doing or saying anything, he insists upon it. But with anyone else—the chief inspector, the production manager, or whoever—it's "Here's the dope," and on to something else. And if someone, regardless of his position, butts in on something that he knows less about than you do, you tell him where to get off.

A few days ago, while Moon and I were at the window checking through some travelers, one of the many vice-presidents stalked up. There was a pile of leading edges on the floor; he nodded at them, looked at me. I am older than Moon; I also dress less roughly. I suppose the v.p. thought I was in charge.

"Nice bunch of edges you've got there," he said.

I said, "Yes, what about them?"

"Get them off the floor this instant! What do you think those racks are for?"

I looked at Moon.

"Tell him to go piss up a rope," said Moon idly.

The v.p. choked, spluttered, and rushed away. A few minutes later our phone rang and Moon answered it.

"Yeah, I told him that," he said. "Only I didn't say pee. Those edges are drilled wrong. We're waiting for a move-boy to pick 'em up."

That was the end of the matter.

I spoke of having turned out fifty planes. The Government has accepted that many, but only a few of them are complete. We're short of props, instrument panels, tailwheels, and dozens of smaller items. A few of the things may actually be in the plant; the majority, I believe, are not. Every day searching parties from Dispatch, Inspection, and Material Control go through. But they rarely find anything any more. No one can be sure that an order we received hasn't been scrapped or loaned to another plant. No one can be sure of anything.

Some of the things that happen in here are nothing less than fantastic. One Monday morning while I was posting my travelers, I ran across three, for a certain type of fairing, that had no count on them. I checked with all the boys, trying to find out who had put them up, and they all denied that they had. I went through the fairing section, piece by piece, and I couldn't find anything that matched the description on the travelers. I checked my books; I wasn't carrying any fairing under those three numbers. I checked with the foremen on Final Assembly; they'd never heard of any fairing like that. Certainly they'd never put any on the planes—I could see that for myself. I began to get cold chills.

According to the travelers, those fairings had been

used from the start. Fifty pieces of each had cleared through me and should have gone on the planes—but they hadn't and I didn't have them. As I say, I didn't even have a record on them. I went to Moon with it. He got kind of pale around the gills and went to Baldwin. Baldwin tore his hair out by the handful and began calling Material Control, and Sheet-metal, Inspection, Dispatching, Painting and Dope Shop. And the various foremen and superintendents came rushing up to his office to study the travelers and—nope, they'd never seen anything like that.

I won't give you all the painful details. Blueprint-crib finally solved the puzzle. The travelers bore work-order instead of finished-parts' numbers. They actually covered only one part which we carried on our books under an assembly number. Some overly-fastidious (and new) routing clerk, averse to the idea of crowding one traveler with the delineation of the hundreds of processes involved in making the assembly, had innocently spread the information through sub-division numbers which he had picked off the blueprint.

Well, I'll admit it. I don't see how I could possibly have anything to be afraid of. But I'm keeping my fingers crossed. It sounds foolish, childish; but it's been my experience that I can avoid a potential disaster by worrying about it enough. Anyway, it's just as well to think that I do have to stay here. Because, of course, I must. At least until I can get my story sold, and Pop settled, and Frankie toned down a little, and—

As to why the Government accepts planes that can't be flown, I don't know. The way I figure it is that we've either got a darned good sales manager or someone in the government procurement office is overly anxious to make a showing.

I'm getting sixty-five cents an hour now. That's supposed to be very good for a man who has been here such a comparatively short time, and Dolling made it very clear that the company wasn't obliged to give it to me. It's as much as Murphy gets; it's five cents more than Gross's wage. I think I'm underpaid, naturally, but I can't say anything so long as the records are in their present shape. It isn't my fault, but I can't say anything.

If anyone has been mistreated here, it's Murphy. That really is his right name. He's half-Irish, half-Mexican. When he ruined his hands fighting, he took what money he had and studied mechanical engineering for two years. Some small, cheap, and not very good school that few have ever heard of. Graduating, he was unable to get a job at his profession and he worked as a messenger, soda-clerk, and whatever he could get to do for a few years. When WPA opened up, he got a job as a cartographer on one of the records' projects. And, with the beginning of defense work, he applied and was accepted here.

I don't suppose he was outstanding as a draughtsman. On the other hand he was probably no worse than dozens of others, and, given time, he doubtless would have become a valuable man. But he didn't mix well, and he looked like a Mexican, and—and he's down here now.

. . . At one o'clock my head begins to swim. I pour out half of the cup of coffee I have saved, and toss it down.

At a quarter of two my head snaps up and I look at the paper in my typewriter. There are two lines more of type than there should be. When I last looked—saw— there were three lines; now there are five. They all seem to be all right though. I get a drink of water and come back again.

. . . *just enough to sleep on and not hear and no morn-ing and write no morning and write but drink and sleep but write . . .*

"Dilly! . . . Oh Dilly!"

Moon is at my side. Not looking at me; not noticing. Moon is good. Much kinder to me than he should be.

"Want to take a walk upstairs, Dilly? Get us some carbon—(or pencils, or take these reports up)?"

I go upstairs. You can smoke up there. You can light up as soon as you hit the foot of the stairs.

Two-thirty, and the rest of the coffee. Three.

. . . *half tonight and half in the morning write and sleep no job job . . .*

The low voice again. It has to be low to get under the noise; you soon learn that you can't get above it:

"Got about ten minutes, Dilly. Dilly, about through? Ten minutes?"

"Huh—sure. Sure. Just about set."

I rip out the five copies: one for us, one for Dispatching, one for Production, and one for the expediter. God,
will he catch it! What about the extra copy—a thousand
times, and you've forgotten. Can't ask anyone. They'll
think you're crazy . . . Material Control? No. Sheet-
metal? Sub-assembly? Factory manager? No, no, no.
Plating, Painting, Planning, Lofting? No! No! No! Drop-
hammer, Plannishing? Oh God, no; what would they
want with it! Punchpress, Sewing, Singing, Praying. . . .

"Dilly, you made a copy for Inspection, didn't you?"

Inspection, Inspection!

"Oh—sure, sure. Taking 'em around right now."

The five-minute whistle blows. Upstairs and back—
four blocks—and five minutes to do it in. They want
you out of here when that second whistle blows. If you're
caught inside without an overtime pass, you can't get out.

". . . matter, Dillon? You tired?"

I sit up. Murphy is grinning sympathetically, and we
are crossing Pacific Boulevard.

"Kind of."

"Kind of a hard day."

"Say, Murph, I know I must have—but did you notice
whether I punched out?"

"Yeah. You punched out all right. I was right behind
you . . . well, here we are. See you in the morning, huh?"

"Yup."

"I may be a little late. Got to bring the wife in, and—"

"Now not too late, Murph! One more ride like that
this morning—"

"Ha, huh! Okay, Dillon. So long."

"So long, Murph."

. . . The whistle is blowing, and Moon is talking to me.

"Want to help me take some stuff down to the express office, Dilly? We can get a couple hours for it."

Two hours of overtime—two dollars. It won't really be working, and that doctor bill of Shannon's . . .

"Why sure. Thanks."

"I thought maybe you and your wife and Frankie and me might do something tonight."

"I don't know about Frankie, Moon. I think she said something about—"

"Aw, she can't always be tied up."

"Well . . ."

He waits for me to say it.

"Well. All right."

SHANNON AND MACK WERE SITTING ON THE FRONT STEPS. Moon, who was preceding me, stopped in front of them.

"Seen any policemen around?"

They grinned and shook their heads.

"Well, there's some in the neighborhood," he declared solemnly, and he fumbled in his pocket and produced two dimes. "You take these and stay out here and sort of keep on the lookout for 'em. If you see any, run in and tell me. I'll come out and beat 'em up."

"Get ice cweam?" said Mack.

"Good ice cream at my store," said Shannon, looking at Moon hopefully.

"Sure," said Moon. "But look out for the policemen."

I said, "Hadn't you better wait until after dinner?"

But of course no one paid any attention to me.

Shannon dashed off, Mack churning along behind her, his usual three paces to the rear. Moon went on into the kitchen and put the packages down.

"Hi, Mom," he said.

"Why it's Mr. Moon," said Mom, pleased. "You would catch me looking like this!"

"Got enough skillets to cook four pounds of pork chops?"

"You didn't get four pounds!" said Mom. "Jimmie, what did you let Mr. Moon get so much for?"

"Now, never you mind," said Moon, opening another sack. "Just get 'em cooked or you don't get any of this sherry."

It was ten years old. I was kind of ashamed of, but more sorry for, Mom—the way her eyes glittered when she tasted it. She's had so few good things, and she enjoys them so much. Only—well, maybe I'm a snob. But what right had he to come into my house and call my mother anything but Mrs. Dillon, and take it for granted that she'd be as glad to get the wine as—as she was?

I guess I've answered my own question. I am too thin-skinned; everyone says so.

He fixed rye highballs for himself and me, getting down the glasses and making himself perfectly at home. We went back into the living room, and he opened the hall door and shouted for Roberta. Well, perhaps *shout* is the wrong word. He never raises his voice very much.

Roberta opened the bedroom door. "Is that you, Mooney? I'm not dressed yet."

"Goody," said Moon. "Come right on out."

Roberta laughed, and above the sizzle of chops and the clinking of glass I heard Mom laugh. I laughed too—Moon was looking at me. And he hadn't said anything out of the way. Moon is all right.

Roberta came in and shoved him playfully.

"Hi, Mooney."

"Hi, Sunny."

She laughed; different from the way she usually laughs. "What're you drinking? . . . Oh phoot! Why didn't you get gin? You know how I like Tom Collinses."

"I didn't know it."

"You did, too. You knew—" She paused, seeing Moon wink at me. "You did get some, didn't you?"

"Did we, Dilly? I can't remember."

"Why you mean thing!" said Roberta, and she pushed him again.

I went out into the kitchen and fixed her a Tom Collins. No; please get that straight. I am not, never have been, jealous of Roberta. Sometimes, when I have been looking for a reason to escape, I have wished that I had cause to be jealous. But I know I haven't—that I never will have. Actually, I suppose, I was angry with myself. Angry because any outsider could make himself more at home than I could.

When I took Roberta's drink to her, I brought along another stiff drink for myself. I began to thaw a little after I'd got it down.

Jo came in and sat down on the arm of my chair.

"Can't you say hello to Mr. Moon?" said Roberta.

"Hello," said Jo.

Moon said, "Hello, Jo. How are you?"

Jo smiled at him silently.

Moon ran his hand into his pocket. "You don't know any dances do you, Jo? I'd give a quarter to see a real good dance."

"I don't know any," said Jo.

"You do, too, Jo," said Roberta. "You know a—"

"I've forgotten, Mother."

"But you've been dancing around here all day! You couldn't have—"

"I'm tired, Mother."

"Jo!"

It was probably a very good thing that Frankie arrived at that moment. She dropped down on the divan next to Moon, pushing her hat back, and kicking off her shoes. She removed the drink from his hand and, gripping her nose with two fingers, killed it at a gulp.

"Ugh! I don't see how you can drink rye mixed."

"Like one straight?" said Moon.

"Well, okay."

He got the bottle and we all had another drink. Frankie had a new story. It was the one about the old king who had three beautiful daughters, one of whom he was going to award to a knight for doing something or other. The question was: Which one did the knight choose. And the answer: None. He took the king. This was a fairy story.

Moon didn't laugh very hard. I got the impression that he didn't like to hear Frankie talk like that, and I wondered what business it was of his how she talked. I don't wonder now because I know that, despite everything, he was in love with her.

"Got a date tonight?" he said.

"Yep."

"Thought we all might go down to Tia Juana."

"Well . . . gee . . ." said Frankie, and glanced at me.

"I'd sure like to go," said Roberta. "You ought to go, too, Jimmie. All the time we've been here and you've never been across the border. Maybe you could get an idea for a story."

I laughed, probably not very pleasantly. "Do you suppose I could get the time to write it, too?"

"Do you good to get out, Dilly," said Moon.

"And it wouldn't do me any harm," said Roberta. "I've not been out of this house in weeks. I may not be as smart as some people, but I'm still human."

"Now, honey," I said.

Mom came in from the kitchen. "If youall want to go, I'll take care of the kids."

"I guess I could break my date," said Frankie.

Well . . .

"Well, it suits me fine," I said. "Let's go."

We didn't eat much dinner. Frankie and Roberta had a lot of getting ready to do, and Moon and I had drunk too much to be very hungry. None of us was drunk, though. Just feeling good. Roberta and Moon and Frankie were feeling good, and I felt less bad than usual.

As we rushed through the night toward the border, Roberta snuggled close to me and tucked my hand under her breast.

"You're not mad at me, are you? I thought we just about had to come."

"I suppose we did."

"Moon's been by so many times, and he's your boss and all, and I thought—"

"We had to," I said.

"Got any money with you?"

"All of seven cents."

"I've got a dollar but let's not spend it unless we have to. We need so many things, Jimmie."

"Look," I said, "whose idea was this, anyway? How do you expect to go down here and spend an evening without money?"

"Moon's got plenty of money. You just let him pay for things."

"I guess I'll have to."

She stiffened in my arm and looked straight ahead, and I knew that I was as bewildering and unreasonable to her as she was to me. I pulled her head down in my lap, and put my mouth over hers. And after a moment her lips parted, and her hands were twining in my hair. She rolled from the waist, bringing her feet up into the seat, and the wind dropped her dress around her thighs, and in the moonlight they were pure ivory. She had no girdle on (I think they make a woman look cramped), only the frilly white panties which she buys—or used to buy—by the dozens because she knows I am disturbed by the potential uncleanliness of colors; and she used no perfume because I object to that for much the same reason. And I thought, bending over her, knowing that her eyes were closed so that mine might be open, how many ways, in this one way—the one way she understood—she had tried to make herself over to my pattern. And I thought how thankless the task must seem to her, and I longed, for the moment at least, to look only on those efforts and their results—to look, to forget, and to want no more.

And I knew, before the wish was full-formed, that I couldn't. I couldn't because I had been down to the bottom and I knew what was there, and I knew each pleasant and deceptive curve of the descent. I couldn't because of a tall overweight farm boy who had entered the first grade when he was sixteen, and who was admitted to the bar at twenty-one; an absent-minded untidy fat man who won 129 of his first 135 cases; a man who forgot to pay grocery bills, but who would borrow money for the *Letters of the Presidents* or *American History in Romance*; a broke and friendless old man who had told me to leave him and go to school.

We didn't stop at the Mexican Customs Office. Moon merely slowed the car a little, honked, and sped by. The two guards, in their multi-buttoned uniforms, looked after us smilingly, although, it seemed to me, a shade crestfallen.

In another two minutes we were entering the long main street of the town.

Moon said Wednesday wasn't a very good night. "We ought to come down some Saturday." But it was good enough for Roberta. She sat up, leaning first out of my window, then hers. Laughing excitedly. Pointing. Asking questions.

"Oh look, honey! Look Frankie! That woman—isn't she a movie star? No, *that* one. Oh she's gone now! . . . Are all those places saloons, Mooney? How do they all make a living? Do you suppose that stuff on the pushcarts is good to eat? I guess there'd be a law if it wasn't, don't you, honey? Oh Frankie"—with a long sigh—"look at those hats! Did you ever — why they're as big as umbrellas!"

"Like to have one?" said Moon, turning the car into the curb.

"I guess not," said Frankie.

"How much are they?" asked Roberta.

"I'll make them give us some," said Moon. "Come on. Leave your hats in the car."

As we got out, a dozen or so ragged children swarmed around us. "Give us penny, misters. Ladies, give us pennies. Penny, penny, penny!" they screamed.

Roberta and Frankie automatically began fumbling with their purses, but Moon pushed us on ahead into one of the dozens of curio and souvenir shops.

"It's not the money. You give one of them anything and we'll have a parade behind us all evening wherever we go."

Moon speaks Spanish or, I should say, Mexican, fluently. The kind of Mexican that the Mexicans speak. He and the proprietor were haggling in a friendly fashion all the time we were trying on hats.

I don't know what he paid for them, but I think it was a dollar each. They weren't as big as umbrellas; they were

177

bigger. There wasn't room for two of us on the sidewalk when we had them on, so we took them off and carried them.

We walked across the street to the "longest bar in the world." There were only a few people in it, all non-Mexican except for the employees; but the marimba band was playing away as vigorously as if the place had been packed.

The girls went back to the restroom and Moon and I had Scotch and sodas. They hadn't returned by the time we had finished them, so we had tequila with salt and lemon. And then because it slid down so nicely, we had another. Things began to get pretty rosy about that time.

A drunk, hatless and with a filthy vest, staggered out on the floor and approached the end marimba player. The latter, a plump elf-like fellow, tried to shoo him away; but the drunk wouldn't be shooed. He kept shouting for "Home on the Range," and the more he was disdained, the more determined he became. Finally he started to climb up on the platform.

The marimba-player moved his sticks off into space a few inches and, without the barest flicker of a smile, tapped out the remainder of the score on the drunk's bald head. The drunk went down on his knees and was hustled out by two waiters.

Well—it doesn't sound funny now. But I laughed so hard that I would have fallen off my stool if Moon hadn't caught me. He wasn't as drunk as I was, I guess. In fact I'm sure he wasn't.

Roberta and Frankie came out and had drinks, and
then we strolled up and across the street to the Mona
Lisa. It's run by Chinese, as many of the places in Tia
are, and the prices are pretty stiff. Of course, you can get
beer for fifteen cents a glass and a shot of tequila for the
same. But you're liable to find that your table is needed
shortly if you do. The hosts of Aunt Jane aren't at all
inhibited about things like that. They feel not the slightest shame in telling you that you're not drinking fast
enough to be a good customer. If you want to fight about
it, that's all right too. You'll never want to brawl again
after you've been in Tia jail once.

Moon ordered Sunrise Specials at fifty cents a piece.
Before they could be brought, Roberta and I got out on
the dance floor, but we needn't have done so. Moon had
made a deposit with the cashier when we came in, and
no checks were ever brought to the table. I don't know
how large the deposit was. Roberta and I could never
make anything more than a rough estimate as to the size
of our bill. But I think it must have been twenty dollars
anyway.

I don't know, either, when Moon and Frankie left.
The place began to fill up, and the orchestra was playing
steadily. We'd go back to the table and Frankie and
Moon wouldn't be there, and we'd just suppose they
were out on the dance floor. For that matter we weren't
bothered about anything much but having a good time.
I was drunk—not staggering drunk, I never stagger; but
totally irresponsible. Roberta, who doesn't have much

capacity, was tipsy. It'd been two or three years since I'd seen her enjoy herself so much. It'd been that long since we could really cut loose without scrimping for a month afterwards. Tonight we didn't have to worry about money.

Well, but money couldn't bring us back those two or three years.

Along about eleven o'clock we were sitting much more than we were dancing, and Roberta kept saying, "I wonder where they could be, Jimmie?"

And I'd say, "Huh?"

And she'd say, "Moon and Frankie. I must say they've got darned bad manners to go off and leave us like this. Where do you suppose they could be?"

"I dunno. Let's have another drink."

After a while I suggested that we go to bed. "You got a dollar," I recalled. "We can get a room for a dollar."

"Jimmie!"

"What's wrong with that?"

"We're going to get some black coffee and something to eat. And you're going to straighten up. . . . Oh, that Frankie!"

We had ham and eggs and coffee. We were on our second pot of coffee when Moon and Frankie returned.

"And where have you been?" Roberta demanded.

Frankie slumped against the bench, wearily. "Oh—what a time we've had. We went outside to get a breath of air, and one of Mooney's tires was going down. So we drove down the street to get it fixed. We finally found one, a filling station, where they did tire work, and got it patched. And then the car wouldn't start. Something wrong with the battery—"

"The switch," said Moon.

"Well, anyway—"

"Anyway, we finally got here," Moon said. "How about another drink? Roberta?"

"No thank you."

"I don't think I want any," I said.

"Jimmie and I have to be going," said Roberta. "We should have gone a long time ago."

"So should I," said Moon. "We'll go as soon as Frankie and I have one."

He and Frankie had double bourbons, straight—and they did look like they needed them—then we left.

The ride home wasn't exactly pleasant. There were probably thirty cars ahead of us at the U. S. Customs Office, and we were almost an hour getting to the head of the line. And the silence, while we waited, was pretty heavy. Frankie got off a joke or two, but they didn't go over. Roberta was mad, Moon was getting, and I was trying, out of a sense of duty, to work up to it.

At last a door on each side of the car was jerked open, and two khaki clad patrol officers turned their flashlights on us.

United States citizens?

Yes.

Birthplace?

We told them.

Anything to declare? Cigarettes, liquor, clothing. . . .
No, no. Well, we did have those hats.

"We won't charge you for those. Let's take a look in your back end."

Moon pulled his bunch of keys from the switch and handed them out.

"How about hurrying it up a little?" he said.

"How about getting out and opening it yourself?" said the guard.

Moon muttered something under his breath and got out. I felt constrained to get out also. I followed him around to the back of the car and watched while he tried each of the keys in the lock. He straightened up for a minute, wiped the sweat from his forehead, and began trying them over again.

"Can't you find the right key?" said the stern-faced gray-haired guard.

"Sure," said Moon. "I'm just stalling you guys. I've got six Chinks and a ton of opium in here."

"Better snap into it."

"Snap into my ass," said Moon.

The younger guard took a step toward him, but the other put out his hand.

"Step in the station, Bill," he said. "And bring out the hacksaw."

"Now you're not going to saw that lock," said Moon.

"Can you open it?"

"No, I can't. I must have left the keys at home."

"Too bad."

The other guard came back with the saw. Frankie climbed out of the car.

"What're you going to do, anyway?"

"We're going to saw the lock, lady."

"Well of all things! What are you going to do that for? We don't have anything in there."

"We don't know that, lady."

Roberta stuck her head out. "If you ask me, there isn't much you do know."

The two guards looked at each other. The oldest one turned to Moon. "Pull over here under the shed."

"Now what the hell—"

"And cut out the cursing. We don't take it."

"But—"

"We can't bother with you now. You'll have to wait until we get rid of these other cars."

We waited. Hours passed and still we waited. As long as the guards could see a car approaching, they made us wait. And then, taking their time, they sawed the lock. It was five-thirty when we pulled up in front of our house in San Diego.

Moon went on home, saying that he thought he'd lay off that day. Frankie said she thought she would, too; she works on a straight salary, not an hourly rate as I do.

Roberta said, "Jimmie, you know you can't work today. What's the use of being stubborn about it?"

I said, "Oh, hell!"

When you're working forty-eight hours, the day you lose is your overtime. My rate was only a little over five dollars a day; but if I lost a day, my check would be short eight dollars. We couldn't get along without it.

I fussed and swore around until she finally dug down in the trunk and got the little brown bottle she'd hidden. Then she went to bed crying, saying that she j-just hoped I blew the top of my d-damned head off.

Now there's nothing wrong with this drug. The trouble is with the people who take it. Two tablets in a glass of coke will put you on such a wildly delicious drunk that you'll never want to come out of it—and you may not. A tablet and perhaps a fraction of one, the morning after, will convince you that you have the hangover problem licked. (And, of course, you never do.) A dose—the same dosage produces different effects on different days —will have you believing that sleep and food are non-essentials.

I started off with half a tablet, and added to it by eighths. At a tablet and a quarter my eyelids snapped open so hard that it was like two doors slamming. There was a lull then, so I took another quarter.

My scalp prickled and the hair seemed to rise and drop back to my head. My back and shoulder muscles flexed themselves. My nostrils trembled and I could smell a thousand scents I had never smelled before. My eyes coned outward, the pupils narrowing, and I knew without really looking that there were exactly 122 bricks in the fireplace and that the corner of the rug beneath the divan was turned up. And I was filled with such furious energy and impatience that to be idle was agony.

Unlike alcohol, this drug doesn't leave you stupid and drowsy. It makes you want to work, and you can literally work yourself to death while under the influence. You are suddenly impelled to do all the forbidding tasks you have been putting off, and you do them well, too, because your mind is wearing itself out at the rate of about an hour per minute.

That day shot past so swiftly that the scenes of its composition, while perfectly clear and unblurred at the time, are impossible to recall—there were so many thousands of them and they were moving so rapidly. For that matter, however, only a few are really pertinent.

I remember:

Asking Murphy if it was characteristic of the Mexican temperament always to be late; whether or not he had ever consulted an oculist about his eyes; and whether or not he did not think it would be better for him to take any job he could get and go back to school for a few years. (Of course, I wasn't trying to insult him. At the time, I simply wanted to know; had to know.)

That Vail told me to mind my own goddamned business and he'd mind his; and that I neither protested nor was disturbed—there were so many things that needed doing.

That I had a huge mass of index cards spread out in front of me; and that I wasn't having the slightest difficulty in operating the typewriter with one hand while I turned the pages of the release books with the other.

That a prematurely gray man, Baldwin, the production manager, was leaning over my desk, frowning:

"I don't know, Dilly. Did you ask Dolling about this?"

"What's the use? He doesn't know anything. What goddamned fool set this system up anyway?"

"I did."

And I remember that when I went outside that night Murphy had gone.

MEMORIAL DAY CAME THAT WEEKEND, AND WE HAD A three-day holiday beginning on Friday. I had time to get straightened out after a fashion. I'd finished my story a few weeks before and didn't have that to contend with. And the folks had decided among themselves that I was "entitled" to a rest. Rest and such things are always spoken of, around our house, as luxuries. Which I guess they are. Around our house. Anyway—

Well, Roberta had said the story was marvelous. And Mom said, well, Jimmie, aren't you glad you tried now? But I knew. It was rotten, unbalanced. The way I felt lay over the pages like a black shadow. We sent it off to MacFaddens first, and when it bounced, to Fawcetts; then, to Moe Annenberg's string, and on to—but it doesn't matter. I didn't care whether it sold or not. In fact, I hoped it wouldn't. I knew that if it sold, they'd be after me to write another one, and the next one would be worse. And having it constantly impressed upon me how much I'd slipped and was slipping would kill that last feeble desire to really write.

But I'm getting off the track again.

The folks decided I was entitled to a rest, so they fixed a lunch and went down to the beach early Saturday morning and stayed all day. And they all got frightfully sunburned. They were going around for days afterward covered with cornstarch and walking spraddle-legged. And I wasn't very sympathetic.

I'd come home in the evening, all jumpy and fagged out from the mess I'd started at the plant, and there wouldn't be anything to eat because no one had felt up to going to the store; and I'd be expected to examine backsides and shake out talcum powder and speak with a sob. I never got so thoroughly sick of looking at hind-ends in my life, and I've looked at quite a few what with changing diapers for two families, and—and one thing and another. I wanted to blister them a lot worse than they were.

"What in the name of Christ were you doing all day?" I snarled. "Standing on your heads?"

"We were trying to keep out of the way so you could rest."

"Couldn't you have done it with some long slacks and an umbrella? Did you think you'd make me feel better by getting barbecued?"

"Well . . . we didn't know it was so hot, and—anyway my slacks were dirty, and Shannon took the umbrella over to—"

"Why didn't you stay under the cliffs then? Good God, girl! I fell thirty feet into the Pecos one night when it was covered with ice, and our nearest camp was twelve miles away. But I didn't just accept things. I didn't say, well, I've got my matches wet and lost my lantern, so I'll have to freeze. I started one of the generators and—"

"Oh don't tell me about that again! We're not all as smart as you are."

"I know why you did it. You wanted to make me feel responsible, sorry for you. You wanted to appear ten times as dumb and helpless as you really are, so that I'd think that I had to stick around—"

"You don't need to stick around me," said Mom. "I'm sorry I even mentioned getting sunburned. Let's not say another word about it, Roberta. I'll go to the store to-morrow night and—"

"No, I'll go, Mom. You feel worse than I do."

The kids would start screaming, could they go along? And pretty soon everyone would forget how it all started. And the next night I'd go to the store again and have to take "just a peek" at the spots that had peeled that day. And it was like that for ten or twelve days.

I hated myself for being that way; they are all more than solicitous about me when I am sick. And I have been pretty sick. I have had the doctor twice in the past month. I didn't want him because I knew how it would turn out, but they called him anyway.

The first time was about two weeks after I got hopped up. I was eating supper when a piece of bread went down the wrong way, and the next thing my plate was filled with blood.

The doctor came and listened to my chest and asked a lot of questions about what I ate and drank and how much I smoked and how many hours I slept. And the following evening I had to go downtown for an X-ray and urinalysis and blood test. They didn't show anything, of course.

He called up a few days later, while I was at work, and gave Roberta the report. Pretty disgusted, he was, I gathered. There wasn't any lung infection; the old scars were healed. There wasn't anything at all wrong with me except that I smoked and drank too much, didn't sleep enough, and didn't eat the right things.

When the folks gave it to me with a lot of "you see, Jimmie" and "I told you so," I thought they were trying to kid me. It was so goddamned funny. I laughed until I got another coughing fit, and everyone said, "Oh Jimmie thinks he's so smart! He knows more than the doctor does." And I finally stopped laughing. They really were sincere. They didn't understand.

I started going to bed—not to sleep—at ten o'clock. I didn't drink anything. I consumed a lot of eggs and milk. I smoked only five cigarettes a day.

Well, that week was about the same as any other, except that I practically stopped sleeping and my digestion was worse than it had ever been. I don't mean that the same things happened. I mean it just wasn't any worse. Maybe some—but not much.

On Sunday morning, about the time I'd gone to sleep, I heard Roberta up stirring around. I sat up and asked her what was the matter.

She said, "Nothing's the matter. I'm just going to church, that's all."

"But it's only four-thirty," I said.

"Well, I've got to walk down there, don't I? Or have you got taxi fare?"

"They were still running busses the last I heard."

"I'm getting sick of riding busses. I'd rather walk."

"And I suppose they don't hold Mass except at six o'clock."

"They don't for people with half a dozen kids to look after. You know I can't go after they get up."

"It's never stopped you before. You went at ten o'clock last Sun—"

"Well this Sunday I'm going now."

She went into the bathroom to fix her face, and I tossed around for a few minutes and finally followed her.

"I've been trying to figure out," I said, "what you were getting even with me for."

She whirled on me, surprised. Yes, actually surprised. For she didn't know, I'm sure. She only felt.

"Now spill it," I said. "What am I charged with? Going outside while you were listening to Walter Winchell? Telling Jo that she probably wouldn't die if she didn't brush her teeth three times a day? Passing Frankie the bread before I passed it to you? Or what?"

She stared at me, getting whiter by the second.

"You know I like Frankie. You know how good I try to be to Mom."

"I think you want them around," I admitted, "even when you're pretending hardest that they're a burden. If you didn't want them, I'm pretty sure they wouldn't be here. They are closer to you than they are to me. You can hold me in line with them. You can hurt me through them, just as they can hurt me through you. You all hold that threat over me constantly."

"Say," she snapped, "just what is this all about, anyway."

"I've got a little off the subject," I said. "I wanted to know what you were getting even with me for. Not that it wasn't about time for you to break over. You've been holding in much longer than I expected you to."

She began unbuttoning her dress. "All right. I won't go."

"No, no. I want you to go. Don't mind anything—"

She slammed into the bedroom waking Mack up, and got in bed. And, of course, he wanted to get in our bed, too, so she was in the position of "not even being able to go to bed any more"; and I was sorry as hell, but I couldn't help what I'd said. I couldn't help it any more than she could help waking me up at four-thirty to go to Mass.

I took Mack out in the kitchen to fix him some breakfast. But I dropped the skillet on the floor, and that
awakened Shannon. So pretty soon all of us were out
there, except Jo and Roberta; and Shannon and Mack
were chasing each other around the table, and I was
trying to explain what the trouble was.

"Well, why didn't you let her go to church?" said
Mom. "Good lord! A person's got a right to their own
belief. She's got the money, I know that. She didn't
give me back the change when she paid the paper
boy."

"It wasn't church. It was—and I'll give you the
change—"

"No, no. I don't want the change. I was just saying
that—"

"But, dammit, she's got money. She's got my whole
check. She's just trying to make me—"

"Oh I know how it is," said Frankie. "But it's nothing any worse than the rows Chick and I used to have
or anyone else has. Jimmie just needs to put his foot
down, that's all."

That is as close as Frankie can come to understanding.
Relatively speaking, Frankie caught more of the Spartan
training and life than I did. She's never known anything but trading punches with chain-store customers
and keeping the desk between her and the boss, and she
pretty much believes that if you get the worst of a deal,
you'll change it when you get tired enough of it.

I finally went back and pleaded with Roberta until I was forgiven, and she went off to Mass at ten o'clock.

At twelve, just before she returned, Clarence and five other Portuguese arrived.

We'd asked Clarence over for dinner because he'd been so good about bringing us fish and the like. But we'd forgotten that it was this Sunday, and we certainly hadn't counted on these others. They were cousins, I believe. When Roberta walked in, her mouth dropped open almost a foot. She did manage to speak and smile before she went through to her bedroom, but it was rather grim.

No, our guests didn't notice. It was beyond their understanding that any friend of another friend could drop into a third friend's house and be unwelcome. I remember Clarence picked me up one Sunday, when he was supposed to have a date with Frankie and she'd gone off, and he toured me around Point Loma. We picked up fresh passengers at almost every block, it seemed, until we were packed in the car three deep. We must have stopped at a dozen houses, and no one seemed to think a thing of our all trooping in. In fact, I gathered that they would have been hurt if we hadn't.

We were pressed with Port—and there's nothing wrong with it the way the Portuguese make it—and if we declined that, there was whisky (the best) or beer or something you did want. And food. Big plates of chicken and ham and tuna; pickles; a half a dozen kinds of bread. You felt that they had known you were coming for a week and had spent the time preparing for you. That's the way they were, are, so they naturally couldn't see why anyone should be disturbed over only five unexpected guests. Tuna fishermen, in case you're wondering, do pretty well for themselves. Those who aren't yanked overboard to the sharks or who don't die from exposure or exhaustion average from five to ten thousand dollars a year. Right now a number of them, like Clarence, have been beached. The Government has bought up a lot of the boats for mine sweepers.

As I say though, there they were and they had to be fed; and we only had enough short ribs and browned potatoes for ourselves. I went around to the little neighborhood grocery and got extra bread and a lot of canned meat—it came to two dollars—and all in all we had a pretty good meal. (Mack, whose appetite is excellent, had to be taken back in the bedroom to "look at a pretty book.") Mom didn't eat and Frankie and I only made passes at things. Roberta stayed in our bedroom.

After dinner our friends didn't want to be rude and hurry away, and they wanted to show their appreciation. So one of them went out and came back with a case of beer and a box of cigars. Each of them drank a beer and smoked a cigar. Then, leaving the balance with us, they left. They were very gentlemanly. I am afraid we rather rushed them out the door.

Well, I wasn't drinking, and I don't care for cigars, and we didn't have any food. The afternoon was practically gone, too, and Roberta had wanted to go to a show before the night prices became effective. We couldn't now, of course. We couldn't even afford matinee tickets. And the house was upset, and the kids were all demanding something to eat.

Frankie bought some lunch meat and canned beans, and they and we ate that. But Frankie thought Roberta was "blaming her" for Clarence. And Roberta was sulking and snappy. And Mom was hurt. She got out the help-wanted ads and called about a dozen numbers where they'd advertised for housemaids and practical nurses. I finally grabbed the paper out of her hands and banged up the telephone and tore out of the house.

When I came back around eight, everything seemed to be lovely. Mack was asleep. Jo was reading. Roberta had made some fudge, and she and Mom and Frankie were gossiping in a very friendly way. Mom said something about, well, here's our wild man. But Frankie said, don't, Mom. And Roberta sat down on the arm of my chair and kissed me.

"Where's Shannon?" I said. "Gone to bed?"

"Why I don't know," said Roberta. "Has she, Mom?"

Mom went back to look. She looked through all the closets and in the bathroom. Shannon wasn't there.

"Oh she's probably gone over to the drugstore," said Frankie. "She'll come home when she gets ready."

"Did you see her leave, Jo?" I said.

Jo said she hadn't.

I had a premonition that something was wrong. I began to get so uneasy that I couldn't sit still, so Roberta and I walked over to the drugstore. We didn't go inside. The druggist was nice enough that time I talked to him, but I got the impression that he didn't regard me very highly. Roberta couldn't go in because she "wasn't dressed." She wasn't there anyway. No one was there but the soda clerk. We could see that from the door.

We walked back home, and Mom was waiting on the front steps.

"Part of her clothes are gone, Roberta. So's that little dressing case of Frankie's."

Roberta slumped. "Mom!"

"I don't know where the child could be, do you? Jimmie, can't you think of anything?"

I didn't know what to think. Once, when she was three, she'd told us she was going away and leave us for good, and, traditionally, we'd said that's just fine, and we'd fixed her a lunch and packed some clothes for her to take; thinking we'd bluff her out of it, you know. It was almost a day before we got her back. A brakie found her sitting in the caboose of a freight that was getting ready to pull out for Chicago.

"I don't know," I said. "She didn't have any money, did she?"

"Not that I know of."

"Well," I said, thinking out loud, "that night we were down to the bay she kept wanting to get into one of the boats. She said she bet she could cross the ocean if—"

Roberta screamed. "That's where she's gone! She'll be drowned! I know she's drowned! My baby, my—"

Then she fainted.

Mom and I lugged her into the house. Frankie started telephoning. She called the Travelers' Aid. The police. The transportation company. She was almost hysterical, for one of the few times in her life, and I guess they could only half-understand what she was talking about because— But I didn't wait for her to finish. As soon as I'd dropped Roberta, I got out and headed for the bay as fast as I could run.

There wasn't any beach there, there at the place where we had been. Just an embankment and a private dock and the mud flats that were already vanishing under the incoming tide. Forty or fifty feet out from the water's edge was a small rowboat, one of dozens that were rocking and leaping with the waves. Something white clung desperately to its side, and strangling, faintly, I could hear Shannon calling.

I knew what had happened. She had walked out there on the mud before the tide started coming in. Perhaps, as the waves began to sweep and crash around her, she had tried to walk back. Perhaps she had been trying to get the anchor undone and had fallen over. Now—

I shouted for her to hold on. Shouting, I slid down the embankment to the mud and plowed into the water. A wave swept me off my feet, and I still kept shouting, and I was strangled. But I came up half-running—trying to run—and half-swimming toward the boat. I got there. Holding on to the edges, I worked my way around to the place where Shannon was.

It wasn't Shannon. It was a piece of canvas. . . .

I was plodding back up the hill, so completely out of my head that I didn't know how cold I was, when I met Frankie coming down.

"Jimmie! What on earth!"

"She's dead," I said. "She fell into the bay and—"

"She's home in bed," said Frankie. "She was with the druggist."

"B-but—"

"You know how much she gets on Jo's nerves. Well, during all the excitement this afternoon, Jo wrote a note to the druggist on your typewriter and signed your name to it, and asked him to look after Shannon for a few days. She said you were going to be out of town, and you knew how much he enjoyed having her, and so on. It was a darned sight better than I could have written; I don't blame the guy for being taken in. As soon as Jo saw all the commotion she was causing, she got scared and told us about it."

"But why—"

"I told you. Jo has a lot of plays she's working on, and she didn't want Shannon around. At least that's all she'd say. She didn't have time to say much before she locked herself in the bathroom."

When we got home, Mom was standing in the door way, very red and apologetic, and a cop was sitting in a scout car out in front. There was another cop coming down the steps, and he was mad and apologetic. And the old man in front of him—a very dignified old codger—was just plain damned mad. He was cursing every breath he drew, but the little girl in his arms was bawling so hard that you couldn't understand what he was saying.

Frankie and I kind of scurried around the procession, and just as we darted in the door, another car pulled up in front. A woman in a blue suit and an overseas cap emerged. She opened the rear door of the car, and a Negro girl—a cute little tot of six or seven with pink-ribboned pigtails and an ear-to-ear grin—got out.

Mom gritted her teeth and told me to take care of Roberta. "I'll settle this."

Frankie started telephoning again.

I made for the bathroom.

Roberta had an insect-spray gun. She was trying to shoot the spray through the keyhole and kick the door down at the same time. She was shouting that she'd kill Jo if she didn't open the door, and that she'd kill her as soon as she did get it open. Jo wasn't saying anything. She was (I knew) sitting on the stool reading. There's always something to read in the bathroom.

Mom got rid of the Travelers' Aid woman, and Frankie finished notifying people that the lost was found, and between the three of us we dragged Roberta into the front room and held her down until she'd cooled off.

Mom told about the cops and the old fellow with the little girl, and the Travelers' Aid woman with the little Negro girl, and it was funny. Funny unless you thought about it from my standpoint. Roberta began to giggle, then to laugh. Mom made a pot of coffee for all hands and told me I'd better change clothes. I went back and advised Jo that it was safe to come out. Roberta shook her a little by one arm in a sort of absent-minded way and that was all there was to it.

I didn't think it was funny, and it wasn't just because I'd got a ducking out of the business. Jo wouldn't feel any different toward Shannon tomorrow than she did tonight. She wanted to get away from Shannon, and she couldn't; so she was trying to get Shannon away from her. And it was pretty obvious that she didn't care how she did it. As obvious as the fact that Shannon wasn't going to change or make herself any less detestable to Jo.

Jo is resourceful; she has the I.Q. of a person ten years older; and there is no use denying that she can be deadly hard and contemptuous of consequences. I couldn't help thinking what a nineteen-year-old girl might do to a—

I shut the idea out of my mind. Things weren't that bad—yet. Jo still felt a deep affection for Shannon. She was proud of her fighting prowess. She'd dress her up and drag her around the neighborhood to plays. Share things with her. So—no, they weren't that bad, yet. But they were bad enough.

Long after she forgot kindnesses, Shannon would remember such things as being shoved off on the druggist under false pretenses—remember and hold it against Jo. Just as I hold things against Marge, now. The violin lessons for instance; her frailties and fawnings and simperings that got her the things I was denied.

Yes, I do hold it against her. I may as well admit it.

It was about three in the morning before I went to sleep, and I have been getting up at five since I started walking again. I didn't think I could make it, but of course I did. There's nothing new about that, so I won't go into details. I won't take up the days individually.

Moon was—well, I'll use the present tense, because things haven't changed any except for the worse—Moon is distinctly cold. There's no more going up to the office for a walk; no more soothing drawl to wake me when I doze off. I'm strictly on my own. Murphy doesn't speak to me. Vail ignores me, which means, naturally, that I get the cold shoulder from Busken also. Gross pretends friendliness but that only makes matters worse. It only makes Moon more cool and watchful.

I don't know whether he is angry because of the way Roberta acted, or whether he blames me for the considerable expense he was put to on our Tia Juana excursion, or whether he is simply on the defensive because of Frankie. Probably all those things figure in it to an extent. The chief factor, I believe, however, is that he thinks I'm trying to put something over on him. He doesn't like it because I didn't discuss this new records system with him before taking it up with Baldwin. He can't conceive of a man going to all that extra effort merely to do a job that needed doing.

I should explain about the system. There's nothing very original about it. I'm simply taking the parts off the release books and putting them on cards, the cards to be filed in chronological order. This does away with any chance of duplications. It makes it possible to locate a part and the data on it in a second instead of fifteen minutes. And there is only one posting to make, instead of from one to thirty as used to be the case. There are two columns per card: one for stockroom inventory, one for the assemblies. Debits and credits are reflected within the balances, not set out by themselves, so the number of parts needed to complete 750 ships can be obtained instantly by adding the two balances—less any "X" items —and subtracting the total from that amount. "X" items are spare or extra parts.

The thing has one serious flaw, or will have when I get it finished. We issue parts and make shortage reports by positions. My cards are filed in chronological order. This will mean that to locate all the cards in one position I will have to search through the entire file of several thousand cards.

I'll have to get around that some way. I've been playing with several ideas, but I can't seem to—

I'm off the track again.

I had to keep up our present records system. I had to work on the new one. I had to have inventories taken, and no one would take them for me. I had to work twice as hard as I had before, and I felt half as much like working. And I had to walk back and forth.

That's the way it was. That's the way it still is.

We got a wire from Marge Tuesday, saying that Pop was pretty sick, and we were all in an uproar for the rest of the week. I mean we had the uproar from that in addition to our customary one. Mom felt that she "just had to go," but she knew that neither Frankie nor I had the money, and she wouldn't let us borrow any, so what was the use of asking us twenty times a night if—

I wanted a drink. I was sick for one. And I didn't know what to do with my hands all evening, sitting around without a cigarette. But I followed instructions.

Sunday night we got a long-distance call from Marge —a collect one because Walter was slowly being hounded out of his job by bill collectors and he'd told her she simply couldn't run up any more bills. Pop was better, well enough to be taken back to the place—and after she'd divulged that, she talked of absolutely nothing at all, to the best of my knowledge, for fifteen solid minutes. Roberta and I had gone to bed, and Mom was doing all the talking or listening. Roberta kept saying, you've just got to stop her, Jimmie; we'll never be able to pay it, and Frankie won't be able to pay it, and we'll be stuck. Now you just go in there and tell her . . .

When Mom came in to tell us what Marge had said, Roberta turned over on her side with her back to her. That made everything lovely.

Then I came home Monday evening and everything was lovely. Roberta couldn't wait until I got in the house to throw her arms around me and kiss me all over the face, and the kids—even Jo—were screaming with excitement. Mack was going away on the choo-choo, and Shannon was going to buy a gun, and Jo was going to take dancing lessons. Mom got the opened letter off the mantel and gave it to me. It was from the foundation.

They had a project (they believed) which would interest me very much. But, before discussing that, they were forced to mention the matter of last year's research. It was not impressive; it definitely was not. The style was stilted; the subject matter superficial. At least, so it appeared to them. But this was doubtless more their fault than mine. They had given me a great deal of latitude in working, and they had not made their wants clear. In fact, there had been some doubt in their own minds about what was most desirable. Now, however . . .

I began to laugh.

Roberta didn't understand. "Isn't it nice, honey? I'm so glad for you."

I kept on laughing. "Stop it," I said. "You're killing me."

"What's so funny?" said Roberta, smiling uncertainly. "I don't see—"

"Why they've 'discovered' that old collection of mine! The one that was published three years ago."

"Well?"

"All they want me to do," I said, "is write like that. Write like I did then. That's all."

And I got down on the floor and rolled.

The doctor came and went and I didn't know about it. I only know that I went to sleep. When I woke up, I began pumping Roberta as to what he'd said, and I couldn't get much out of her for a while except that "he asked all about you and everything."

"He didn't mention anything about three months of absolute rest, did he?" I said.

"Well, he did, but when I told him—"

"I know."

"I don't want you to work so hard, Jimmie. I don't know what I can do about it, though."

"I know you don't," I said. "Have you got the whisky yet?"

"What whisky?"

"The whisky he told you to let me have."

"I didn't know what kind—he did say you mustn't drink too much, Jimmie."

"What about cigarettes?"

"You mustn't smoke too many of them either."

"That's damned good advice," I said. "I'll have to remember it."

"I hope you will, honey. I get so worried—"

"One more thing. He told you there wasn't anything organically wrong with me at all?"

"That's just what he said, honey. He said if you'd just keep quiet, and not worry, and not get excited about things. And eat more. And not smoke and drink so much, and—"

"Why, then I'd be all right."

"Uh-huh. You will mind him, won't you, honey? You'll do it for my sake?"

I nodded. I couldn't laugh any more, and I was too tired to get up and beat her.

William Sherman Dillon, well-known inmate of the H——
Sanitarium, and former millionaire oil-man, politician, and
attorney, died at his residence early Sunday morning after
gorging himself on the excelsior from his mattress. At his
bedside was his wife, who had to be, his daughter Margaret,
who didn't know any better, and several imbeciles who
wanted to taste the excelsior themselves. While the will has
not yet been probated, it is understood that the entire estate,
consisting of unpaid bills and a heritage of lunacy, is to go
to Mr. Dillon's son, James Grant Dillon, prominent hack-
writer and aircraft flunkey of San Diego, California. . . .

Ha, ha, ha, ha, ha! You don't like that, eh? You don't
like it? Well, drown me out, then. Send me outside to do
some work. Try to send me out. You can't run away this
time. No, by God! You think you've run away, and that
I'm stuck as I've always been stuck, but by God—

No.

NO!

No, I didn't mean that.

I'll scratch it out. (Scratch? Cats? . . . No, no cats.
The grounds are fully protected against cats and other—
er—predatory creatures.)

I'll rub it out.

I'll hold on to myself, I've been kind of goddam

crazy, Pop, and I—I don't know when I am and when I'm not. I just want to know, that's all. I want to know if there is something I have not seen and cannot see or did not or could not put together. Nothing more.

I'm not mad. I'm not angry, I mean.

I'm just—

Eh? Can you make it a little louder, Pop? I know we used to—but you don't need to keep your voice down in here. Let it roll out as it used to roll through the court-rooms. Raise it like thunder above the thunder of a drilling well. Shout and roar and pound the table as if you meant it, and if anyone doesn't like it, we will beat their goddam heads and leave them there for dead. Goddam their eyes.

No, I guess it isn't a very nice song. I forgot you didn't like songs like that. What was it you liked? "I Will Take You Home Again, Kathleen"? "Humoresque"? "On the Banks of the Wabash"? Yeah. Nice violin pieces. I never played the violin, you remember.

Have a drink? Have a cigarette? Aw, go on. Little drink never hurt anyone. Remember I told you that once before. Remember that Sunday morning when I fell down on the front porch and almost bit a hole in the planks, and you carried me into the bathroom, eyes filled with disgust. Yeah, I knew what you thought of me. I never got so drunk that I didn't.

And you always called cigarettes coffin-nails. Going around with a coffin-nail pasted in my lip. *Pasted*—I'll never forget that. Yes, I drank until I never fell down and I smoked coffin-nails. But I never had gravy on my clothes; no, goddamit, I never had that. My clothes were a damned sight better than yours ever were, I saw to that. And I supported the family ten times better than you'd ever done. And my manners were better. I didn't sit down at the table and gobble up everything in sight. I didn't walk through doors ahead of people. I didn't keep breaking in when someone else was talking. Goddam you, I was better! I showed you I was, and I made you like it. . . .

Ahhh, you never! You never had a thought for anyone. Marge, maybe, after you'd got all you wanted for yourself; and she'd saw away on that damn fiddle until the sky was green and you'd sit with your eyes closed, tapping on the arm of your chair, and no one dared to say a word. . . .

I'm not sore. I just want to approach this thing from the—the scientific viewpoint. That's the right word, scientific? You should know. You always knew, and I had to stop and think. And why in the hell shouldn't it have been that way? I'll tell you a thing or two.

Those two years you were in Mexico—finding a copper mine, and sinking the shaft, and getting the machinery hauled in by burro; and then not being able to move your ore. Ha, ha. Not being able to move it, because the bandits had goddam well made hash out of the railroad, and—

Those two years:

I was wearing dresses, and I laughed when I saw the

sun, or the trees making shadows on the grass, or a spar-
row hopping through the dust. I laughed because it was
good to laugh. There was no bad, only error. (Like the
Christian Scientists, Pop.) And I slept long hours, and
I was still fat with mother-fat. Then snow lay on the
ground, and in the cold room where Mom watched by
the window a little girl and I tossed a ball back and forth
by the hour—a ball made out of an old stocking; and
there was nothing so funny as when it rolled under the
bed or fell behind the door, and I wondered how the
little girl could ever bear to stop. And then the snow was
green, and we were like the others now—not the big
others but the others that were bigger than we were, and
we did not need sleds and warm boots and mackinaws.
Barefoot, we walked down to the grove and we laid sticks
upon the ground and I sat on the ground with them,
holding back my laughter with my hand, and the little
girl frowned and she was the teacher. And I laughed
when the clods fell around us, and the little girl ran this
way and that and tried to climb the trees; ran in circles,
crying and screaming until her eyes rolled white in her
head; ran because there was nothing to do but run; ran
because Mom was at the house and she was not at the
house. And I laughed because everything was laughter.
There was the smell of fresh earth and yellow dust, and
a great pile that was a mountain of gold (like Pop is
going to find); and the gold spouted downward from a
pipe in the sky, falling around my head, mounting above
my feet like golden sand, above my waist and shoulders.

And I was looking into the man's eyes, far above, and he was looking down into mine, and I knew that we were playing a game, that he was going to hide me beneath the gold; and I could not understand why Mom came racing across the field nor why the man's teeth bared like a frightened dog's. But I knew that everything was good, and I laughed. Then the grass was white again, and the stocking-ball was strange and no longer funny, but there were other things of laughter. The closet that was a cave, and the bedsheets that could make a ghost, and the frosted window that was a slate, and the cracks in the floor, and the snow sifting in at the eaves, and the wind whispering in the chimney, and the broom with its whiskers, and an old newspaper between the mattress and springs, and . . . And a big bear that was tired and had to rest now, and two little bears that had to go to sleep, too, and when you wake up it'll be daylight. Many things, and some to laugh at. And then the grass again, the snow and the grass, and then only the grass. And there was a long table where the others sat, and Mom going from the table to the stove, from the stove to the table, from the pantry to the table. And we could not be seen because we had made king's X's in front of us, and we smelled all the things, and counted the bites the others took, and sometimes I could forget why we were counting—sometimes—and it was funny. And there was a cupboard, and the little others, the little others who were still bigger although we were bigger (and that was funny) would reach down great brown loaves and smear thick slices from them with jams and jellies, and watch you as you watched them stuff their mouths. And then you were hiding behind the doorway, the plate of tarts you had found in front of you—the plate that had been so easy to find. And then you saw the woman, the woman who looked like Mom, and you smiled up at her because she was smiling. And you did not notice the brown flecks that moved along your hands, that swarmed up your arms. And then there were needles in your throat, and in the top of your mouth, and your tongue was on fire, and your lips puffed, and the flecks marched in and out of your nostrils, and they stood outward from your face like acrobats, burying their furious fiery heads in your flesh. And you knew that she did not know, you thought that she knew something that you did not, because you were crying and she was laughing. And you tried to tell her, and she only laughed. Then the leaves turning brown, and the water in the pails slopping over your feet, tickling them, and your shoulders and arms, drawn tight and numb, tickled also. The great baskets of fuzzy cobs for the stove tickled your chin, and you laughed at that. Laughed at those things. And then somehow the tickling became pain, the laughter weeping; and you no longer saw the shadows, the sun, the sparrows in the dust. And the snow fell, and your shoes were too tight, and your coat dragged upon the ground, and you wondered at the shortness and the longness of the days, and you wondered why you could not sit in the room with Mom and you were told why. You were told, and you could

not understand. There was food and warmth and sun-
shine and the sparrows hopping from foot to foot, and
you knew that these things were better than the things
you had. But when you told them, they only laughed.
They laughed now. They. Sometimes you laughed at the
little girl, but when Mom noticed she pressed her lips
together and shook her head. And you began to know
that it was not funny when, after the little girl had sat
for hours, a day, rigid, frightened into immobility, her
eyes rolled back into her head and the urine spurted
from her pantslegs. It was not funny to you, and you
did not want them to laugh when you could not. You
hated them for being able to laugh, and you began to
hate her for making them. Then, and then, the straw
cushions of the day coach, the shaded lanterns swinging
from their hooks, and your image floating along in the
night outside, dancing along with the clicking of the
rails, and staring in at you sullen-faced, laughterless. And
the woman across the aisle, the friendly motherly woman
with the ostrich plume: Can't you smile for me, little
boy? My, my! What make 'ums look so mad? . . .

What make 'ums look so mad! God! You with your
fat dignity; and me with my toes permanently over-
lapped, and my body outgrown my organs so that I
could never eat what I needed; and what you might call
my soul—ha, ha, my soul!—turned inward because I
knew how unbeautiful it was. Inarticulate, and awkward,
and angry. Angry; raging; suspicious. Not pleasant to
have under your eye. Something that could carry golf

clubs, and telegrams, and be kept out of the way as much
as possible, and—

Never mind.

*It wasn't that, Jimmie. I will have you know now that
it wasn't. You were so pale and brooding, and I wanted
you to be strong and mix with other boys. I knew that
Marge had broken, and I did not want you to . . .*

Oh, never mind.

*Yes, and when you got off the train I was shocked
and outraged. When I saw Marge, when I saw you, when
Mom told me things . . . I did not know there were
people like that. I suppose I did know; but I had never
thought of them as touching us, me and mine. I tried
never to think of things like that. They made me—*

I know. I'm the same way.

*And I didn't know it would be so long. There were so
many things I hadn't anticipated. The peons were bound
to the land, the dons; no matter what we paid them they
got no more than a subsistence, so they didn't care.
When the shaft was halfway down, they let a dump-pail
filled with dynamite drop, and ten of them were killed.
By the time we'd indemnified the dons, and their families, and—*

Yeah, you told us all about it. You had a tough time,
I guess. But, why the hell—why the hell in the first place,
Pop? I don't remember, but I can read. And Mom has
told me and you have told me. You were doing all right
before. Why the—

When I went into law, there were only two other things to go into: medicine and school-teaching.

But you were so damned good, Pop! There wasn't a lawyer in the Southwest that could come up to you. Not even Bill Gilbert, or Temple Houston with his flowered vests and ten-gallon hat, or the blind man, Gore, or Moman Prewitt. None of them. I don't know whether it was what you said, or the way you said it. Frankly, I used to get so sick of reading and hearing about you when we didn't have—but let that go. I don't know whether you knew a hell of a lot of law—although I don't see how you could have—or . . .

No. I didn't know the law as well as I should have, and I knew that I could never know it. I was afraid every time I stepped before a jury; timid, afraid for my client. My size was with me, and I had a good voice, and I was terribly afraid of losing; that was all I had. It wasn't enough. I lost six cases. . . .

Everyone has to lose some time. Only six out of a hundred and—

Only six cases. . . . If I had known what I should have. . . . As it was, I dropped four men through the trap, and sent two over the road.

Oh, hell . . . well, I know how you might feel. But you could have got out of it. Used it to step into something else. You could have been United States Attorney for—

I never pled a man's case unless I was convinced he was innocent. I wouldn't try to convict him unless I was sure he was guilty.

You could have gone to Congress. I was looking back through an old newspaper today—one Mom had saved—a yellowed special election-edition. And there was your picture everywhere: Bill Dillon in a lion-tamer's outfit, and the western half of the state a cowering lion; the western district a dove, eating out of your hand, a monkey on a chain, sitting on your shoulder. And there were pages about you. They took you apart and put you together again, and—and it was a non-party paper—they couldn't find anything that wasn't good. Why didn't you—

Yes, I think I would have liked that. I thought I'd told you why.

You told me so many things so many times. I began shutting my ears pretty early. I don't mean anything. I suppose, seeing so many people, you forgot when you'd told a story and when you hadn't.

Well, I was from the North and so was my campaign manager. Our fathers marched with Sherman to the sea. My middle name was Sherman. In all modesty, I think I could have won without a manager, but this man was my friend. Well, our state, particularly my district, was strongly rebel in its sympathies. However, that wasn't the reason I'd never obtruded my full name and background. I wouldn't deceive anyone about them. I simply liked Bill Dillon better, and I was content to let old hatreds die. But—I had a three-car railway train traveling over my district, with a band and campaign workers and various influential people. On election day each one of those railway cars blossomed forth with a banner: WILLIAM SHERMAN DILLON. Moreover, the band played "Marching through Georgia" at every stop.

A double cross?

No, I don't think so. I don't like to think so. I suppose my manager felt that the election was in the bag anyway, and he'd just let the rebels know the Yankees had won another war. Of course we lost by a landslide.

No one could be that dumb! Why didn't you stop him? You must have known about it as soon as it began.

It was my name. "Marching through Georgia" was a good piece; there was nothing dishonorable or indecent about it. I couldn't deny my name or the piece that my father marched to in helping to liberate the slaves.

Oh, my God! Free the slaves!

It is what I believed. Right or wrong, I believed in it. You will find this, Jimmie: To get even as far as I did, you must believe in something; believe in it so firmly that it is part of you, so much that you would no sooner think of changing it than you would of twisting your arm out of shape or cutting off a leg.

You say that. All the stinkers and grafters and nitwits that get into office, and you tell me—

I'm not talking about them. They can. We couldn't.

Yeah—but Pop. The money. Us. What right did you have to marry and bring children into the world and—

What right has anyone?

But—I know. I know how that is. Of course, you don't plan it that way. You think everything is going to be swell, and—

Yes, and in his love for his family a man will do all the things that he shouldn't and do the one thing that he should when desperation drives him to it. I was a lawyer, a politician, an insurance salesman, a little bit of everything. I didn't get into the oil business soon enough. I was too old to learn the things one had to know to exist in it.

Pop, did—did you hate us very much?

I did. I had come in from the outside, and I was different from you. The things I had to tell bored you, bored your mother. I had learned to push in front of people, to raise my voice, to interrupt when an interruption seemed necessary. In my environment food had not been dallied with and clothes had been to keep you covered; and I was absent-minded; and there were times when I preferred reading to talking, because I enjoyed reading and I knew what a terrible thing it is not to know enough. And because I was different from you and would not be as you were, you hated me and in self-defense I hated you. You ringed me in with my failures, and each action of mine that was unlike yours you snatched up and laid on top of this ring. And in time I was walled in with nothing but failure to look at. And from my prison I peered cautiously out at you—angrily at first, then boldly, then cautiously. And I began to think perhaps I was wrong, perhaps the things I thought right were wrong and the wrong right, and I began to lose something called character. Yes, I knew about the money; I smelled the whores and the whisky. But out of your eyes you despised me, and I could not speak because there were no ears to hear, and I was no longer sure. You were, as you have pointed out, supporting the family ten times better—

I didn't mean that, Pop. Honest to God, I didn't mean it.

You meant it, and it was true. True and damnably false. But I couldn't be sure. I couldn't talk to you. Perhaps—but I don't hate you that much. I don't hate you at all, now. Food. You drink. Mine was food. When you are walled in, you do something.

It must have been hell, Pop. To have been a big man, to have been something—

Yes, and may you never know that hell, Jimmie. Because I love you, now. I hoped you would die out there on the pipeline. I had taken your money because I thought I would shame you by not taking it, and you had shamed me instead. I thought you were mean, rotten to the core; a dirty blob of scum that floated by virtue of its own filth. You came back and I sank even farther within myself—

I wanted to talk to you, Pop. I wanted to tell you about the stories.

I know that now; I never understood you, and I could not take the time for understanding. There were so many things to do, and— But you came back. It started all over again. Then you came to me and told me about the magazine, about going to school. . . .

And you made me, Pop. You stood there before the empty house with the locked doors and without a penny in your pocket—damned little anyway—and there was a smile on your face as we drove off.

Yes, we understood each other then. Twenty years too late. It was not your fault or mine. Circumstances had made us different and we were too long in adjusting ourselves. . . . Well, and then you married and settled in Oklahoma City, and I was working as a janitor there. And it was like beginning life all over again. Like it, but not the same. The things I had to tell you were interesting, true, but I had lost my sureness of them and I could never bring it back. And I was surrounded by doubts as to how far I should move a hand or foot, and I had to think when I spoke because there were so many words to choose from and so many had been laughed and sneered at. I would see your impatience when I began to speak—and so I spoke less. I was slow when I walked, and so I—

Pop . . .

But it was nice. I can't tell you how nice, how much I appreciated it. We would sit there in your apartment in the evenings, and I would close my eyes, and Jo would climb up onto my lap. And Roberta wouldn't notice when I called her Mom, and Jo would be Marge, and

*you would be—Jimmie, of course. Your voice was husky
and you were big, but a boy's voice should be husky and
he should be big. And then, later—farther down the
years—Jo and I would walk. And we talked and walked
the same—*

Jo worshiped you, Pop. When she heard that you
were dead, she broke down. She's in with Roberta now.
Would you like to see her? *Jo! Roberta!*

And we—we talked and walked. . . .

Only one of us could go, Pop. I sold the story, but
there was only money enough for one. That was the
reason I didn't come. It wasn't because I was ashamed of,
hated you, for eating the—

And we talked and—

I didn't mean it about Marge. I know now. I know
about the violin lessons. I know why you—Pop!

And we—

Not yet, Pop! Seventy years and thirty-five years, and
we didn't speak, and Jo and Roberta are coming, and
I want to—

And—

Pop! POP! . . . O Christ, just for a minute . . .

"Come to bed, honey. Want me to fix you a little
drink? You've not had much. Want to take a drink and
come to bed?"

"Pop was here. He's been talking to me."

"There, there, honey."

"He came to take me for a walk," said Jo. "He was shaved and he had a haircut, and he had on a suit without any back."

19

MOM CAME IN EARLY LAST WEEK. SHE SHARED EXPENSES with some people who were coming this way in a car, so the trip cost her only twelve dollars. She was pretty much worn out. They drove straight through without an overnight rest, and she hadn't eaten much. She couldn't have eaten very much. She didn't have the money to do it with.

Pop had a burial insurance policy for a hundred dollars, but the stuff they furnished for that price wasn't even decent. The cheapest thing she could get next to the hundred was a hundred and fifty—"and it wasn't at all bad"—so she had ordered that. She'd paid ten dollars down and signed a note for the other forty. And then there had been the lot to buy, and that was ten dollars down and a note for a hundred and ninety.

"There were a lot of people there, Jimmie. Pop's picture, one of the old ones they'd taken when he was running for Congress, was in the paper and there was quite a long piece about him. People I'd never seen before, real well-dressed people, kept coming up and speaking to me and looking into the casket. And there were all kinds of flowers."

"How was Pop dressed?" said Jo.

"Never mind," I said. "I'm glad you did things right, Mom."

"Well, I felt like we couldn't do much less. But we've got those notes to pay. They come to twenty dollars a month all together—"

"And don't worry about that either," I said. "We'll take care of the notes."

I expected Roberta to stiffen up and say something, and I was prepared to say something back. But she didn't. She didn't say what I expected her to.

"No, don't you worry a darned bit, Mom," she said. "I thought as much of Pop as I did my own father. I only wish we could do more."

And I squeezed her hand and was proud of her; and Mom kind of took a deep breath as if she'd just jumped a chasm.

Frankie didn't say much. She started to cut loose once, but I stopped her with a look. Frankie's motto is there's no time like the present, and I didn't think Mom was in any condition to hear what she had to say. On top of everything else, she was worried about Marge. Walter's about to lose his job—or says he is—and he blames it on Marge.

The next night when I got home, Frankie was already there. She'd taken sick down at the office. And Mom had been told, and she was all torn up about it.

I will say this: We don't have many inhibitions. You can't have when you live as close to each other as we do.

Anyone can discuss anything at any time, and everyone feels free to put in his two cents' worth.

The powwow began as soon as I hit the door, and it continued on into the night until the chief participants, Jo among them, gave up and went to bed. And, of course, we talked about everything under the sun except the subject at hand. And, of course, we didn't get anywhere.

Mom said I shouldn't have let Frankie do it; I should have been looking out for her.

"And how should I know what she was doing?" I said.

"Yes, Mom, how could we know?" said Roberta. "We looked up all of a sudden and they were gone. They told us they'd gone to get a tire fixed."

"Well, Jimmie ought to have talked to her," Mom said. "I warned him a long time ago that she was going to get into something like this."

"Oh, Mom," said Frankie, "you know I wouldn't have paid any attention to Jimmie! The way he—"

"What?" said Roberta. "Why not?"

"Nothing," said Frankie. "I was just saying that I was twenty-five years old. If I don't know what I'm doing by this time, I never will."

"Well, it's a fine mess," said Mom, her mouth working. "It just looks like there's always s-something to—"

"Oh what's the use of getting in such an uproar?"

"But what are you going to do? You can't send for Chick, can you?"

"Heavens, no! He's not that dumb."

"Well what, then?"

"What do you think, Jimmie?"

"Why, the usual thing, I suppose."

"You mean a prescription or—"

"No, medicine won't do you any good. Not if you're really caught. You're sure you are, are you?"

"I know I am."

"I don't know why you had to get in such a fix," said Mom. "I'll declare, Frankie! The way I tried to—"

"You'll have to get a doctor."

"I can't seem to find out about any. I've been kind of feeling my way around with some of the other girls. But—"

"I told you we'd find one. I've never been—" I stopped, and avoided Roberta's eyes. "I'm pretty sure we can find a doctor. But it'll cost to beat hell the way things are out here now. They're all getting by so good, and they won't touch it unless you make it worth their while."

"Fifty dollars?"

"That's depression rates. We might get it done for a hundred."

Frankie flexed her bare toes and looked down at her fingernails. "I guess I could get it if I had to. Some loan-shark would let me have it, probably, at 100 per cent interest."

"You'll not do anything of the kind," said Mom. "My goodness! You talk as if hundred dollars grew on trees, child! We'll just make that fellow Moon pay for it, that's all. Jimmie, you just tell him he'd better get the money and get it quick or he'll wish he had."

"No, don't do that," Frankie. "I don't want you to."

"I'd look fine telling him he had to come through," I said. "The first thing I'd know I'd be walking down the road talking to myself. I've got about a month to go before I'm eligible for unemployment compensation. I don't care what happens after that, but I'm sticking around until then."

Roberta looked at me. "Oh," she said, "so that's it! That's what you've been thinking about when you sat around here evenings looking off into space. If you think for a minute, James Dillon, that I'm going to skimp along on fifteen or eighteen dollars a week when you could be making—"

"It'd be around twenty. And you could have it all. I'd go off some place and kind of get straightened out, and—"

"No sir! No sir-ee! Any time you go, I'm going right along with you. You're not going any place unless the family and all of us go, too. Get that idea out of your head right now."

"But if I could get away, and start writing again—"

"I guess if you really want to write, you can do it here. You sold that last story, didn't you? Well?"

"Yes, I sold it. I sat in here and picked it out at fifty words a night. And I average ten cups of coffee and a package of cigarettes to every line. I didn't write. I just kept reaching out and throwing down handfuls of words, and I moved them around and struck out and erased until I secured combinations that weren't completely idiotic. And in the end I sold the thing to a fourth-rate magazine. I can't do it again, I won't do it again."

"I thought we were going to talk about me," said Frankie.

"Why Jesus Christ," I said, "I don't see how you can ask me to! What if you'd been a singer—not a great one but pretty good—and you knew how a thing ought to be sung, but your voice was cracked—you needed some repairs before you could sing again. It was in such bad condition that it was plain hell for you to listen to it, and you knew it was at least as bad to others. So you weren't singing. You couldn't, and the effort of trying left you so sick and discouraged with yourself that if you kept on you would never recover. Well then, under those circumstances, would you still take engagements? Would you—"

"I would if I could get a hundred dollars," said Mom.

And Roberta said, "Jimmie's always been like that, Mom. Why one week when he got five hundred dollars for two little old stories, he was going around pulling his hair and swearing and saying that he was ruined, that he'd forgotten how to write. You'd've thought the world was coming to an end. . . . Now you know you did, Jimmie! You know you've always been like that."

Well—I guess I have. I guess every writer has. But there was a difference, a difference that only another writer can understand.

"Oh, see here," said Frankie, "can't we stick to the—"

"And that's another thing," I said. "When and if I do start writing again, there's going to be no more of this crap. I'm getting plenty sick of writing with a picture of a cop and a kindergarten tot pasted on my paper carriage. Never again, you understand? All of you get that through your heads. I'm going to write what I want to write, and the way I want to write it."

"Another book, I suppose," said Roberta.

"Lord deliver us," said Mom.

"All right," I said, "maybe I will write another book. What's so funny about that?"

"Nothing, as I remember," said Frankie. "But I thought we were—"

"I'll say it wasn't funny," said Roberta. "You remember, Mom? He'd come home from work at night and you'd've thought he was walking in his sleep. He'd sit down, and maybe he'd speak and maybe he'd just stare at you; and if you said anything to him, he wouldn't answer, or what he would say didn't make sense. And half of the time you'd think he'd been in a wreck—his clothes all sloppy and his vest buttoned up wrong, and cigarette ashes and coffee stains from one end of him to the other. He always wore such good clothes, too. It just made me sick to look at him."

"Oh God," I said.

"Yes, oh God," said Roberta. "That's what I used to say. He'd finish his supper—and it didn't make any difference how nice it was he never noticed—and then he'd fuss and fidget around and get his typewriter out and put it right down in the middle of the table before I could get the dishes off. It didn't make any difference if I'd finished my coffee—"

"And then the dirt-daubers would start coming in," I said. "There was—"

"That's what he called my friends, Mom. Dirt-daubers. They were real nice ladies, too."

"Women, Mother," said Jo.

"Will you shut your mouth?"

"There was that four-eyed bitch," I said, "that was always telling you you ought to make me help with the housework. And that half-wit you'd met over at the grocery store. And that droopy-drawered gal—I don't think you ever told me her name; I don't think she knew what it was herself. And you'd get in the other room and talk just loud enough so that I'd know you were talking, but not so that I could hear what you were saying. And it would go on, by God, for hours."

"Yes, Mom," said Roberta. "I'd have company in, and I never knew it to fail there'd be collectors coming to the door all evening and I'd have to go and talk to them with everyone listening. I couldn't let Jimmie go because he'd either swear at them or promise them the world with a ring around it to make them go away. I tell you—"

"Oh I know how it was," said Mom. "I know how Pop—"

"I got so mad I wanted to kill him sometimes. All he was getting was a teeny little old fifteen-dollar-a-week-advance, and we just barely had enough money to get by on, and he could have been making all kinds of money. MacFaddens wanted him to do a serial, and Gangbusters was calling him long-distance and sending wires, and Fawcetts was begging him to go to that governors' convention and pick up ten or twelve little editorials on crime-prevention—it wouldn't have taken any time at all and he could have gotten seventy-five dollars a piece for them—"

"Well I finally gave in," I said. "I rushed the book on out."

"Rushed it, the devil," said Roberta. "You talk about being slow, now. You couldn't have been any slower and written anything at all. I thought I'd go crazy. And—and Sunday was the worst day of all. We couldn't go any place. We'd hardly get out of bed before Jimmie's friends —they weren't my friends, I'll tell you!—would start coming in. And they'd be there all day, drinking coffee and scattering cigarette ashes all over everything, and— and you'd have thought it was their place instead of ours! They'd flop right down on my clean bedspread and sprawl around on the floors, and go to the toilet—and you could hear them going, Mom. They'd go in there and leave the door wide open and holler in to the front room when they had anything to say. And if they wanted something to eat, they just went right into the kitchen and helped themselves. There was one fellow that always wore dirty old corduroys, and I know he hadn't had a bath in years, and he was the worst one of all. One Sunday I had half a roast I'd been saving and he got it and brought it into the front room with the salt and pepper shakers. And I want you to know that he sat there, shaking salt and pepper all over my clean carpet, and he ate every bit of it. Gulped it right down, Mom, sitting right there in front of everyone, just as unconcerned as—as anything. I never got so—"

"If I remember rightly," I said, "he paid rather handsomely for everything he ever got from us. He was just about the best painter in the Southwest. Before he went to Washington to do some murals, he gave us a portable electric phonograph and a complete set of Carl Sandburg recordings and—"

"Don't mention those records," said Roberta. "I never got so sick of listening to anything in my life. I heard them from morning until night. Every time Jimmie couldn't think of anything else to do; when he was tired or nervous or cross—and he always was when he was working on that crazy book—he'd get those records out. And of all the disgusting filthy— That's where he got that 'Foggy, Foggy Dew' business, and 'Sam Hall'—"

"They're old English folksongs. You can't expect—"

"Old English folksongs, my eye! I guess I know when I hear filth, and I certainly heard those things enough."

"Well, I got rid of them."

"Yes, you got rid of them! After I—"

"I got rid of them, and the people, and the book."

"And after you'd put me through all that, the book wasn't published!"

"Wasn't it?" I said. "I'd forgotten. It must have been quite a disappointment to you."

"Well," said Roberta, "I couldn't help it."

"Funny how it slipped my mind," I said. "But of course I wasn't really interested in the thing."

Roberta's mouth shut, and there was the old helpless puzzled sullen look around it. "I don't know why I can't ever say anything—"

"You're doing fine, honey. You've said quite a bit."

"Jimmie," said Frankie, "give up. What I want to know is—"

"I think that's the thing to do, Jimmie," said Mom, plucking absently at a safety pin in her dress.

"What—give up? I already have."

I knew that wasn't what she meant. She'd been having a long discussion with me—even if I hadn't heard it— and she (we) had reached a satisfactory conclusion. I knew it, but I wouldn't admit it. That is one trick of Mom's that exasperates me.

"Do what?" I said. "What are you talking about anyway?"

"Why—about the story. We can send it to this last magazine, they liked your work so well, and we could have a check back inside of a month. Frankie would pay you back, of course, but it would save borrowing from . . ."

I looked at her. I looked at Frankie and Roberta. Jo was grinning. Everyone else, apparently, seemed to think it was all right. Mom had pulled a rabbit out of a hat. She had dived down into the muck and come up with a diamond.

"Well, I will be goddamned!" I said. "I will be damned by all the saints and Christ and Mary. Willingly, by God. They can damn me individually and collectively, and I will not say a word. They can come in pairs and squads and regiments, in trucks and sidecars, on roller skates and bicycles, and they can damn me to their heart's content! What in the name of—"

I got the bottle out of the kitchen and had a slug.

"Don't pay any attention to him, Mom," said Roberta. "He's just acting crazy."

"Now look," I said. "Once and for all, I am not—"

"Jimmie! You're spilling that stuff all over the rug!"

"—I positively will not write another story. I'll peck horse-turds with the sparrows—"

"Jimmie! You dirty thing!"

"I'll swill slop with the hogs; I'll peddle French post-cards; I'll bend over bathtubs—"

"Jimmie!"

"I'll adopt Frankie's triplets or whatever she has and give them the same thoughtful and tender rearing I'd give my own. But I will not—I utterly by God will not write another story!"

I sat down again.

"He means he won't write another story," Frankie remarked idly to Roberta.

"Oh," said Roberta.

"Well," said Mom. "I don't see why not."

I choked on the drink I was taking.

"Mom," said Frankie.

"Well, I don't," said Mom. "Of course, this isn't the best place in the world to write, but you can't always have things just like you want them. Why look at the way Jack London did, Jimmie! He—"

"Now just a minute," I said. "I want to introduce a piece of evidence. Will you look at this for just a minute?"

Mom looked at the black-and-white photostat and handed it back. "I don't see what your birth-certificate has to do with it."

"It establishes the fact that I am not Jack London? It proves conclusively that I am not Jack London, but a guy named James Dillon? It—"

"You'd better stop acting so crazy, Jimmie," said Roberta. "You know how you'll get."

"No, you're not Jack London," said Mom, fumbling faster with the safety pin. "Jack London didn't give up just because he didn't have everything right like he wanted it. He wrote on fishing boats and in lumber camps and—"

"Yes, and I wrote in caddie houses and hotel locker rooms and out on the pipeline; I wrote between orders of scrambled eggs and hot beef sandwiches; I wrote in the checkroom of a dance hall; I wrote in my car while I was chasing down deadbeats and skips; I wrote while I was chopping dough in a bakery. I held five different jobs at one time and I went to school, and I wrote. I wrote a story a day every day for thirty days. I wrote—"

"I think we'd all better go to bed," said Roberta. "Come on, hon—"

"I will not go to bed!"

"I didn't mean anything," said Mom. "I was just saying—"

"You didn't read your Jack London far enough. He began slipping off the deep end when he was thirty. Well I'm thirty-five. Thirty-five, can you understand that? And I've written three times as much as London wrote. I—"

"Let's skip it," said Frankie.

"You skip it! Skip through fifteen million words for the Writers' Project. Skip through half a million for the foundation. Skip through the back numbers of five strings of magazines. Skip through forty, fifty, yes, seventy-five thousand words a week, week after week, for the trade journals. Skip through thirty-six hours of radio continuity. Do you know what that means—thirty-six hours? Did you ever sit down and write thirty-six hours of conversation? Conversation that had to sparkle; had to make people laugh or cry; had to keep them from tuning to another station. Did you? Did you?"

"Please, Jimmie . . ."

"Of course you didn't. Why should you? What would

it get you? What did it get me? Shall I tell you? You're
damned right I shall. It got me a ragged ass and beans
three times a week. It got me haircuts in barber colleges.
It got me piles that you could stack washers on. It got
me a lung that isn't even bad enough to kill me. It got
me in a dump with six strangers. It got me in jail for
forty-eight hours a week and a lunatic asylum on Sunday.
It got me whisky, yes, and cigarettes, yes, and a woman
to sleep with, yes. It got me twenty-five thousand re-
minders ten million times a day that nothing I'd done
meant anything. It got me this, this extraordinarily
valuable, this priceless piece of information that I'm
not . . ."

I opened my eyes and said, "Jack London."

I was sitting on the divan. Roberta had her arm around
me. Frankie was holding out a drink.

"I'm sorry," I said. "I guess I slopped over."

"I didn't mean you hadn't worked hard," said Mom.
"I know how hard you've worked."

"You'd better go to bed, Mom," said Frankie. "I'm
going to turn in as soon as—"

"No, I'm all right," I said. "Now that we've buried
the dead, let's take up the living. What do you think
we'd better do, Frankie?"

"Well—what do you think about Moon?"

"I don't know. He spends a lot. He might not have it."

"Yeah. I know."

"You could borrow the money if you had to? A hundred bucks is a pretty stiff loan for a shark."

"I know that, too. I could get part of it, though. Maybe I could get part of it one place and part another."

"You're not going to, though," said Mom. "And that's final."

I couldn't see, at the time, why Mom was so dead set against it. Frankie's got money from sharks before. And this was certainly an emergency.

"Why not, Mom?"

"Because there's other—because that Moon can just be made to come across."

"What if he won't?"

"Well, he'll have to."

"Oh, for—well, we don't have to decide anything to-night," I said. "We don't even know of a doctor yet, anyway."

20

WE ALL WENT TO BED, AND JO KEPT GETTING UP TO GO TO the toilet. And Roberta lay taut and silent. Hurt, now that the excitement was over. After a while:

"Jimmie."

"Yes."

"Are you asleep yet?"

I wanted to say yes, yes, I'm asleep, but I knew I hadn't better. "No, honey," I said. "I'm still awake."

"Well—Jimmie—"

"Yes."

"Did you mean all those things you—"

"No, honey. I was just raving. You know how I get."

"You said some pretty mean things, Jimmie."

I patted her on the bottom. Her nightdress was up, and it was bare. She turned, facing me.

"You really didn't mean them?"

"No."

"And you really do love me?"

"That's one thing you can count on. No matter what I say or do or where I am, I'll always love you."

And it was and it is true.

I had my mind on that—the abstract—and I didn't notice when she wiggled closer.

"You don't act like you loved me."

"I'm sorry, honey."

"You—you never kiss me or pet me any more."

"I'm sorry, dear."

"Well, you don't, Jimmie."

"Sorry."

She leaned over me and pressed her lips against mine in a long kiss, and her shoulder straps were down and one of her breasts slid under my armpit.

"Good night, Jimmie."

"Good night, honey."

Thinking. And worn out. And I had no more emotion to spend.

I was thinking of why I couldn't talk to Frankie; of how she had got to be like this.

A little girl who was big for her age, a little girl with yellow hair who was thirteen in years and eighteen in size; whose eyes were as innocent and blue as a ten-year-old's. Walking down Commerce Street, the little girl and I . . .

"Who was that woman that spoke to you, Jimmie?"

"No one."

"You know lots of women, don't you, Jimmie? Every time we go down the street—"

"Forget it."

"One of the girls in the coffee shop wants to come out to our place and live. I told her she couldn't sleep with you because Pop—"

"Don't talk to those tramps."

"A man gave me a whole dollar last night, and he's going to give me another one tonight. Can I put one of them in my bank?"

"I guess so."

"And he said if I'd meet him after work, he'd give me five dollars. He said—"

"You point the son-of-a-bitch out to me! I'll have him rode."

"But he's a nice man, Jimmie! He said he knew you and it would be all—"

"Just point him out."

And a big girl, living with relatives, taking magazine subscriptions from door to door, selling Christmas cards, going to school more and more infrequently. A big girl who could walk into a garage or a barber shop or a warehouse and hand back as good as she was given. A girl who studied *Harper's* and who read the *New Yorker*, who memorized good English and wisecracks because they were valuable to have.

And a woman. An overweight overdressed woman with blondined hair and too much lipstick who sat behind the cash register in coffee shops and barbershops and cigar stores:

"Hi-ya, Jack. What you got up your pantsleg besides your sock?"

"Say, Frankie, you got to hear this one. This one'll slay you."

"Just a minute . . . How do you do, Mr. Pendergast. Was everything satisfactory?"

"Very. Something for you."

"Thank you, so much . . . Now what were you saying, Jack?"

A woman who knew there was something wrong and wanted to get out of it. A woman who would marry the first man who came along to get out of it. A woman who could never feel anything very deeply, regard anything very highly.

I sat up.

Roberta raised her head.

"Where are you going?"

"Just to the bathroom."

"Oh. When are you coming back?"

"Do you have to go?"

"No. I just wondered."

I got my cigarettes out of my pants and went into the bathroom. I stood in front of the mirror and blew smoke out at myself and looked sinister, and heroic, and solemn. No reason. I just did it. I sat down on the stool and started thinking, and somehow a crazy story I'd read came into my mind. *Crazy* isn't the right word. It was by a writer named Robert Henlein, and it was one of the finest pieces technically I've ever read. Here's the gist of it:

An inmate in a private nut-house is talking to a

psychiatrist. The latter is drawing him out, trying to get at the basis of the persecution complex from which the inmate is obviously suffering. The lunatic is firmly convinced that the whole world is in a conspiracy to make him do things he doesn't want to do. Everyone is plotting against him, and they always have. When he was a little boy (he relates), the other children dropped their games when he came around, and stood off by themselves, whispering and looking at him. When he entered a room where adults were talking, they stopped until he had left—

The psychiatrist laughs: Well, there's nothing very unusual about that.

Oh, but that isn't all, says the nut. When I entered college *they* wouldn't let me study the things I wanted to. *They* made me study the things that—

But you had to be equipped for a job, says the psychiatrist. Their judgment of what you needed to fit into life was probably better than yours.

No, it wasn't, insists the lunatic. When I got out, I got a job, and it didn't make sense, and *they* made me stay there against my will.

They? Who are *they*, anyhow?

Well, my wife and my employer and all the Others. Maybe you were in on it, too.

I see, says the psychiatrist. But how do you mean—the job didn't make sense?

Why it just didn't. I slept all night so that I could be

rested enough to go to work in the morning, and I got up and ate breakfast so that I'd have strength enough to get through until noon, and at noon I ate so that I'd have strength enough to get through the afternoon, and I went home at night and ate and slept again so that I could go to work the next morning, and the money I made was just enough to keep me strong and rested so that I could work so that I'd be strong and rested so that—

The psychiatrist throws up his hands: But those things are true of any job.

No, no, says the patient. No, they're not. There is work that does make sense. I know there is, if I could just find it. *They* are keeping me from it. *They* keep putting things in my path. Making me see things that aren't real. Trying to make me do something I don't want to do.

The psychiatrist shakes his head sadly and gets up and walks out.

Then comes the final scene:

The man's wife, his employer, his college teachers, and a host of other demons—yes, demons—are in conclave. There *is* a plot.

He's getting on to us, says the wife. I think he's going to run away again. What'll we do this time?

Let him go, says the psychiatrist. We'll get him back. We always get 'em back.

I guess I don't tell the thing very well. But if you

read it, it'll stick in your mind for days. You get to
wondering—

"Jimmie."

I jumped.

Roberta was in the doorway. Her breasts were completely bared, and her gown was hiked up. But I was
thinking, and she often sleeps that way, with the thing
just tied around her middle, when the weather is warm.
Her breasts are so full that the gown bothers her, it
seems, and she likes to spread her legs wider than it will
allow, so she sleeps that way. I've asked her why she
doesn't do without a gown, because there's not much
left to expose. But she says she gets cold there, and
maybe she does. My unspoken theory is that she simply
knows the value of understatement.

"Aren't you ever coming to bed?"

"Oh sure. Right away."

"Well come on, then."

She went back into the bedroom, and I sat there a
moment longer, thinking about that crazy story that
wasn't crazy. And then she hollered again and I went in
to her, but I was still sort of dreaming.

I lay down and—

And there was a Fury upon me; sobbing, mad with
impatience, shivering with heat: an angel-Fury with
cream-yellow thighs who had made herself over, and who
would never be able to unmake herself. A Frankenstein
monster with silky lashes and a white smile, with breasts
that turned outward with their fullness.

"You better! You always better! You hear me? You better! What would I do if . . . Not—now. . . . Don't . . . answer . . . now . . ."

I don't think I had realized until then how impossibly hopeless it all was.

21

I HAVE BEEN RIDING WITH GROSS. I COULDN'T VERY WELL get out of it. He knew that I didn't have a ride, and he offered to haul me back and forth for nothing (I wouldn't let him do that, of course). And I needed a ride. I couldn't have made it walking much longer. I take a quart vacuum bottle of coffee to work instead of a pint, and, what with the knowledge that everyone there would like nothing better than to catch me asleep, I have kept from dozing off. But I couldn't walk any longer.

I'm sure, of course, that Gross isn't putting himself out any merely to favor me. I'm just about to get my new system set up, although I've not solved that one problem I spoke about, and he knows that Baldwin is pleased with it. And, in me, I think, he sees someone on whose coattails he can ride.

But clubbing up with Gross hasn't helped me any with Moon, personally, that is. I think he is doing all he can about Frankie. He wasn't at all bad when I first spoke to him about it.

He stood rapping my desk with a ruler, looking off absent-mindedly toward the final-assembly line. At last he said,

"You're sure it was my fault, Dilly?"

"I'm sure," I said. And nothing more. When you've lived like we have, when you put yourself on a spot of this sort, you've got to take that kind of question.

"I guess it was, all right," he said. "How much do you think it'll take?"

"A hundred dollars, anyhow."

He nodded. "You think you can get it done for that? When my wife was—"

"I'm not sure," I said. "I just supposed we could."

"Well, I think I can get a hundred."

"You ought to be able to," I said, taking courage.

He nodded again. "It looks that way, don't it, Dilly? I'm running better than seventy-five dollars a week. But I'm paying for that car, and we bought us a houseful of furniture here a while back, and I've been sending money to my brother's folks. It looks that way, but when you try to lay your hands on even a hundred dollars—all in one chunk—it's not easy."

"We'll have to have it, Moon."

"I said I'd try to get it. I'm pretty sure I can."

Well, it was a couple days later that I started riding with Gross, and as soon as Moon learned of it he got me off in a corner.

"Did you tell Gross about this?"

"Of course not," I said. "Why the hell should I, Moon?"

He didn't say anything for a minute, and when he did, he didn't answer my question.

"Are you after my job, Dillon?"

"After your—!" I burst out laughing.

"Are you or not?"

He was serious. I couldn't believe it, but he was.

"No, Moon," I said. "I positively am not. Why—what in the name of God would I want with your job?"

"You're drawing seventy-five cents an hour. I'm getting twice that much."

"But I don't like this work, Moon."

"You'd like a dollar and a half an hour wouldn't you?"

"Not if I had to stay here to get it. I'm a writer—at least I used to be. If I took your job, it'd mean I couldn't ever get away. I wouldn't have the excuse that I could make more writing. It would be the end of my writing."

"How much were you making before you came here—on this fellowship you told me about?"

"Twenty-one hundred a year."

"Well, but my job pays almost twice that much."

"I know, Moon," I said. "But—"

"But what?" he said, staring at me somberly.

"Why, goddammit, didn't I just tell you—"

"Keep your voice down. Are you trying to tell everybody in here about it?"

"I'm through talking," I said. "Think what you want to."

A few days later he came around again.

"If you don't want my job, what are you working so hard for? Why'd you want to learn blueprints and set up this new system and—"

"Would you rather I hadn't?" I said. "Would you rather I just sat here and let things go to hell like they were going? If you would, just say so. I'm getting pretty goddamned tired of working my head off for a bunch of numbskulls who don't appreciate it and won't lift a finger to help me."

"I just asked, Dilly."

"And I told you. Think what you want to, do what you want to."

I am pretty confident of one thing: He doesn't dare fire me. He might make things so uncomfortable for me that I couldn't stay, but—I don't think he would even do that. We've been inquiring around, you see, and 250 dollars seems to be about the minimum for the job we need doing. And Moon is undoubtedly figuring on my paying a good share of it. If I lost my job . . .

I have already seen one man "crowded down the line" —a new man in our department. It was a vicious and fascinating piece of business.

He was an honor-graduate from high school. Perhaps that was the trouble. Perhaps he was a little too eager to show his knowledge of things in general, for that is one way of getting your ears knocked down very quickly in here. Knowledge is taken for granted here. You don't flaunt it. You use it. He hadn't been here three days before I was aware that everyone had it in for him. And that he wasn't going to last.

Moon, say, would set him to sweeping the floor. When

he got up in the Purchased-Parts Department Busken would call him over to help shelve some parts. The kid would have worked at this for an hour or so when Moon strolled around.

"I thought I told you to sweep the floor."

"Well—Mr. Busken asked me to—"

"Well—hurry it up."

It was then Busken's turn:

"All right. Go on. I won't ask you to help me again."

"Why? What's the matter, Mr. Busken?"

"Go on. I didn't think you'd go around griping to Moon just because I asked you to give me a hand."

Naturally, that alarmed the kid. He didn't want people mad at him. He insisted on staying and helping, working frantically so that he could still get the floor swept. And invariably when he did get the broom in his hands again, there was Murphy or Gross needing assistance.

If he hesitated:

"Hey, Moon! What's the matter here? Can't I have a little help?"

"Sure you can. Grab ahold there, Shorty. You won't get your hands dirty."

If the kid didn't hesitate, but grabbed ahold at once:

"When are you going to get this floor swept?"

"Well—Mr. Mur— Right away, sir."

That night, of course, the floor wouldn't be swept.

Dolling brought the kid's dismissal slip down the third week of his probation. It said:

General attitude? . . . . . . Sullen
Helps others? . . . . Unwillingly
Competence? . . . . Seldom completes assignments
Remarks . . . . Wholly unsatisfactory

And it was all true. But I don't think a brighter, faster, better-natured boy ever walked into the plant.

It is even easier to "crowd a man down the line" in the assemblies. The parts for the different positions are being changed constantly. Time-study may learn that a part that has been put on in Position 1 can be better handled at Position 3. And when a new part is turned out, it may have to be put on "at the door" or "in the yard," because the planes have progressed that far and they cannot be returned, say, to Position 2 where the part would normally be integrated.

Under these circumstances it is obviously easy to make a competent man look the opposite (although it is seldom done, now, because of the shortage of skilled workers). And when he is called on the carpet, he has no alibi. There has been another shift in parts. He has no more to do than he should easily accomplish.

I feel extremely sorry for the time-study men. Life for them is utter hell. They go from department to department, timing the workers in their various operations. And no one likes to be timed, and everyone makes it as difficult as possible.

The worker may flatly refuse. "Get the hell away from me. I don't want to be bothered now."

And the time-study man may not reply in kind, or call the foreman—except as a last resort. He must time the process, yes, but it will be very bad for him if he causes a skilled worker to throw down his tools and walk out. Anyone can tell time; everyone cannot run a rivet-gun or assemble a control column.

He laughs, pleasantly. "Got to keep 'em flying, huh? Want me to drop back after lunch?"

No answer.

"Ha, ha. Like to have me drop back after lunch?"

"I don't give a damn what you do."

He comes back after lunch: "All set? Ha, ha. Fine, fi—"

"Get away from me!"

"Please. I've got to—"

"You heard me. Clear out!"

The time-study man calls the foreman. "I'm sorry. Your man won't let me time him."

"Oh yeah? What's the matter, Bill?"

"Aw the son-of-a-bitch keeps getting in my light, Mac."

"Yeah? . . . Look, you. You go back to the office and tell 'em if they want this process timed, they can send a man down that knows how to do it. Now scram!"

And so it goes.

Time-study men come and go rapidly. Today I saw one, a poorly dressed hungry-looking fellow of about forty-five, who probably will not be here very long. Someone had constructed a replica of a sanitary napkin from gauze and waste, dipped it in red paint, and stapled it to the back of his coat. He could see the men grinning as he passed and feel something flopping and splashing against his rear. But he couldn't see it or reach it, so he concluded, I guess, that the men were merely in a good humor and that the other was his imagination. When the office sees him, I imagine they'll let him out. If not, I'd think he'd be too humiliated to come back.

Down in the foundries it is even worse. The drop-hammer men like nothing better than to catch a time-hound in the narrow aisle between their implements. Then it is—*bang! bang! bang!*—and the jolts are enough to throw him off his feet and the pressure enough to deafen him.

He has white-hot washers dropped into his pockets. Oily waste is speared to his coattails and set afire.

And he may find—the guards may find—when he leaves that night that he is carrying out some expensive tool or part.

Yes, they know—the office knows. But no one is going to discharge or even reprimand an essential worker because of a time-study man. I said once before that you could get away with anything here if you were good enough; but I didn't mean it literally. I do when I say it now.

I have never yet gone into the toilet when there was not someone asleep on the stools; the sleepers were (and are) particularly numerous during the afternoon. The guards used to take their badge-numbers, and it would mean a three-day layoff. But now they wake them up and that is the end of the matter. It used to be that you could hardly find a place to smoke at noon because of the restricted areas and planes in the yard (you aren't supposed to smoke within twenty feet of a plane). Now, however, if the guards see you smoking where you shouldn't be—and they don't go out of their way to see you—they approach very slowly so that you will have time to finish before they arrive. No more tickets are handed out for such things as running in the aisles. The incessant practical joking is generally winked at. A riveter will take a paper cup of water and pour it into the tail-cone where his bucker-up lies prone and helpless. The guard sees it, takes a step forward, then remembers and turns away. I feel pretty sorry for the guards, too.

I think I told you of the guard who accosted me when I first went to work here. Well, a few days ago he came up to my window, and he was no longer in natty khaki and Sam Browne. He was wearing unionalls—just another parts boy.

I looked at his badge.

"What do you want with nose-over posts? They're not put on at your station."

"Well—my lead-man sent me after them."

"Who is your lead-man?"

He told me.

I gave him a suspicious stare. "Where is he now?"

"Well—I don't know just where right now."

"Better find him. And make it snappy. We're all here to work, you know."

Yes, I think he did recognize me; and I felt ashamed of myself afterwards. He'd already been punished enough for lacking tact and diplomacy.

I don't know.

I don't know why I can't like the job better, get interested in it. Working conditions couldn't be better. The pay is at least fair. Everything within reason that can be done for the worker is done. We're turning out four planes a day now, but we have the men to do it with. The speed-up has slowed down. I don't have to worry about my past bobbing up.

It's not pleasant to work in a department where the others are unfriendly, but I've worked where the atmosphere was much colder and not minded particularly. I minded, but it wasn't enough to make me want to get up and pull out. Of course, those were writing jobs and—

Still, I don't know.

Out in the yard at noon when a plane goes over, everyone looks up. They stop eating and talking to look up at a plane that they have seen in the plant at least a thousand times and the counterparts of which are all around them. And then the discussions about torque and drag and potential efficiency, and the arguments anent the merits of liquid- and air-cooling, and the minute comparisons of the different kinds of rudder tabs and shock-struts and tail pants and—God knows what all. And the little groups drawing diagrams in the dust and slapping their notebooks, and—well, goddammit, it's crazy. It's infuriating. You'd think there was nothing more important in the world than—

Oh, sure. I do know.

It doesn't make sense to me any more than polishing a paragraph for two hours would make sense to them. I don't want it to make sense. If it ever does, I will give up. That will be the end.

Yes, and I am going to get out of it. I will get out of it. As soon as I see Frankie clear of this mess, I am clearing out. They can all do what they please, but I am leaving, I mean it.

If I only knew what to do about Roberta; she is the main problem. I had always thought before that I was the only one who was that way. But now I know that she is, too. And I don't know what she would do. I know there would never be any other man for her.

And Jo has been extremely nervous lately. She seems to sense that I am about ready to take flight, and she will not leave me alone for a minute. She is on the arm of my chair, squeezing my hand, bringing me things, and talking to me from the minute I get home until I go to bed. We can hardly make her go to bed any more before I do. I don't know what Jo would do if I left. I am the only one there who understands her and speaks her language.

Then Shannon. I think I could do something with Shannon if I had the time. Perhaps if I could get her off by herself for a few hours each evening—I don't see how I could, but—

And Mack is trying to learn some new jokes. They still deal with biteys, and they're hardly hilarious. But if he doesn't have anyone to encourage him, he'll never make any progress. Mack looks a lot like the pictures of me when I was his age. He'll grow into one of those big slow extremely sensitive boys. And he's going to need a sense of humor. He's going to have to have it.

And Mom's heart has been bad. I'd hate to think that anything I did made it worse. Made it fatal.

I've been thinking. I might take a room some place here in town. Something just big enough for a typewriter and a table and a bed. I could do my own cooking and washing, so it wouldn't cost very much. I don't think I'd mind writing another thriller if I knew I could use the money to get into some real writing. Roberta could have my unemployment compensation, and I'd finance myself with a few pulps. Of course, it would be kind of difficult living right in the same town with them and not seeing them. And if I did see them, why—

Oh I don't know.

Things could be worse, I guess. Mom has been hinting that Marge should come out. Walter has had his salary attached by about a dozen different creditors, and they've barely got enough to live on, and he's treating her pretty wretchedly, it seems. But I put my foot down there. I simply had to. . . .

Well, there goes the telephone. But Moon is catching

it. And, evidently, I'm going to catch it about something. I wonder—

"You tell your mother not to call me here any more, Dillon."

"My mother?"

"Yes, your mother. If she calls down here one more time, why—why you'll—she'll—"

I got off my stool. "What?"

"Well—she just can't do that, Dilly. We're not supposed to get outside calls in here. You know that. If that'd been a girl on the switchboard that didn't know me—"

"I didn't know Mom was going to call you. If I had, I'd've told her not to."

"I'm doing all I can, Dilly. You know I am."

"Mom's getting worried, Moon. So am I. You can't let these things go forever."

"I know it, Dilly. I went to two different loan places last night, and I couldn't do any good. I owe so much money they don't think I'm a good risk. Besides they're afraid I might be—"

He broke off the sentence, and a look that I could not define came into his eyes. "Don't say anything more now. Your fr— Gross is watching."

When Gross drove me home, he asked me what Moon and I had been talking about. Gross isn't at all reticent about inquiring into things that he wants to know. Particularly when they are none of his business.

"Nothing," I said.

"I thought I heard him say something about your mother."

"Well."

"Does Moon go to your house quite a bit?"

"No."

"You've got a sister, ain't you?"

I can't like the guy. I feel sorry for him, but I can't like him. So of course I had to be thrown right up against him where I couldn't get away.

"What did you eat for breakfast?" I said. "Did you and your wife get together last night? How much rent do you pay? What kind of underwear do you have on? Do you think it'll rain, and what in the hell will you do about it?"

He grinned sheepishly. "I guess I'm always butting in where I hadn't ought to be. I just like to talk."

We didn't say anything more until we stopped in front of the house.

"I do appreciate riding with you," I said. "Are you sure a dollar a week is enough?"

"Oh, sure. I'd carry you for nothing, Dilly. You're the only friend I got in the plant."

"See you in the morning then," I said. "Good night."

Mom was peeling potatoes, and by the way her hands were moving I knew that she was building herself up to jump me before I could say anything to her.

"I called that Moon fellow," she announced. "I told him he'd better show up here with that money or it would be too bad. The idea of a married man running around—"

"Moon's doing all he can, Mom," I said. "And you mustn't call him down there any more. It'll just make him mad."

"He won't get any madder than I am," said Mom.

"But you mustn't, Mom. You might cause him to lose his job. Then we would be in a pickle."

"I thought you said they thought so much of him they wouldn't let him quit?"

"They do; they did. But if someone keeps calling down there when he's trying to work—"

"Well if he don't want to be called, he'd better get the money."

I poured myself a drink. "There's no use arguing, I guess."

"No, there's not."

"We'll have to face it, Mom. Moon can't get the whole two hundred and fifty. I think it'll be a darn tight squeeze for him even to get half of it. We may as well make up our minds that Frankie is going to have to borrow part of the money."

Mom rinsed the potatoes, covered them with water, and placed them on the stove. She got hamburger out of the icebox and began making it into patties.

"She'll have to, Mom," I said.

"She can't, Jimmie."

"Why not? She always has borrowed when—"

"Well"—Mom turned and looked at me defiantly—"she's got to borrow money for Marge to—"

I put my glass down with a bang. "Mom! Are you out of your mind? How the hell—what will we—oh, my—"

"She's already sent it, Jimmie. And if Marge isn't welcome here, if you can't make a place for your own sister when you've got a good job, and—"

Her veined red hands went up to her eyes, and I did not curse or storm. The curtain had risen again, and I saw those hands transforming bits of bread into fish and steamboats; saw them slipping food from her plate, food that she was starving for, to take up to the cold room so that a little boy there might laugh a little longer. And I saw the little girl again, smiling, patient, tossing a ball by the hour, a ball made from an old stocking . . .

"She'll be welcome, Mom," I said. "Anything I've got she can have."

And I meant it. And there wasn't much else to say.

22

YES, THE CHILDREN ALWAYS DID STAND OFF BY THEMSELVES
and whisper when I approached. And grown people did
stop their talk when I went into a room. Well, there's
nothing very unusual about that. I didn't know how to
play. I was shy and sullen and I made people uncomfortable.

The first thing that really meant anything—that inclined me to think that something or someone was working against me—happened when I was fifteen; after I'd
been hopping bells for a few months.

I didn't go to school that morning. I waited downtown at the street-car stop where I knew Pop would get
off; and when he did, I grabbed him and took him into a
restaurant, into one of the booths. He was freezing up
toward me, even at that time, but he saw that I wasn't
drunk, just excited, and he came along.

"Pop," I said, "did you ever hear of a man named
S—?"

"I knew him very well," said Pop. "He and I and
President Harding crossed the country together on Harding's private train. Let's see . . . Gaston Means was in
the party, too, and Jake Hamon—"

"Never mind that now," I said impatiently. "What became of S—?"

"No one knows. He was president of a small insurance company. After Harding's death he disappeared with a million and a half dollars in negotiable securities. They never found either him or them."

"How much would the bonding company—or the security company or whatever it is—pay to get that stuff back, Pop? How much?"

"I should think they'd pay 10 per cent gladly. Say a hundred and fifty thousand."

"That's the way he figured it," I said. "Our share would be seventy-five thousand. That's what he told me, Pop."

Pop looked at me sharply. "Who told you?"

"S—. He's here in town, Pop. He's at the hotel. And he's on the snow. I took him up a— I took him up some cigarettes last night, and he kept looking at me and asking questions, and finally he asked me if my name was Dillon, and if you weren't my father. And he said you were the only man in the world he'd trust. And Pop, he'll tell us where the stuff is hidden. And all he wants is half of the reward and a promise that they won't prosecute him, and—and it'll be all right, won't it, Pop? You'll do it, won't you?"

I was afraid that he'd say no, because being broke hadn't changed him a bit. But he'd been a lawyer, and he knew that things like that were done every day. And it was a lot better for the stockholders to get part of their money back than none at all. So he said yes, he'd act as intermediary. And then he began to get as excited as I was. He'd put the money in trust for me, he said; well, maybe he'd borrow a little of it if I wanted him to. . . . And I said oh no, Pop, I want you to handle it all. And he straightened up, looking kind of proud and pleased and sure of himself. And I knew that everything was going to be all right between us—for all of us. That it wasn't too late then to make a new start.

I was supposed to be standing on the corner of Eighth and Houston Streets at seven-thirty that evening. Alone. S— would come by in a rent-a-car and pick me up. And we would drive from there to the Trinity River Viaduct on the north edge of town where Pop would be waiting. S— was no sucker, even if he was walking the mountain tops. In case of a double-cross, I'd be thoroughly mixed up in the deal. Another lousy bellhop trying to pull something crooked. He trusted Pop, yes, but he trusted him a lot more with his son as security.

I went home. I told Mom I was too tired to go to school and to wake me up at six that night—I wanted to go to a show. Pop and I thought that story was best. Mom wouldn't understand things, and she'd be scared, and Marge might spill something.

Well—Mom called me at nine o'clock that night, after Pop had got worried and phoned the house. Mom said I was sleeping so soundly, and she guessed I needed my rest a lot more than I needed to see a show.

That was the last of S— needless to say. He checked out without bothering to take his baggage.

I went to Lincoln. I enrolled in the College of Arts and Sciences which was the logical—the only practical—place for me to enroll. Then I went around to the two newspapers and applied for a job, and they laughed at me heartily. Why they had applications from graduate students in journalism who were glad to work for the *experience!* I went to the Western Newspaper Union, not knowing that they only handled boiler-plate stuff, and they laughed heartily also. But a girl in the office took pity on me (or I wonder if it was pity). One of the biggest farm journals in the country was in Lincoln. Why didn't I apply over there?

I did.

I walked in there in my brown Kuppenheimer suit and my snap-brim Stetson, and I was carrying a tweed topcoat I'd paid ninety dollars for. And the PBX girl said why certainly, any of the editors would be glad to talk to me.

I was ushered upstairs and introduced to a young man of about my own age, and he said yes, it was entirely possible that they could do something for me. He was going to the University himself. Several of the editors there were. Just a moment and he'd call some of them in. . . .

He called them in, and by God they acted like they were glad to meet me! They wrung my hand and looked at me like I was something good to eat, and they insisted that I "come out to the house" for dinner the next day, Sunday.

Well, hell, I didn't know about those things. I supposed maybe they all rented a house together to cut down on expenses. Two of them came by in a swank roadster and got me, and they took me out to the house, and it looked like they had about a hundred other guests. And I began to get wise then that I'd put my foot in something. But I still didn't know what it was all about.

I didn't know until I'd had a swell dinner and five or six stiff drinks; until I'd been shaken by the hand and slapped on the shoulder and talked to by about fifty guys of the kind that I'd always wanted to talk to—or thought I had. Then in a small room upstairs, with half a dozen of them crowded around me, encircling me:

"But don't you like us, Dillon?"

"Why—why, sure. And I appreciate your being so nice to me. But—"

"But what? It's surely not the money, is it? You're the type of man who's used to the better things of life. You couldn't get decent board and room for much less."

"Well—but I really need a job, right now."

"Didn't we tell you we'd help you? That's what we're here for, to help each other."

"And I'm already enrolled in Arts and Sciences."

"We get enrollments changed every day. Don't need to worry about that at all. And even if you weren't coming in with us, you ought to switch to Agriculture. You can still get English and Journalism, and—and you'll really be prepared to do something then. You know how it is, yourself. You tried to get a job on the newspapers here. The only place that could give you a—any encouragement was the farm magazine."

I surrendered in the end. I hocked half of my wardrobe to get the immediate cash necessary to be pledged, and they enrolled me in the College of Agriculture. And I had a swell time from then on. Oh, swell.

The good brothers taught me how to clean out the furnace and wash dishes, and every six weeks the "scholarship committee" applied barrel staves to my backside in an exasperated effort to make me remember the distinguishing points between rye and barley—or something else equally nonsensical. And I cut open the guts of turkeys looking for symptoms of blackhead. And I felt hens' butts and tried to guess how many eggs they would lay—and they didn't like it. And I cribbed so many problems in farm physics that I lost any sense of being a cheat.

Well, how could they get me a job on a farm paper, dumb as I was?

They got me a job in an all-night restaurant. I got the others myself.

Hell, in case you're interested, is actually the College of Agriculture of the University of Nebraska. You can take my word for it.

I was going with Lois. She was wearing my pin. We hadn't started fighting yet. I was very much in love with her and very humble. I knew that when I became uncomfortable or wanted to lash out, it was only because of the money angle, because I was on the defensive. I knew that if I could show any tangible assets, if I could assure her folks that I would complete my four years and have something for emergencies, their attitude would be completely different. They weren't unreasonable. They simply didn't want her to lose her head over someone who already had more than he could take care of, and who, admittedly, acted on impulse rather than logic.

I knew this. And—then—I knew they were right. And . . .

I almost didn't open the letter. I thought someone was trying to sell me some stocks and bonds, and I didn't want any. But I did open it, and it was from Blackie Martin.

Blackie and I hopped bells together. He was a kind of stand-offish kid, and he didn't stay at the hotel long. But he'd always liked me, and after he went to New York, he'd dropped me a card now and then. I didn't always write back. The only time I'd written since I'd been in Lincoln was right after I joined the fraternity— when I wrote everyone I could think of on the fancy house stationery. I suppose he got the idea that I was in the money.

He knew something. He wouldn't say how, but he knew it. Cord Motors was going to take a hell of a jump.

I was to get on it with as much as I could on as narrow a margin as I could. I—we—could clean up. He'd trust me to give him his split. He "knew I was honest."

Well, I started to laugh it off; but I couldn't do it. Something told me that it was straight goods. Blackie wasn't given to popping off, and I knew he'd always liked me. Everything fitted. He was working for a broker, he was on the level, and he liked me. And I had a hundred and fifty in the bank.

I'd been saving it up to repay the student-loan I'd gotten when I first enrolled in school. The thing was long past due, and they'd been riding me pretty hard. I'd even drawn a check for the full amount the day before, and I'd intended mailing it. But they didn't have anything but three-cent stamps at the confectionary across from the "house." So I hadn't. I'd be damned if I'd spend an extra penny for those birds.

Well, I went down to the bank and I drew a check to "Cash" for the hundred and fifty. And the guy that had been standing behind me when I got it followed me right to the door and stopped me. He was one of those big bony guys with a head like a quail-trap, and a little button of a nose, and a come-to-heaven smile, and the seat of his blue-serge pants looked like he'd been carrying books in it. I don't know where guys like that come from. I don't think they're born. And I can't figure out how they always get on the boards and committees of this and that and the other; how they always manage to run things. They do though, by God.

"Ha, ha, Dillon," he giggled. "I'll bet you were looking for me, weren't you?"

"Now you don't need to get sarcastic," I said. "I'm going to pay your damned loan."

"Don't swear, Dillon. I might lose my temper. Ha, ha. Give me that money."

"Ha, ha," I said. "I'll send you a check tomorrow. I've got to pay a hospital bill with this."

"You won't need a hospital now, Dillon. Ha, ha." And he took the money. He clawed it right out of my hand.

I don't know which made me maddest at the time— losing the money, or walking into a fast one like that.

I knew by the end of the week when Cord jumped twenty-eight points in a day. If I'd had 150 shares at a dollar margin—but I didn't have. When Blackie Martin wrote me, I marked the letter "Moved, address unknown" and sent it back.

I know I mustn't start thinking that way. But it's hard not to at times. I didn't need anyone to help me. I've never wanted anyone to. All I've ever asked is to be left alone. And no one will ever leave me alone. Someone is always doing what's best for me; making me do what I should do, from their standpoint.

But I mustn't begin thinking that it was deliberate. That, baldly, there is a plot against me. It is becoming harder not to, but I know I must not.

I must not!

23

MOON HUNG UP THE PHONE. BEFORE HE COULD SAY IT, I said.

"I can't stop her, Moon."

"Did you tell her I'd tried every place and couldn't get the money?"

"Yes, I told her."

"Well what does she keep calling for then?"

"She's old, Moon. And she's mad and worried. You know how you'd feel."

"But it doesn't do any good to keep calling, Dilly. It'll just get me run out of here. And if I'm fired with that on my record, I can't go to work any place else. Not in any kind of a job."

"I don't suppose she cares much, Moon."

The moment the words were out of my mouth I knew I'd said the wrong thing. But it was true. Mom's viewpoint was that she had everything to gain and nothing to lose by cracking down. She might force him to come through. If he didn't, if he did lose his job, she'd partly evened scores. She'd tried to get Frankie to call, too, and even to come down to the plant. Of course, Frankie wouldn't.

"That's just what I thought," said Moon. "I thought you said you didn't want my job."

"You should think it. I've only told you about fifty times."

"What makes your mother keep calling for, then?"

"I'm through talking," I said.

"Well, if—"

"I said I was through talking."

He turned away. "You won't get it even if I am canned. I'll see to that."

I didn't answer him. Travelers were piled on my desk a foot deep. I still had some of the old inventory to transfer from the release books to the cards. Under the old system, you might show the same part in more than one place; for instance, in "Left-wing" and "Right-wing." That is why, partly, things were balled up so badly. You couldn't keep the thing evened up. The rack men would throw out parts for, say, the right wing, when you were carrying your inventory on the left, and, according to the records, you didn't have the parts to throw. . . . Well, I have had to pick this stuff up—some parts are used in dozens of different places—and it hasn't been easy.

Moon went upstairs, I suppose. In fact I know he did because he didn't use the telephone. When he came around again, he said that Production wanted a shortage report on every position by three-thirty.

"That's fine," I said, without looking up. "It won't hurt them to want."

"You're not going to get them out?"

"You know I can't."

"You used to be able to. You could do it when we were using the old release books."

"And I can do it now," I said. "In a few days, at least. Right at the moment I don't have any way of sorting my cards into positions."

"Fine system you dreamed up," he said.

And I began to boil a little. That system is—it's almost like a piece of writing. It's a damned sight better than the one they had. I told him so.

"As soon as I'm able to sort the cards I can turn out reports three times as fast as I used to."

"The office wants 'em now."

"Did you tell them they wanted them?" I said. "You went up there and got them to tell you to have me get out the reports when you knew I couldn't?"

"Are you going to do it or not?"

"No, I'm not."

"We'll see about that," he said, and headed for the stairs.

I was watching the clock. It was just five minutes before the phone rang.

"Dilly?" It was Baldwin.

"Yes."

"Can you come up here a minute?"

"I can," I said. "But if it's about those shortage reports, you'd better come down here."

He hesitated. "Okay. Be right down."

I dropped the receiver and snatched up the scissors

and a handful of blank cards. I'd had the idea in my head for days, but I'd never got around to working it out.

Moon unlocked the gate and Baldwin came skimming in ahead of him, pockets bulging with papers, bursting with impatience as usual.

"Now what's the matter here? Moon tells me you refused to obey orders. Why can't you get out the shortage reports? What's wrong with—"

"In the first place you don't need shortage reports," I said. "I watch this stuff coming and going, and I know what I'm talking about. You don't need them."

"That's what you say," said Moon.

"That's what I say," I said.

"Now hold up," said Baldwin. "Let's get to the bottom of this thing. Supposing we did need shortage reports, now. Why couldn't we get them?"

"I've got no way of sorting my cards. The parts were listed by position. Now we carry them chronologically and alphabetically."

Baldwin frowned and shook his head. "Not so good. I didn't—didn't you think of that when you were setting these cards up? God, if we can't get them by position, they're no good to us!"

"All we need," I said, "is a simple sorting device—"

"Oh no you don't!" said Baldwin, and his frown deepened and Moon tried to suppress a smile. "That stuff costs to beat hell! We'd never get an okay for one of those machines. Besides, they've got to be installed to fit the system, and it would take forever to get one—"

"I don't mean to buy one. I mean to make one."

"Make one? How the—"

"Look," I said, picking up the handful of cards. "It's as simple as this. Here's a card for each of the positions. The cards are slotted at the bottom in twelve places, a slot to each position. Starting at the left, all the slots are uniform except one which is lower than the others. On the next row it's the same way, and the next, and all the way across. In each row eleven of the slots are alike; one is lower than the others."

I picked up a pencil and slid it under the first row of slots. "This is Position 1," I said, and I raised the pencil. And Position 1 card rose up and the others remained stationary. I did the same thing on the other rows. "All we need is a file with a sliding lever running beneath it. It would probably cost all of a couple of dollars."

"Say," said Baldwin. He took the pencil and ran it back and forth in the slots. "Well I'll be damned," he said.

Moon cleared his throat. "You're just using a few cards now. It won't work with two or three thousand."

"Why not?" said Baldwin.

"It just won't."

"I guess you and I went to different schools," said Baldwin.

He looked from Moon to me. "What's the trouble between you birds, anyway?"

"No trouble," said Moon.

"Everything's okay with me," I said.

"Well—I'm glad to have you both here, but you'll have to tie the fights outside, understand? Good. Moon, we'll let those shortage reports slide."

And he was on his way again.

Moon and I didn't speak for the rest of the day.

I hate it about Moon. He was kind to me here when I needed kindness badly. I feel somehow that it is I who have put him behind the eight-ball instead of the other way around.

Marge was sitting on the steps that lead down to the walk (almost all San Diego houses are on terraced lots). I had wondered how long it was going to take her to get there. At first she had stood in the doorway, then on the porch; then she sat on the porch steps. And now she was down to the street.

I told Gross good night abruptly and slammed the door as Marge arose. For a moment we were like two people who meet on the street and can't determine which way the other is going. In actions, that is. I knew which way Marge was going, and I kept in front of her. She rose on her toes and peered over my shoulder as Gross's car roared away angrily.

"Now, Jimmie!" she said, stamping her foot and showing the whites of her eyes. "Why do you always do things like that?"

I could understand her being cross. She was dressed in green—a leaf-green tweed sports coat, sea-green street slacks, green socks, and snakeskin oxfords that had cost twenty-two dollars and a half. I knew what they had cost because Walter had written his last note to her on the back of the bill, and she had showed it to us. Her hair was freshly tinted. Her face was a flawless cream and pink mask. It must have taken her at least six hours to fix herself.

I slid around the question. "Did you want to go some place?"

She brightened at once. "Let's do. We'll all go. Frankie's sick and Mom will have to take care of the kids. But you and I and Roberta could go, and maybe you'd see someone you knew. Or maybe Roberta wouldn't want to go. Not an expensive place, Jimmie. Abe Lyman's at Pacific Square and it only costs two dollars and a half, and we wouldn't need more than a cocktail or—"

"I'm afraid we can't even do that, Marge," I said. "We'll try to figure out something for Saturday."

"But it wouldn't cost hardly anything, Jimmie. And you said—"

"I've got to finish that story, too. You know that has to be done."

"Well," she said. "All right. We'll really go some place Saturday? You promise?"

"I promise," I said, rather desperately.

"Can I go over to the drugstore now and get a coke? I'm about out of cigarettes, too, and—"

I gave her what change I had in my pockets, and she counted it out meticulously—although not very accurately—and wrapped it in her handkerchief. "Now you remember that, Jimmie. I'll pay you back as soon as I get some."

She started up the walk.

"Just a minute, kid," I said. "Why don't you go over after while? After dinner?"

"Why can't I go now?"

"Well, you can," I said, "but—" I hardly knew how to put it. "Well, Shannon's over there and she doesn't— you wouldn't enjoy yourself. Having to take care of her, I mean."

"Oh. . . . Well. I'll wait."

We went up the steps together. "And do something else for me, kid. Please don't go next door to use the telephone any more."

"Why not, Jimmie?"

"Because they know we have a telephone. And that boy works down at the plant. It makes things kind of embarrassing for me. Please don't do it again."

"I guess there's not much I can do," she said in a small voice.

She went into the kitchen. I went on back to the bedroom. Roberta was examining a pair of hose.

"You'll have to buy me some new stockings," she said. "I had these hanging in the bathroom and someone wiped a mascara brush all over them."

"All right," I said.

"I don't know why anyone has to do things like that."

"I'll tell her to be more careful."

"No, don't say anything to her, Jimmie. She can't help it, and she *is* your sister."

"Now what the hell *is* this," I said. "You get me worked up to do something, and then—"

"Well, she is your sister, Jimmie."

Mom came in. "What did you say to Marge?"

"I didn't say anything to her. I just asked her not to go over to the drugstore right now and not to use the telephone next door."

"Well, I'm getting out of here," said Mom. "I'm packing up my clothes and getting out tonight. I put up with the work and the noise and people biting my head off every time I open my mouth, but I'm not going to stand by and watch you mistreat Marge. I—"

I went into the bathroom and turned on the shower. Frankie pushed the door open.

"Oh. You in here?"

"No," I said. "This is my spirit getting ready to take flight. My spirit's got some sense."

Frankie chuckled. "What's the trouble with Marge?"

"The same thing that's always been the trouble with her."

"Don't be too hard on her, Jimmie. She can't take it."

"All right. I forget."

"I called the loan company today. You can get the money."

"You didn't tell Mom? She'll raise hell with Moon, and it won't help any."

"No, I didn't tell her. Think you'll finish the story tonight?"

"I suppose."

"Look, Jimmie. Is Roberta sore about all this? You know I'll pay you back just as soon as—"

"No, she's not sore," I said, truthfully. "On the contrary, she's damned well pleased."

Frankie looked blank. "What do you mean?"

"You figure it out. It'll give you something to think about besides your sins. And get out so I can take a bath."

I don't believe I took one. I had the shower turned on and my clothes off. But, looking back, I don't believe I bathed. My piles were unusually bad, and I stood up on a chair and got to examining myself in the mirror. And then—I believe—I put my clothes back on again and went out.

I don't remember eating supper either, although I suppose I did. I know that when I was back in the bedroom writing afterwards, I had the sensation of having eaten a great deal more than I should have. I had never thought I would see the time when anyone could isolate himself mentally in our house, but I guess I am beginning to.

At eight-thirty the page in my typewriter was numbered 18, and half-way down was the symbol—30—. I pulled the sheet out, slipped it under the bottom of the others, and reached for a bundle of manuscript envelopes. I didn't want to look at it again. I couldn't rewrite it. I suppose it was that fastidiousness which makes certain criminals averse to handling the implements of larceny any more than they have to.

Jo was lying on the bed, eyes wide. "Are you going out now, Daddy?"

"Yes."

"When will you be back?"

"You go to sleep."

"Can I go with you?"

"NO! And once and for all, go to sleep!"

She turned over on her side. I gave her a little pat as I went out, but I don't think it helped much. She's not used to my hollering at her.

"Going out?" said Roberta.

"I've got to mail this manuscript."

"Why don't you go along with him, Marge?" said Mom. "You've not been out all day."

"Oh I guess I'd better not," said Marge, raising a magazine in front of her face.

Roberta said. "Now you just go on, Marge. It'll do you good to get out. I don't care about walking or I'd go."

So I said, "Sure, Marge. Come along."

Marge put down the magazine. "Do you really want me to go?"

"Of course I do. But hurry, please."

She was fifteen minutes "getting ready." Don't ask me what she was doing. Roberta gave me fifty cents for stamps; and I drank half a glass of whisky and smoked two cigarettes.

Finally, Marge came out and said she hated to go looking like that, but—

I grabbed her by the arm and got her outside.

I walk very rapidly. After we had gone three blocks, I became conscious that Marge was dragging back on my arm.

"Going too fast for you?"

"Well—how far are we going, Jimmie?"

"To the Post Office. It'd take forever to transfer around there on the bus."

"Well hadn't we better take a taxi?"

"Marge," I said, "can't you—" Then I caught myself. "Honey, if I had the money, you could have a dozen taxis. Don't you know that you never had to ask or hint for money when I had it? I want you to have fun. I don't want to deprive you of things. I'm not stingy—"

"Of course you're not stingy!" she exclaimed. "No one'd better say you are around where I am. I told Walter that if he was just half as good to me as—"

"Well, all the money I have is just enough for postage."

"But I've still got that sixty-five cents, Jimmie—"

"But Marge! You've— I've— Look. We won't go all the way to the Post Office. We'll get some stamps along here some place and mail it. It'll still go out in the morning."

"But we won't get to see any people then, Jimmie."

"Well—well, maybe we will."

We tried two drugstores and neither of them would

sell us stamps. They had them, undoubtedly. But we didn't want to buy anything, so why should they sell them to us?

Then I happened to think of a chain liquor store down the hill toward the bay which I had occasionally—well, damn frequently—patronized. They had stamps, and they couldn't very well refuse to let me have some.

It was about seven blocks down there. With all the walking around we did, we might as well've gone to the Post Office. I mailed the manuscript in a corner box, and we started back up the hill.

"I'm awful tired, Jimmie," said Marge. "Can't we sit down for a minute some place?"

She was looking at a beer and cocktail bar half a block or so up the street. A place with a cinder drive and a tremendous neon sign and awninged windows. Its patrons were chiefly aircraft workers. That was reason enough for me to stay out of there. With Marge.

"I'll tell you what," I said. "Sit down on the curb and rest a minute. Then we'll go on home and I'll mix highballs for all of us, and we'll roll up the rug and dance. How will that be?"

Marge has moments of awareness. They are becoming rarer, but she still has them.

"Jimmie," she said, "what do you think I'd better do?"

"How do you mean?"

"You know. I'm no good for anything. There's nothing I can do, and there's nothing I can do about it. I tried to read those books and magazines you got for me because I thought if I could know some of the things you know, we could talk together again like we used to—and you'd like me better. B-but"— She drew a deep breath— "I couldn't even do that. I don't even have the sense to kill myself. Somehow, I still want to keep on living. Tell me what you think I'd better do."

"You really want to know?"

"Yes. But if it's anything like studying—"

"I think you ought to march right down here and have a drink and listen to the music a while."

The taut intense look—the awareness—vanished. She almost clapped her hands.

"Something just *told* me I ought to come along with you tonight," she declared. "Here, you take my sixty-five cents."

The place had a little dance floor and a coin phonograph and booths in the rear. There were only a few couples there besides us. Most of the business was at the bar out front. I dropped a nickel in the juke box, and we had a brief dance. Then the waitress was there with our drinks.

She shifted impatiently from foot to foot while I fished out sixty cents. I had seven cents more, change from the stamp money, but I wanted a nickel for the phonograph. Anyway, I didn't like the waitress' looks any more apparently than she liked mine, and a dime tip was enough.

I laid the money on the table, and she still waited.

Finally she snapped out, "One dollar, please."

"What for?" I said.

"For your drinks. What do you think?"

"Rum and cokes are twenty-five apiece. The sign out on your bar says so."

"That's at the bar. Back here they're fifty cents."

"You can take mine back," said Marge. "I didn't really want—"

"We don't take drinks back."

"Well you'll take these," I said. "Sixty cents is all I've got."

"Say," she said, "what kind of a gyp is this? I got to pay for them drinks myself. I got to pay for them before I brought 'em back here to you. You come in here an' order drinks an' . . ."

The music had stopped, and everyone was watching us. Watching and listening. It was my pet nightmare come to life. I got nervous and started to pick up my drink, and the waitress snatched it out of my hand.

"No, you don't! I'll throw 'em down the drain first! You gimme that money, an' if you ever show up in here again—"

"What goes on, Mame?" It was Gross.

"Oh, hello, Butch. This guy's tryin' to get out without payin' for—"

"Aw nuts," said Gross. "These people are friends of mine." He opened his billfold and shoved something into her hand. "Bring me a drink and then bring us another drink all around."

The waitress took the money and glanced sidewise at

me. "I'm sorry, mister. There's so many guys come in here, an' I got to pay out of my own pocket . . ."

"That's all right," I said. I knew how it had been with Frankie.

Gross sat down and, naturally, I introduced Marge.

"You're a lot better looking than your brother," he said. "Dilly, you're sure she's your sister? She's not your daughter, now, is she?"

Marge ducked her head and looked up at him kittenishly. "Now Mr. Gross! Jimmie's only three years older than I am. You shouldn't say things like that." She gave him a delicate tap on the arm.

"Oh that's all right. Dilly won't get mad. Dilly's the best friend I've got."

It may have been true, relatively speaking. Anyway, I couldn't very well deny it to his face. And I was grateful for being pulled out of a hole.

They danced, and then they kept on dancing, and I noticed that Marge's jaws were moving pretty steadily. But—well, I sat there smoking and drinking and my mind drifted off onto something else. A dozen other things.

When I came out of it, it was eleven-thirty.

Marge didn't want to leave then, but a reminder as to how Roberta was going to feel induced her. Gross drove us home.

"If you'll wait just a minute," I said, "I'll get you the money for those drinks."

"What's the matter?" he said, an ugly note creeping

into his voice. "Ain't I good enough to buy you a drink?"

"We're both working for wages," I said. "You need your money as much as I need mine."

He didn't say anything. Marge said afterward that I was "awful cool" toward him and it was no wonder I made him mad. But I don't think that had anything to do with what happened. He saw a chance to push himself ahead at my expense and he would have done it, eventually, no matter what I said or did.

I got the money and virtually pulled Marge out of the car. And we started up the walk to the porch. Then I saw that Gross had stopped the car and was rolling down the window. I hesitated, thinking he had something to say. He did have.

"Good night, Comrade," he called.

And his mean cackle floated back to us as he raced away.

I grabbed Marge. "What did you tell that guy?"

"W-why nothing, Jimmie. I was just telling him about the books I'd been reading and he wanted to know why, and—yes, I did tell him about how you got out here. . . ."

24

HE DIDN'T COME AFTER ME THE NEXT MORNING, OF course. I was sure he wouldn't, and I didn't wait for him. I wouldn't have gone at all if I hadn't been afraid not to. I was sure that if I stayed away, Gross would spill everything he knew (and I couldn't find out from Marge just how much he did know). I thought that if I was there, within reaching distance, he might think twice before he said anything. I should have known better. Physically, at least, there wasn't any comparison between Gross and me.

I couldn't eat anything. I didn't have any stomach. I took a couple of stiff drinks, but they stopped at my tonsils and made a round trip before I'd gone a block.

I got through the gate safely and went inside. It was almost seven but there wasn't anyone in the stockroom that I could see. I sat down on my stool and sort of pulled myself together. Then the whistle blew, and I saw Gross stick his head around the corner of a rack at the far end of the room. I stared straight at him, and he marched boldly out. Behind him came Moon, Murphy, and the others.

I turned around to my desk and waited. Went to work. There wasn't anything else to do.

They all kept away from me that morning. All except Murphy, that is. About ten o'clock he came around to look at a card. As he studied it he said from the corner of his mouth:

"I'm taking off at noon. If you've got anything at home you want to get rid of, give me a note and I'll do it for you."

I didn't have anything. If I had, I wouldn't have fallen for a gag as old as that. At least, I thought it was a gag.

"Thanks," I said. "I don't have anything I'm afraid for anyone to see."

"Okay. I know how you feel."

I didn't go outside at noon, badly as I wanted a smoke. I was afraid my legs would tremble if I walked around very much. And, somehow, I felt safer inside.

One o'clock came. Two. Two-thirty. One hour to go. And I knew I wasn't going to get through it. The skies were going to fall before I could get out of there.

Suddenly I didn't care if they did. I ceased to be afraid. I had worried all I could and been afraid all I could, so I just stopped. Perhaps you've had the same sort of thing happen to you.

Three o'clock.

The phone rang. Moon picked it up. He has been very quick to answer the phone since Mom started calling. I hoped it wasn't Mom this time. I knew it wouldn't affect what was going to happen to me, but I just didn't want her to call. I didn't want to go out of there with Moon hating me any more than he did.

"How about a shortage on wing, Dilly?" he said phlegmatically. "Can you get it out?"

I nodded. And then, because I wanted to get everything in order, because as long as I live I will have to make changes, do things I think should be done, I said:

"Why don't we have a Purchased-Parts shortage to tie in with it? I've been thinking lately why worry about plant parts when we don't have the rivets and other stuff to put them together with?"

"All right," said Moon. "You go tell Vail to give you his shortages."

"Don't you think you'd better tell him?" I said.

He turned away without answering.

I got off my stool and walked up to Purchased-Parts. Vail was weighing up bolts on the computing scales. Busken was sacking.

"What do you say, Red?" said Vail.

"How about giving me a shortage on wing?" I said.

"What do you want with it, Red?"

"I want it to—"

"Want it to send to Russia, Red?"

"Now look here," I said. "Moon told me to—"

Then I jumped three feet in the air.

I turned, half-squatting, sick with pain. I don't think anyone can know how much those piles hurt. Busken was holding the broom, giggling, still fencing at me with the end of it.

"He, he! Mustn't jump so high, Red. Might drop a bomb out of—"

I snatched the broom from his hands and brought it down on his head. Rather, I aimed at his head. He threw his head back and the tough sharp straws swept down across his face. Instantly it was bleeding in a dozen places.

I was sorry, of course, as soon as I'd done it. But Vail had to choose that moment to say the thing that infuriates me more than any other.

"Why don't you pick on someone your own size?"

So I let him have it, too. And I did get him in the head.

Then Gross was trotting up, pushing his way around them. This was what he had been waiting for—the chance to put himself in good with everyone.

"Let me get him, guys. Just let me get ahold of the Red son-of-a—"

I swung on him. Not with the broom, but with a two-pound sack of bolts. I don't know why it didn't kill him.

Then the guards came.

25

"WHEN DID YOU JOIN THE COMMUNIST PARTY, DILLON?"

"Late in 1935. I forget the month."

"What was your motive in joining?"

"The usual one, I suppose. I was pretty disgusted with the old-line parties."

"There wasn't any other inducement?"

"Well, yes. There was usually some good conversation. I like good talk."

"You weren't paid any money?"

"On the contrary."

He wasn't as old as I was, the FBI man. He had yellow hair, combed straight back from his forehead, and the blandest blue eyes I have ever seen. That is, they appeared bland until you met his gaze square-on. Then you saw that they were something else.

"Is Dillon your right name?" said the plant chief-of-police.

"You've seen my birth certificate."

The chief brought the front legs of his chair down to the floor with a crash. His finger shot out.

"I asked you if Dillon was your right name!"

"Let's let Mr. Reynolds handle this," said Baldwin, frowning at him. And the FBI man took up again:

"Now you dropped out of the party you say?"

"Yes. In the spring of '38."

"What was your reason?"

"It caused trouble at home, for one thing. My wife and children are Roman Catholic."

"Weren't they Roman Catholic when you went into the party?"

"That wasn't the only reason. A number of the people I'd known had moved away. It didn't seem the same without them."

Reynolds stared at me, and I couldn't look away from him.

"What was the real reason you dropped out?"

"I've told you."

"No you haven't."

"All right," I said. "I was beginning to drink pretty hard about that time. They didn't want me as a member."

"You were kicked out then?"

"No. I took some hints."

The chief leaned forward. "If it hadn't been for that, would you still be in the party?"

Baldwin said, "No one can answer a question like that, Chief. I couldn't decide now what I might have done in the past under different circumstances. I'm no longer the same man that I was then."

"Besides that," said Reynolds, a faint flicker of a smile

on his lips, "I don't think Mr. Dillon would give us an answer that would prejudice us against him."

I didn't say anything. His smile disappeared.

"Had you ever done any aircraft work before you came here?"

"None at all."

"You knew nothing about it?"

"No."

"Let me see Dillon's employment record, Baldwin."

Baldwin handed him a sheet of typewritten paper. Reynolds studied it.

"What would you say about this record? Is it unusual? Good or bad?"

"It's exceptionally good. I'll even say that we've never had a new man who did as well."

I think he realized that he was hurting me, even as he said it. But, after all, the opposite would have hurt also.

"Now, Dillon. You'd never been in aircraft work before, you say, until you came here. And yet you are drawing more money than men who have been here two years and longer. You know more, you're worth more, presumably. How do you account for that?"

"It may be," I said, "because I needed money worse than they did. Most of them are single. I'm married, have children and other dependents."

"I need money, too, Dillon. But it wouldn't turn me into an A-1 aircraft man."

"Well, I've held some pretty good jobs before I came

here. Certain abilities can be used in one place as well as another."

"Yes, but—"

"Dillon does mostly paper work," said Baldwin.

Reynolds said, "What do you pay your clerical workers in the office, Mr. Baldwin?"

"Well—twenty a week or so."

"And Dillon is getting twice that much. Why?"

"Well . . . I didn't mean to say that he doesn't have to know anything about aircraft—"

"He has to know a lot, doesn't he?"

"Well— Oh hell. Yes!"

The chief crossed his legs and leaned back against the wall. I couldn't see him smile, but I knew he did.

"When I came here," I said, "I filled out an application blank. It gives my past employment record."

Reynolds nodded. "It shows you as a free-lance writer most of the time for the past twelve years. You were your own employer."

"Do you mean by that," I said, "that during the time I was writing I was also doing aircraft work?"

"You could have been, Dillon."

"Well I wasn't."

"Now you are no longer a Communist, you say?"

"I not only said it—I'm not."

"You severed all connection with the party in 1938?"

"Yes."

"All right. But despite that fact, the Communist Party

supplies you with a new car and the money to travel halfway across the continent. So that you could go to work here."

"Now wait a minute—"

"A man who stands convicted of criminal syndicalism and who is now under ten-year sentence gave you that car and the money to come out here on. Why?"

"I'm not answering that question," I said.

"You don't have to, Dillon. You can have a lawyer if you want one."

"I don't want one. But I don't want to be asked the parallel of whether I've stopped beating my wife yet. I've told you how I got that car."

"Tell me again."

"I met Mike Stone in the Post Office. I told him I wanted a change in scenery, that I should really carry on some of my research in another area. He introduced me to his attorney who gave me the car to deliver here. Not to keep, but just to deliver. That's all there was to it."

"But why should Stone have cared whether you got here or not? You weren't in the party any longer. Why should he want to do you a favor?"

"Why not?"

"Don't ask me questions. I'm asking you."

"I've answered. 'Why not?' is the only answer I can give. It wasn't any trouble. The car had to be brought back here, and Stone knew I wouldn't wreck it or run off with it. That's all there was to it."

The chief spoke up. "Fellows drive cars in here from the Middle West all the time, Mr. Reynolds. It saves freight charges. The dealers back there are glad to give a man his passage and a few dollars for driving a car out here."

I was surprised. I began to feel a little more comfortable, too. But Reynolds seemed not to have heard.

"Mr. Baldwin," he said, "I believe you've had a great deal of trouble in your stockroom. Parts getting lost, mislabeled; unfinished parts and parts that belonged to other departments being stowed away in there, and consequently causing expensive delays. When did this trouble begin?"

"Well, six or seven months ago."

"Or about the time Dillon went to work here? . . . Just a minute."

The door opened and another man, a man who somehow looked like Reynolds, poked his head in.

"Nothing," he said. "A few books but they were all from the Public Library."

"Thanks, Jack."

The door closed again.

"About your question," said Baldwin. "Yes, our trouble did begin about the time Dilly started to work here. But that was also about the time when we were really getting into production. We'd received our first large Government orders. Before that an order for a dozen ships was an event. Everything was snarled up six or seven months ago. Every department was in a jam."

"Are they still?"

"Well, we're pretty well lined out now, but—"

"You're still having trouble in your main stockroom, however?"

"Yes, but that's the nerve center of the entire plant! And—and Dilly's just about to get things straightened out in there. He's set up a new records system that should remove a lot of the trouble."

"But it hasn't yet? Things are still far from what they should be?"

Baldwin admitted that they were.

"Now these discords and disputes between the various workers in the department? When did they begin?"

"Well . . ."

Baldwin scuffed his feet against the linoleum and lighted a cigarette. He exhaled a cloud of smoke and tapped the cigarette nervously into a tray.

"Mr. Reynolds, you're making out a very bad case against a man who, at the worst, has only been misguided or too impulsive. Those quarrels can be attributed almost entirely to this fellow Gross. He's a tale-bearer and trouble-maker from the word go, but he's a husky devil and he's clever. Dilly's been catching the brunt of things that Gross started. Personnel shoved him off on us, or I'd've canned him long ago."

"I took over Gross's job, you see," I said.

"Yes," said Baldwin, "and Gross tried to get Moon fired one time."

"And he looks down on Murphy because Murphy is part Mexican."

"That Murphy is quite a kid," said the chief, idly. "I saw him fight a couple o' times."

Reynolds glanced at his wrist watch, and I thought he sighed slightly. "We don't seem to be making a great deal of headway," he said. "Dillon came out here under circumstances that were suspicious—and yet weren't suspicious. There were serious mixups from the time he went to work—but there might have been anyway. They haven't ceased yet—but they will. Everyone in the department has been fighting and quarreling—but that could be Gross's fault." He looked around at us. "I think I might add that it's practically impossible to obtain positive evidence of sabotage. The saboteur has to keep on working if he's to be of any real value. He can't pull a trick or two and skip out. He's got to be clever. He's got to do one thing and appear to be doing the opposite."

"Dillon is on the spot and he isn't on the spot," said the chief. "It all depends on which way you're looking at him."

"Yes. I won't say that he's on it, but it would be a lot better if he could take a step in another direction."

"Well," said Baldwin, "I don't know that I can say anything more than I have."

"How about—what's his name?—Moon? The lead-man. Is he still around?"

"I thought you'd already talked to him," said Baldwin.

"Only in a general way when I talked with the others. Is he still around?"

"I'm not sure that he is. It's pretty late and—"

"He's here," said the chief. "I thought you might want him. He's waiting downstairs."

"Have him come up, please."

The chief went out. Reynolds sat staring at me. Baldwin lighted another cigarette from his first one.

"Mr. Reynolds," he said.

"Yes?"

"Well, about Moon. He's been somewhat jealous of Dillon. And I know he's vindictive. I don't believe that . . ."

He left the sentence unfinished.

"I see," said Reynolds.

And I knew what he saw. Nothing that you could put your finger on. The suspicious linked with its antithesis. Proof, and no proof.

And I knew that no proof was necessary in these times. Only a belief in the mind behind those bland blue eyes. Only a charge. Conviction would be automatic.

Moon came in, half of a huge red apple in his hand. He took a bite as he laconically settled into the chief's chair, and, chewing, he looked the FBI man up and down. He didn't seem to mind looking into his eyes. His stare was as hard and straight as Reynolds'. Reynolds smiled faintly and shifted his gaze.

"You know why we've asked you to come up, Moon?"

"Yes," said Moon, flatly. He turned the apple half a revolution and raised it to his lips.

"You've had some very serious trouble in the stockroom, Moon. It began at the time, or about the time, Dillon came here. Now—"

Moon held up his hand. He gulped and swallowed. "Jus'—just before Dillon came here I was trying to quit. Didn't give a damn what happened. I let everything go, including that Gross guy. Dilly stepped right into the middle of a first-class mess."

"Oh," said Reynolds. "Maybe you'd rather finish your apple before—"

"I can talk all right," said Moon. "It'd been a lot better for Dilly if he'd let things slide. Everyone would have liked him better. Wouldn't do it, though, so here he is."

"I see," said Reynolds. "Now you've had the chance to observe Dillon very closely. You and he work largely in the stockroom, while the others spend much of their time outside. Did any of his actions ever strike you as being suspicious? Was there ever anything in connection with his work that seemed suspicious?"

Moon studied the remainder of the apple. He tossed it into the cuspidor. Thoughtfully he stared at the floor.

"Well—I don't know. I don't know whether you'd call it suspicious or not."

The FBI man leaned forward. "Explain exactly what you mean."

"Well—I used to think he was going to blow the place up."

"Blow it up!"

"Uh-huh. Used to sit on that stool so long without going to the toilet I was afraid he was going to explode all over us."

There was a dead silence.

Then Baldwin brought his open palm down on the desk and began choking and strangling on his cigarette. Reynolds reddened; but he grinned.

"I guess that's all, Mr. Moon. Thank you for coming in."

"Don't mention it," said Moon. And he strolled out, his hands swinging limply at his skinny shanks.

Baldwin wiped his eyes.

"I think it's pertinent to tell you that Moon is leaving us. He's been called back into the Navy. We could have had him deferred, but he wanted to go. So we didn't try to hold him. We tried to keep him from leaving once before, and it didn't work out so well."

"Very interesting." Reynolds got up and held out his hand to me. "We'll try to get together again under more pleasant circumstances."

I shook hands, not saying anything.

Baldwin said, "You'll get to see Dilly, all right. He'll be around. He's taking over Moon's job."

26

WHEN I REACHED THE TOP OF THE HILL THAT NIGHT,
the corner, Moon was waiting for me in his car.

"Thought I'd say adios," he said, as I got in and sat
down. "Would have brought you home, but I thought
it might not be a good idea."

"You just about saved my neck," I said.

"Yeah? Well, I guess I owed you something, Dilly.
How's Frankie?"

"She's going to be all right."

"I wish I could have done what I should have. I liked
Frankie, Dilly. It wasn't just another one of those
things."

"I know. I know how it is."

"Want a drink?"

"I guess not, Moon."

"I guess I don't either."

"I'm sorry you're leaving. I hope I'm—we're not the
cause of it."

"I'd've probably gone anyway, Dilly. I've been looking
for an excuse for a long time."

"You know I didn't want your job?" I said. "You know
I'm not going back?"

"Don't let me keep you from it, Dilly."

"It isn't that."

He nodded. "I ought to've known you'd be too smart. You've got some good tricks, Dilly, but they wouldn't carry you there forever. And it would be all the harder on you afterwards."

"Yes, and that isn't all, Moon."

He waited.

"I don't know," I said. "Probably I'll never be able to explain to anyone. Not even if I wrote a book . . ."

___ **No Beast So Fierce** by Edward Bunker $10.00   0-679-74155-0
___ **Double Indemnity** by James M. Cain $8.00   0-679-72322-6
___ **The Postman Always Rings Twice** $8.00   0-679-72325-0
    by James M. Cain
___ **Fast One** by Paul Cain $9.00   0-679-75184-X
___ **The Big Sleep** by Raymond Chandler $10.00   0-394-75828-5
___ **Farewell, My Lovely** by Raymond Chandler $10.00   0-394-75827-7
___ **The High Window** by Raymond Chandler $11.00   0-394-75826-9
___ **The Lady in the Lake** by Raymond Chandler $10.00   0-394-75825-0
___ **The Long Goodbye** by Raymond Chandler $11.00   0-394-75768-8
___ **Trouble Is My Business** by Raymond Chandler $9.00   0-394-75764-5
___ **Dead Lagoon** by Michael Dibdin $12.00   0-679-75311-7
___ **The Dying of the Light** by Michael Dibdin $9.00   0-679-75310-9
___ **The Last Sherlock Holmes Story** $10.00   0-679-76658-8
___ **I Wake Up Screaming** by Steve Fisher $8.00   0-679-73677-8
___ **Black Friday** by David Goodis $7.95   0-679-73255-1
___ **The Burglar** by David Goodis $8.00   0-679-73472-4
___ **Cassidy's Girl** by David Goodis $8.00   0-679-73851-7
___ **Night Squad** by David Goodis $8.00   0-679-73698-0
___ **Nightfall** by David Goodis $8.00   0-679-73474-0
___ **Shoot the Piano Player** by David Goodis $7.95   0-679-73254-3
___ **Street of No Return** by David Goodis $8.00   0-679-73473-2
___ **The Big Knockover** by Dashiell Hammett $13.00   0-679-72259-9
___ **The Continental OP** by Dashiell Hammett $12.00   0-679-72258-0
___ **The Maltese Falcon** by Dashiell Hammett $9.00   0-679-72264-5
___ **Red Harvest** by Dashiell Hammett $10.00   0-679-72261-0
___ **The Thin Man** by Dashiell Hammett $9.00   0-679-72263-7
___ **Ripley's Game** by Patricia Highsmith $11.00   0-679-74568-8
___ **Ripley Under Ground** by Patricia Highsmith $11.00   0-679-74230-1
___ **Ripley Under Water** by Patricia Highsmith $11.00   0-679-74809-1
___ **The Boy Who Followed Ripley** $11.00   0-679-74567-X
    by Patricia Highsmith
___ **The Talented Mr. Ripley** by Patricia Highsmith $11.00   0-679-74229-8
___ **A Rage in Harlem** by Chester Himes $8.00   0-679-72040-5
___ **The Laughing Policeman** $9.00   0-679-74223-9
    by Maj. Sjöwall and Per Wahlöö
___ **The Locked Room** $11.00   0-679-74222-0
___   by Maj. Sjöwall and Per Wahlöö
___ **The Man on the Balcony** $9.00   0-679-74596-3
    by Maj. Sjöwall and Per Wahlöö

VINTAGE CRIME / **BLACK LIZARD**

___ **The Man Who Went Up In Smoke** $9.00   0-679-74597-1
    by Maj. Sjöwall and Per Wahlöö

___ **Roseanna** by Maj. Sjöwall and Per Wahlöö $9.00   0-679-74598-X

___ **After Dark, My Sweet** by Jim Thompson $7.95   0-679-73247-0

___ **The Alcoholics** by Jim Thompson $9.00   0-679-73313-2

___ **The Criminal** by Jim Thompson $8.00   0-679-73314-0

___ **Cropper's Cabin** by Jim Thompson $9.00   0-679-73315-9

___ **The Getaway** by Jim Thompson $10.00   0-679-73250-0

___ **The Grifters** by Jim Thompson $8.95   0-679-73248-9

___ **Heed the Thunder** by Jim Thompson $10.00   0-679-74014-7

___ **A Hell of a Woman** by Jim Thompson $10.00   0-679-73251-9

___ **The Killer Inside Me** by Jim Thompson $9.00   0-679-73397-3

___ **Nothing More Than Murder** $9.00   0-679-73309-4
    by Jim Thompson

___ **Now and On Earth** by Jim Thompson $9.00   0-679-74013-9

___ **Pop. 1280** by Jim Thompson $9.00   0-679-73249-7

___ **Recoil** by Jim Thompson $10.00   0-679-73308-6

___ **Savage Night** by Jim Thompson $8.00   0-679-73310-8

___ **South of Heaven** by Jim Thompson $9.00   0-679-74017-1

___ **A Swell-Looking Babe** by Jim Thompson $9.00   0-679-73311-6

___ **Texas by the Tail** by Jim Thompson $9.00   0-679-74011-2

___ **The Transgressors** by Jim Thompson $8.00   0-679-74016-3

___ **Wild Town** by Jim Thompson $9.00   0-679-73312-4

___ **Blue Belle** by Andrew Vachss $11.00   0-679-76168-3

___ **Born Bad** by Andrew Vachss $11.00   0-679-75336-2

___ **Down In the Zero** by Andrew Vachss $11.00   0-679-76066-0

___ **Hard Candy** by Andrew Vachss $11.00   0-679-76169-1

___ **Sacrifice** by Andrew Vachss $11.00   0-679-76410-0

___ **Shella** by Andrew Vachss $11.00   0-679-75681-7

___ **Strega** by Andrew Vachss $11.00   0-679-76409-7

___ **The Burnt Orange Heresy** by Charles Willeford $7.95   0-679-73252-7

___ **Pick-Up** by Charles Willeford $9.00   0-679-73253-5